SLAY RIDE

YOU'D BETTER WATCH OUT

L.A. Birchon

**OXGATE
BOOKS**

Copyright © L.A. Birchon 2023
All rights reserved.

Cover design by Milan Jovanovic.

The story, all names, characters, and incidents portrayed in this novel are fictitious. No identification with actual persons (living, deceased, or undead), places, buildings, and products is intended or should be inferred.

No animals were harmed or exploited in the production of this book. Not even bees.

https://labirchon.com

Also by L.A. Birchon

The Mayfly

The Rules of Time Travel

Sign up to the mailing list to download *The Mayfly* for free!

https://labirchon.com

For Lizzy

1

Christmas is always a bloody horror show for Nish.

And it's been Christmas since at least June because Nish works in advertising. Influencer outreach, to be precise. The wave of momentum he's been building all these months has finally crashed online like a consumerist tsunami.

TikTok is flooded with the Grumpy Krampus challenge. YouTube is inundated with ring-lit baby-faced thirty-year-olds doing step-by-step tutorials on how to get that Grumpy Krampus look. Viral videos of children fighting in a playground over a Grumpy Krampus have spurred a minor moral panic.

There's been a shortage of the ugly toys as demand has spiked. Desperate parents have been out-bidding each other on eBay as shops sell out. The One Show filled a whole ten minutes of primetime TV with a weeping mother who had failed to secure a Grumpy Krampus, the sole occupant of her terminally ill son's wish list for Santa. Heart-breaking stuff. Clips of the denouement – Marcus Rashford surprising the child with a limited edition gift-wrapped Krampus – had trended online for a week.

It's all been great for business. The toy manufacturer's Sales Director joked he'd not seen so many exponential graphs since the start of the pandemic.

Nish had asked his boss for some kind of financial reward for a job well done. His boss had slapped him on the back as if they were great pals. 'If it were down to me, I'd give you an extra lump of coal. But there's the climate crisis to think of. Know what the business's goal for 2030 and your bonus have in common? Net zero.'

Not that Nish had held up much hope his hard work would be recognised. This was advertising after all and Nish's boss had contrived to combine Don Draper's worst character flaws with the inferiority complex of a man who moves in the right circles but went to the wrong school.

There's no bonus and no rest for the wicked. Nish has been working on Easter for at least a month. And come January forward planning will start for Halloween – or Goth Christmas as it's known in the trade.

But for now, it's Christmas Eve at long last. After on-off lockdowns, tier systems, bubbles, rules of six, hand-washing, hand-clapping, and hand-wringing, this is the first normal Christmas in two long years. Finally, normality is back in sight.

And with normality comes a backlog of seasonal celebrations. Nish has almost lost count of the number of Christmas parties he's had.

First there had been the whole-company do in a hotel ballroom with finger food and drinks vouchers that the CEO insisted showed how the organisation treated its staff like family. As if to demonstrate the point, two fights had erupted and a long-suspected office affair had been revealed as a result of a faulty lock on the disabled toilet.

Then there had been the department Christmas meal, which had navigated the thin line between the different dietary needs of the team, geographical convenience, venues with space for twenty people, and the meagre entertainment budget remaining.

After that had been the team drinks, standing room only in a crowded bar and self-funded since the expenses budget had been completely rinsed.

And then, with the mandatory events out of the way, there were the pre-Christmas meet-ups with people Nish actually chooses to spend time with. Friends who all wanted to catch up before the big exodus from London, everyone heading back to families scattered far and wide.

He'd almost forgotten how the big Christmas getaway could feel like an impending apocalypse. But – *whisper it* – he'd quite enjoyed the cancelled Christmases of lockdown. Those long lazy days where he could lounge around with no particular plans. Go wander London's deserted streets, enjoying the novelty of feeling like he was walking through a scene from 28 Days Later. He could FaceTime his family for a bit – and then escape, his duties dispensed with.

But this year, it would take more than a zombie apocalypse for Nish to escape the call home for Christmas. His family might be practising Hindus, but his mother has appropriated the Judeo-Christian festive tradition with a fervent vigour. The extended family gathers. Gifts are exchanged. There's an enormous meal. And there's *always* a row. But not while the whole family is there to watch, of course.

After the extended family has departed, full and contented, headed back to their successful and fulfilling lives, things will really kick off. Once his mother has firmly established that yet another cousin has become a doctor, that his second cousin has been promoted (again) and is driving a Tesla, that another cousin is getting married in the summer, that his aunt and uncle are now grandparents to two children, and that a second-cousin-twice-removed is moving his whole family closer to his parents to see them more and provide care in their dotage, she will be alone with Nish and his father and a mountain of washing up and a lifetime of disappointment. It's then, as Nish is helping his mother load the dishwasher and soaking the roasting trays, that she'll fire the opening shot on the traditional argument: 'And what about you, Nish?'

By this she means: Why didn't you want to be a doctor? Why aren't you a director? Why don't you have a car, let alone a Tesla? When will you have a wife? When will I have grandchildren? When will there be a family to move closer to me? What have I done that makes you want to deny me these basic human rights?

They'll argue. He'll feel inferior and ungrateful. She'll wish that she'd had more than one child so they could afford to have a failure in the family. An uneasy truce will be called on Boxing Day and his father will look at him with the kind of sympathetic disappointment that says 'If you did just one of these things, she'd be happy. Why make life harder for yourself?'

And then Nish will leave on the first train back to London, replaying the argument in his head as the countryside zips past.

'How was your Christmas?' colleagues and friends will ask. 'Fine,' Nish will say, followed immediately by 'Yours?' to avoid further scrutiny.

Yeah, Christmas was always a bloody horror show alright, and that was before *this*.

Nish emerges from the underground into the vast atrium of Paddington station. The iron arches of the station roof curve into the distance, tracks glinting in the half-light of deserted platforms.

'Twas the night before Christmas and the station concourse was quiet... Too quiet.

There's not another living soul in sight. The thick coat of snow that has settled on the glass roof reflects back the station lights. A bauble-bedecked tree stands glistening in silver and red, topped with a blue neon star. And behind that is the departures board, showing an assortment of trains – the last route out of London before Christmas – all cancelled.

Nish had checked – he had *checked* – and they had been fine. Maybe running a bit slow, maybe warning not to take too many chances, but they had been running. Yet there, at the end of the board, is his slow train to Bristol. The word 'cancelled' flashes in all caps, like a headline about woke culture gone mad.

Is this a Christmas miracle, Nish thinks? A chance to escape the annual ritual humiliation? Or, does this make everything worse?

Two scenes flash through his mind.

In one, he has the shared house to himself and is tucking into a Christmas lunch of leftover Dominoes while playing GTA in his boxers.

In the other, his well-meaning aunt asks his mother: 'How's Nish?'

She sighs and announces to the family: 'Oh, still in the same job, still no car, still unmarried, and now incapable of catching a train. After all these years of Covid and cancelled plans, he can't be bothered to come home. Tell me, what did I do wrong to deserve this?'

Yeah, it definitely makes everything worse. This is a crime for which he will be punished each year. 'Ah, make it this year, did you?' 'Nearly didn't recognise you in person.'

Nish lets his bags drop to the floor, raises his face to the sky and bellows a cry of anguish, channelling Charlton Heston in the closing scenes of Planet of the Apes. His voice echoes and reverberates around the cavernous space. A flock of shocked pigeons takes flight and wheels above the empty platforms.

He doesn't feel any better for the outburst, but some of the tension has gone from his body. It is what it is. He's going to have to call his parents, offer his profuse and profound apologies, and face their disappointment and humiliation head-on. He takes his phone out and is about to dial when—

'Excuse me, are you here for the train?'

'They're all cancelled,' Nish says. He hates how resigned he sounds. His super-successful cousin wouldn't take this lying down. No, he'd somehow make it through the snow. But not Nish the quitter.

'Then you're just in time.'

This time Nish looks up from his phone. The woman standing beside him is middle-aged with tufty white hair dyed blue. She's plump and short, kind of androgynous, with the pasty skin of someone who works night shifts and eats beige food from a work canteen. She wears a day-glow tabard over a Christmas jumper, a pattern of flashing sequins depicts a turkey with a tail fanned out and decorated with baubles, a bit like a peacock. On the fluorescent jacket is a GWR logo.

This isn't another disappointed passenger, this is – *whisper it* – salvation.

'Rail replacement bus, I'm afraid,' she says. 'But better than the big day ruined, eh?'

A smile breaks out on Nish's face. 'You're my Christmas miracle!'

2

Nish follows the woman through the deserted station, past the shuttered W.H. Smith, to a side-road where a dirty white minibus is waiting.

'Aren't rail replacement buses usually larger?' Nish had pictured a coach. Something straight out of Summer Holiday, minus a youthful Cliff Richard. But this, well, you'd struggle to fit more than twelve people.

'Last one we had available,' the woman, who turns out to be a bus driver, says. 'We've never had to put on so many buses. Do you think the great British public would forgive the railways if they didn't pull out all the stops on Christmas Eve? Especially after the last couple of years. Threw everything at Operation Save Christmas, didn't they? So, here you are, last bus out of Saigon.'

The bus driver slides open the passenger door and Nish ducks as he enters. Inside, the air smells of stale booze and someone's snoring.

'… I'm telling you babe some people don't think Die Hard's a Christmas film…'

The last words of conversation trail off. Nish looks pleadingly to his fellow passengers as he searches for an available seat. There's an Asian woman in her twenties, a bulging rucksack occupying the space next to her. There's a white man in his late thirties wearing skinny jeans, a Ralph Loren shirt buttoned to the collar, and a preppy jacket. He sits with a protective arm round a hard-shell suitcase. Behind him is a white woman of a similar age and a bag overspilling with luxuriously wrapped presents. There's a single seat, but it's occupied by a very large teddy bear, safely strapped in. The teddy bear has a smug look stitched onto its face. And then, at the back is the source of the smells and sounds. Nish can just about make out the slumped form of a portly man spread over three seats and out for the count.

Nish waits for a beat of three. He hopes that things will become sufficiently uncomfortable for one of his fellow travellers to make space for him. Everyone studiously avoids his eyes. Except for teddy, who couldn't look happier with his predicament. The count passes three, so Nish continues counting to five and braces himself for the inevitable climb to ten.

'Why don't you sit up front?' Skinny Jeans says, a hint of Essex wide-boy to his voice.

'Elf and safety,' says the bus driver, knowingly. Nish wouldn't be surprised if, hidden by the tabard, there's a 'hilarious' is-it-problem-drinking-or-is-it-my-whole-personality slogan on her Christmas jumper. Gin-gle bells. Let Christmas be-gin. My Christmas a-gin-da.

Skinny Jeans is about to protest when Nish says 'If we can move teddy, I can—'

'Where's he going to go?' Skinny Jeans says, an aggressive edge to his voice. 'He's a five-foot stuffed toy, you can't just plonk him anywhere.'

'He could ride up front,' Nish says. 'Shotgun.'

Both Skinny Jeans and the bus driver begin their well-reasoned protestations at this completely and outrageously inappropriate suggestion. The Asian woman sighs just loud enough to be overheard and slides her rucksack into the footwell by her feet.

'Thank you, that's very kind of you,' Nish says, looking at Skinny Jeans the whole time.

The bus driver counts the passengers, pointing at each in turn, silently forming the numbers with her mouth. Five. 'Still need a few more. I'll go find them, so just you wait here a little longer,' she says.

She's about to slide the door shut when Skinny Jeans speaks up. 'Oi, oi, oi, no mate. We've been waiting ages for this one. Besides, there's no more room at the inn.' He gestures round the seats of the minibus. Teddy looks ahead from his single seat, arms and legs spreadeagled as if he's riding a rollercoaster.

'Just three more people. Won't take long, I promise,' the bus driver says.

'Look around you,' the woman sitting behind Skinny Jeans says, a matching dose of estuary saturating her accent. 'There's no one. Place is dead. The train would've long gone.'

'The sooner I find them, the sooner we're on the road.' There's a strict edge to the driver's voice, but also a note of desperation. 'Have just a bit more patience, please.'

'Nah, screw this.' Skinny Jeans goes to stand. 'Come on Jess, we're getting outta here.'

'How we gonna get there, Steve?' Jess gestures with expensively manicured hands towards the bag of presents and five-foot teddy bear.

'I dunno, get an Uber, find a Zipcar, bloody walk. Anything's better than just sitting here like a lemon.'

'You wouldn't,' the bus driver says.

'Steve,' Jess says, urging caution.

But Steve is already out of his seat, unbuckling the bear.

'You won't find another way to leave,' the bus driver protests. 'Not with the weather like this. Not on Christmas Eve.'

'Just you watch me, mate,' Steve says. Teddy wriggles playfully in his seat as Steve struggles to free him.

'Steve,' Jess says, casting an imploring look at the closest figure she can find to authority.

The bus driver glances around, her control over the situation crumbling. Outside, the station is deserted. There's not a soul to be seen. Reluctantly, she makes a decision. 'Alright, alright. You're right, no one else is coming. Let's get this show on the road.'

'Yeah?' Says Steve, finally having unclipped teddy from the seatbelt.

'Yeah,' the bus driver says. 'You win. There's just the five of you tonight.' She gives the assembled travellers one last pensive look, as if mulling over some particularly tricky mental arithmetic.

'Alright,' Steve says, snapping the seatbelt back in place.

'Teddy makes six,' Jess says, flashing the bus driver a grateful smile.

Nish shares a look with the woman in the seat next to him. Her fine features are sketched out in the dim light of the minibus. She rolls her dark eyes. He smiles, sensing that he's only experiencing a fraction of the Jess-and-Steve show.

The defeated woman in the day-glow tabard slides into the driver's seat with a long exhalation of breath. She clips on her seatbelt and grips the steering wheel hard enough to turn her knuckles white. A moment passes before she turns the key and the engine judders to life, vibrating through the body of the minibus.

The radio comes on blaring Christmas music. 'Bah humbug, now that's too strong!' sing The Waitresses.

They drive through London's quiet streets. They pass red busses and black cabs, shops shut and dark with January sale signs already up in the windows. Christmas lights flicker from lampposts. Shimmering snowflakes and cantering reindeer and exploding crackers sketched out in LEDs. The roads glisten wetly, fresh grit crunching under the vehicle's tyres.

The Asian woman next to Nish puts on noise cancelling headphones and closes her eyes.

It's only as they cross Hyde Park that Nish really sees the snow. At night, the park is usually a black hole in the middle of the city, darkness stretching out beyond the event horizon of the streetlights. But not now. A thick layer of snow has settled over the grass. It ices the bare branches of the trees. The park is a dull and dirty orange as the snow glows with London's ambient light pollution.

They turn on to Kensington High Street and stop briefly at traffic lights. Ahead is a bus stop. Three people wait with hard-shell suitcases, hugging themselves against the cold.

As they wait for the light to turn green, Nish sees the distinctive outline of a stag in a shop window. It is cast in silhouette by the lights behind. The shop is closed and, in the background, two shadowy figures are man-handling a life-sized Santa to be put away for another year. The deer's nose glows red and its head and antlers rise as if to look back at him. The movement is so subtle and fluid he feels a surreal moment of dread. But then the illusion breaks, the display is animatronic.

The light turns and the minibus lurches forwards, only to come to a rapid halt, skidding a little as it does so.

'Easy mate,' says Steve, finding himself thrown forward in his seat.

A red London bus has pulled in at the stop ahead to collect the three shivering travellers. The driver mutters something under her breath before watching the bus signal and pull away.

Other than this close call with one of the few functioning elements of the public transport system, there's little other traffic and they make quick progress. The road widens out and rises as it becomes a motorway.

Darkness surrounds the minibus as London slips behind.

Nish checks his phone. There's a message from his father asking if he's going to be late. There's no question about whether he's going to make it, even though all trains out of the city are cancelled and the country is coated in snow. He'll probably never hear the end of it, but he'll remind them that he's better late than never. For what it's worth. This will just be one more symptom of his negligence as a less-than-dutiful son.

He messages back to say he'll give them an ETA as soon as he knows. He idly checks the BBC News. The main headline is: 'First white Christmas in London since 1999'. Bookies are due to pay out. In fact, they'd stopped taking bets the week before, when the Met Office had issued yellow weather warnings. The news quotes a woman looking forward to her payout. 'I felt it in my bones that this was the year,' she declares. 'So much for global warming, eh?' she gloats at the end of the interview. The BBC, committed to impartiality, reports without comment, but includes a link to a climate change explainer.

There's a selection of newspaper front pages. Flights across the UK have been cancelled. Trains out of Paddington and Waterloo have been cancelled and reduced services have run from Kings Cross and Euston. Gritters are out in force, but roads are blocked. Officials have issued guidance to travel only if absolutely necessary, and if you must travel, pack blankets, water and food. And maybe a spade. 'SNOWFLAKES!' declares the *Daily Express*. 'Not driving home for Christmas' mourns the *Daily Mail*. 'Climate disruption strands festive travellers,' announces *The Guardian*. 'Cold snap hits sales,' warns the *FT*.

There's a link to another BBC article: 'Santa well-prepared for travel chaos, leading scientist'. Sadly lacking in other distractions, Nish hate-reads the article, barely credulous about the elaborate lies the national broadcaster is complicit in at this time of year. 'Santa's plans won't be disrupted by a bit of snow,' said an eminent scientist from Cambridge University's Scott Polar Research Institute. 'His advanced technology allows him remotely monitor children's behaviour and wakefulness year-round, and we understand that the elves have been revising his route in real-time as parents' travel plans change. There's no need to worry, but according to my calculations the reindeer are going to need to expend around fourteen percent more energy in these weather conditions. So leave out an additional carrot to keep them going – and maybe an extra tot of brandy for Santa, because baby it's cold outside.'

See, Nish thinks, here's the thing with Santa Claus: he's an agent of capitalism through and through. The more frugal Father Christmas, with his pagan origins, has been chewed up and spat out by American consumerism. Dressed by Coca-Cola, deployed by brands across multiple media channels – from traditional to social – saturated through culture, and perfected over time with remorseless Darwinian logic to tap into pester power. Even pious old C.S. Lewis couldn't resist the siren call when Father Christmas rocks up in Narnia garbed in red with a sleigh-load of classically sexist presents. A sewing machine for Mrs Beaver? Seriously.

But it's Christmas Eve and soon enough that old guy is going to be put to sleep for the year. He might be good for business, he might pay Nish's bills, but the sooner he gets gone the better.

'You've taken a wrong turn, mate.' Steve, the man in skinny jeans, shouts to be heard over the radio.

'What?' the bus driver shouts back.

'Wrong turn,' Steve brandishes his phone, glowing in the dark to show a course plotted on Google Maps. 'You should have stayed on the motorway.'

'Bit of a diversion. There was an accident ahead.'

'Google's not showing anything.'

'Takes time to update, doesn't it?' the bus driver says, cheery now. 'It's going to take forever for the services to come out in this weather on Christmas Eve. Don't want to get stuck behind that.'

Steve grumbles assent.

The distraction has broken Nish's chain of thought. The snow-covered countryside around them is a shade lighter than pitch black. He can just about make out the horizon. Trees and hedgerows are negative black spaces cut out of deep navy blue. Through the front window he can see thick snowflakes caught in the headlights, curving towards the minibus as they drive onwards. It looks like they're moving at warp speed, even as the vehicle slows. The wipers brush fat splots from the windscreen before they can melt.

The drunk at the back snorts loudly, mumbles as if he's

about to wake, but settles down again and is soon back to more rhythmic snoring. Nish has got used to the alcohol-tainted air, but now he's reminded of the drunk's presence he can't ignore the smell of stale spirits.

Nothing better to do, he turns back to his phone. He's done with the news, so he starts scrolling through his social media feeds. Loading symbols spin, videos jerk to a halt after a fraction of a second, blank boxes mark where an image should be. The signal is terrible, even as the phone insists there's a trace of 4G. He gives up and watches the snow through the windscreen.

The woman next to him looks at her phone, starts fiddling with an app. Nish glances across, drawn like a moth to the source of light. She's navigating through a set of statements, stopping to pause and reflect on each, as if turning prayer beads.

Made a searching and fearless moral inventory of ourselves.

She pauses, her finger on the screen for a few moments, before flicking it away to the next.

Admitted to God, to ourselves and to another human being the exact nature of our wrongs.

Nish finds himself surprised. But what had he expected? A chain of WhatsApp messages and group chats finalising plans for New Year's Eve? Swiping through Tinder profiles, trying to find a distraction for Betwixtmas, the yawning chasm between Christmas and New Year? Browsing previews of the Boxing Day sales? Something about her youth, the way she dresses, the mundanity of a rail replacement bus on Christmas Eve stopped him from imagining she would be religious. Just goes to show you never know the richness or texture of someone else's inner life.

The screen is jerked out of his sight. He feels the woman looking at him – in the dark he can only see the whites of her eyes.

'Oh... Sorry, I wasn't— I didn't mean to, I...' his voice tails off as he realises he doesn't have a good explanation. 'It's kind of like a pub, you know, when your eyes are just drawn to a screen, no matter what.'

She gives him an impassive stare. Or, that's what he imagines he's on the receiving end of.

'Long drive, huh?' He says, squirming on the hook.

She heaves out a breath and says, 'I'm an alcoholic.'

Her words are fast and quiet. He almost misses them over

the roar of the road, the snuffling from the drunk on the backseat, and the squeak of the windscreen wipers.

Nish remembers the Sales Director slurring 'You ain't going nowhere till I've bought you a drink,' forcing a Jägerbomb on him before he could catch the tube home.

'It must be a tough time of year,' he says.

She laughs humourlessly. 'No kidding.'

'I mean, how do you escape from it in the run-up to Christmas? I'd have to live under a rock or something. Just, well, all the people who want to meet up after work, or go for a boozy lunch, or have a cheeky half before the train…' He pauses for a moment. 'Sorry, I'm rambling. I— I didn't mean to look. And you didn't have to…'

'One of the steps,' she says. 'Admit to yourself, then admit to others. I'm going to have to get used to it. I'm going to a retreat this year. Bunch of strangers dealing with our problems in a country house over Christmas. The first night is a group confessional. But since I'm going to be late, I might as well start with you. Not like I'm going to see you again if it goes badly.'

'Sounds like the perfect setting for a murder— Wait, am I the first?'

'You're not my first,' she says. There's an awkward moment while the double entendre hangs between them. She laughs, breaking the tension. 'Family, close friends, they know. Some knew before I did. But I guess you're the first total stranger, you know, out in the wild.' There's a pause before she adds: 'How was it for you?'

Nish heaves out a breath, a smile tugging at his lips. 'Good – I mean, heavy – and I was feeling guilty and bad about myself and all – but… Well, I've not done this before, which I guess makes you my first. How did I do?'

'You were just great,' she says with faux dismissiveness. 'Could have done with fewer reminders that I now need to live like a hermit. So, maybe work on that.'

Nish's laugh is cut short as the minibus jolts over something uneven and the driver slams on the brakes. A piercing feminine scream comes from behind. They're both forced forwards in their seats as the minibus skids on ice, jerks over more uneven ground, and then comes to an abrupt halt.

'Sorry 'bout that. Everyone alright?' the bus driver says cheerfully.

'What the bloody hell?' Says Steve, his voice rasping and dusky. He clears his throat and rubs at his neck.

Jess watches Steve with wide eyes in awe. 'I ain't never heard you make a sound like that, babe.'

'Okay folks, I'm just going to check what that was and we'll be back on the road soon as you know it.' There's a blast of icy air as the bus driver swings the door open and steps out into the snowscape.

'You alright?' Nish asks the woman next to him.

'Yeah, just a bit shaken. I wasn't ready for that.'

Nish sits back in his seat, heaves a sigh. 'Yeah, tell me about it. Don't know what's worse – the whiplash or the tinnitus after…'

She laughs.

'I'm Nish, by the way' he says. 'Nice to meet you.'

'Effie,' she says. 'Do we shake hands now or something?'

Before they can resolve this great quandary of etiquette, the bus driver reopens the door. Her face, cast in the dim yellow light of the cab, shows a strange repressed excitement. 'I've got some good news and some bad news, folks. Which do you want first…? Well, bad news first, eh? The sweetener to follow will soften the blow. That's the traditional way. Well, we're stuck here. Sorry. A tyre's blown and the axel looks like it's thrown. I'm going to need to call the recovery service. But, good news: there's a pub. The lights are on, so looks like somewhere warm we can wait.'

Nish checks his phone to see the time. It's just gone nine, but the glimmer of 4G has now disappeared. Maybe the pub has wifi and he'll be able to keep his parents updated? By the light cast of his screen, he catches the look on Effie's face. It takes a moment to make the connection, but then he understands. A pub. This is the last thing she needs.

'You'll be alright. I'll keep an eye out for you,' he says. 'Unless that's unhelpful. And not in a creepy stalker way. I'm not Sting.'

Her smile is forced. 'And this is why I don't play the lottery.'

'At least things can't get any worse,' he says.

'Guess you've not seen The Hills Have Eyes.'

The passengers slowly climb out of the minibus. The road curves out ahead, climbing up a hill in the distance, caked in pristine snow. Beside the road there's a steep bank capped with a thin leafless hedgerow and a few bare oaks.

There's some debate about whether to leave bags and

presents in the minibus, but a consensus quickly emerges as they stand in the cold waiting for the driver to rouse the drunk.

'Who's going to nick stuff out here on a night like this?' Jess says. 'It's Christmas Eve. Thieves got families too, you know.'

'No good hanging around, I could murder a pint. C'mon, I'll race you. Last one to the bar's buying!' Steve claps his hands together and climbs through a gap in the hedgerow to take the shortest route towards the pub. The snow is deep and reaches up to his shins. His purposeful stride soon becomes a slow frog march.

Jess staggers after him.

'It's bloody freezing, babe!'

The cold bites at Nish's face and hands as he carefully climbs up the gnarled roots of the bank. The snow continues to fall with a white noise like radio static. In the distance, hazed by snow and shrouded in darkness, he sees a small cluster of low stone buildings. Nearby a church spire towers over rows of snow-dusted yew trees, its small graveyard surrounded by dry-stone walling iced with a thick layer of snow like a Christmas cake. And there, across what must be a village green, is a pub.

Not just a pub, but a picture-postcard, quintessential, archetypal countryside pub. A wide, low building of honey-yellow stone, with outcrops of gable-ended dormers peeking out of the snow-capped roof. Nish can just about make out the shape of picnic tables in front of the pub and a low picket fence. A swing-sign hangs in a high wooden frame at the perimeter of the beer garden. The ground floor lights are on, glowing, warm and inviting behind shutters. A plume of smoke carries out of the chimney, low in the air and drifting on the wind.

Effie climbs up behind him.

'They'd better have some chestnuts roasting on that open fire,' Nish says.

Effie says nothing. She heaves out a ragged sigh, her breath frosting.

Steve and Jess have become little flailing figures, arms wide to keep their balance. Their giggles echo and distort across the expanse. The snow flattens perspective making it impossible to judge distance. The village green stretches and warps, becoming a vast desert, the pub a far-off mirage of safety and comfort.

Meanwhile, the driver has managed to rouse the drunk. He staggers out of the minibus, bleary and uneven, like a newborn foal. He looks at the scene around them, blinks twice, swipes idly at the falling snow. 'Where dis?'

'C'mon, just need to get you inside for a bit while we wait for someone to fix the bus,' the driver says with forced cheeriness. She shuts the sliding door and presses the lock button on a key fob. The minibus beeps twice, its indicator lights casting orange haloes in the falling snow.

The bus driver pauses for a moment and peers closer at the drunk. 'Say, don't you have a familiar face now? Do you look like someone famous?'

'I dun… Wha?' The drunk mutters, confused and disorientated.

'Okay, walk with me and we'll get you somewhere warm. You remind me of someone, but I can't for the life of me remember who. It'll come to me, I know it will. There's a pub over there. I'll expect you like pubs don't you?' The driver ushers the drunk up the road rather than over the green.

'You okay?' Nish says to Effie. She's staring with foreboding at the pub.

'I'm going to have to be. How long do you think we'll need to wait?'

'Where even are we?'

Effie looks around, taking in the rest of the scene. Behind them, the deep tracks from the minibus's sudden stop are being filled in by the settling snow. To one side is a road sign. Effie steps down from the bank to get a better look, careful not to lose her balance.

'Little Slaughter,' she says, loud enough for Nish to hear.

'Wha choo say?' The drunk shouts, stopping in his tracks some way down the road.

'Just the village name,' Nish calls back.

The driver tries to quietly cajole the drunk onwards, but he's stubbornly rooted to the spot.

'Wha?'

'This village. It's called Little Slaughter.'

The bus driver reaches out to take the drunk by the arm, but he's fast and strong. He pushes her into the snow. She falls back spreadeagled in the powder as if making a snow angel.

Freed, the drunk staggers back up the road, his feet skittering and sliding on ice.

Nish's brain is very slowly processing the strangeness of this turn of events. He steps down from the bank, gingerly plotting a route to intercept the drunk, but the man's too fast. The drunk steers wide and passes Nish in a whiff of stale spirits.

'You're going the wrong way,' Effie says.

The drunk pauses momentarily to glance at the village sign then back at Effie. His eyes are wild and wide, bloodshot, with pupils like saucers.

'Der gon kill ush all!' The drunk's voice cracks as he screams his warning.

Effie blinks twice.

'Stop him!' the bus driver shouts from further up the road.

The man breaks into a run, staggering through the compressed snow left by the minibus with surprising speed. 'Save yerselves!' He shouts into the night air.

And then he's gone, vanished into the blizzard.

3

Inside the pub, the air is warm and dry and laced with woodsmoke. A fire burns and crackles in the inglenook fireplace. The unmistakeable aroma of roasting meat wafts through from the kitchen.

Despite being the very essence of cosy Christmas comfort and cheer, the inn is virtually empty. The weather will have encouraged people to stay at home.

The building is hundreds of years old, but well-maintained. For centuries, the wide lounge would have been two rooms – a bar for the men and a family saloon for the women and children. But it's been opened up to become a long lounge with gnarled brick pillars. Old blackened oak beams stretch across the ceiling, decorated with garlands of dried hops. The walls are roughly plastered, tinted off-white with traces of nicotine from before the smoking ban. Horse brasses, Toby jugs, and framed vintage photos cover virtually every spare surface. A hunter's horn hangs from one beam. Nish pictures riders in white and red dismounting their horses, surrounded by a sea of foxhounds, to quench the thirst they built chasing their quarry through the countryside. The windows are shuttered from the inside with wooden blinds, painted off-white to complement the shade of the walls. Two slot machines glitter incongruously in a corner.

The pub is decked out for Christmas. There's a fake pine tree – one of the old-fashioned kind that doesn't even try to disguise the fact it's made from plastic and wire – laced with flashing lights and gold tinsel. Presents spill from underneath, boxes in fusty paper held together with yellowing tape. An ancient angel perches on top, her crown brushing the low ceiling. She looks for all the world like a repurposed toilet roll doll with her wide square skirt concealing the tip of the tree.

Stockings – boot-shaped faux footwear in gaudy reds and greens, rather than hosiery – hang from the walls of the deep fireplace. Homemade paper chains loop between the exposed beams.

The effect is of an austere Christmas past revived with sincerity rather than kitsch irony.

At the bar, one of the pump clips advertises a seasonal special. A cartoon reindeer brandishes a vicious dagger, with its antlers arranged into an elaborate crown and a glowing red LED for a nose. The beer is named 'Rudolph's Revenge', an imperial ale weighing in with the kind of ABV that bushy-bearded craft ale aficionados might describe as 'full-bodied', or 'punchy', or even 'challenging'.

Steve and Jess stand at the long oak bar, being served by the landlord, a man wearing a monocle and the kind of purple jacket you might more commonly see on a daytime gameshow host. As with the Christmas decorations, the effect is sincere rather than ironic.

It's been a long time since Nish has been away from the heavy, tired irony of hipster London. There's something refreshing about people who are doing a thing without drolly rolling their eyes about how they are 'LOL doing a thing'.

A sweaty pint of Rudolph's Revenge sits on the bar in a dimpled glass tankard. The landlord finishes fixing a bowl of gin and tonic, light on the ice, heavy on the gin and gives Steve the price.

'Bloody hell, d'you know how much that'd cost in London?'

'From the big smoke, eh? Travelling home for Christmas are you?'

'Something like that,' Steve says, holding out his phone.

The landlord looks at the phone for a moment, then back at Steve. 'Cash only, governor.'

Steve is stumped. 'Cash?' he says, as if processing an alien concept. 'Mate, I haven't carried cash in years.'

'What are you, the Queen?' It's a joke, yet there's a hard edge to the landlord's voice. But then he has a change of heart. 'Sorry, where's my Christmas spirit? These are on the house.'

'Really?' Jess says, pausing in the act of rifling through her handbag.

'Been a good couple of years for the pub,' the landlord says. 'You city folks coming all this way out for socially distanced walks in the countryside. Plenty of space on the village green most of the year round. Served takeaway drinks from the beginning of the pandemic, then started doing food outside soon as we could. You lot loved it. Couldn't get enough of our country air and hospitality. Perhaps it's all change now things are opening up, but I reckon people'll be back, filling their lungs with our clean country air. So, Merry Christmas.'

'Well, cheers,' Steve says. He raises his glass and takes a slurp.

'Wouldn't kill you to leave a good review on Trip Advisor now would it?' the landlord says.

'Five stars, the minute I get some signal.'

'Signal's been terrible since the fire.'

'Fire?'

'The 5G radio mast. Caught alight one night, most mysterious.' The landlord offers a sly grin. 'If the World Economic Forum think they can infect us with their plandemic, they've got another think coming.'

'You showed them, mate.' Steve laughs uneasily. 'Here, you got Wi-Fi at all?'

'We're a pub. If people want to look at their screens all day, they can stay at home.'

Jess and Steve take their drinks and look for somewhere to sit. The tables have been brought together to form a long row, places set for food. Crackers sit beside each place. Dotted along the tables are individual candles wrapped in tinsel, miniature fire hazards to keep diners alert. Four villagers sit at the tables closest to the fire, dressed like familiar, yet unplaceable, caricatures.

The vicar is perhaps the least out there. He's in full black smock with a tidy white dog collar. He might look in keeping with the sleepy village vibes, were it not for the fact that he's in his early 30s with a buzz-cut, easily over six-foot tall and built with the kind of muscular athleticism and year-round tan of a man used to hard physical labour. It's not impossible that he's the village vicar, it's just very, very unlikely.

Next to him is a young blonde woman, squeezed into a bright red dress with a décolletage like the swell of two perfectly baked Victoria sponges at a village fete. The amount of flesh she's showing is inversely proportional to her proximity to the raging fire.

Opposite her is a pale white woman in her thirties, but dressed like a grande dame several decades more senior. Her outfit is entirely white, with hints of faded glamour. She wears a white jacket, a ruffled silk blouse, a vintage cream stole that may even be real fur, and drips with pearl earrings and necklace. So committed is she to the look, she's dusted her brown bob with chalk to give herself an almost spectral appearance.

And finally there's a robust elder statesman, in his sixties, perhaps. Certainly old enough to be approaching retirement or recently retired, but with a kind of outdoorsy vigour that belies his age. He's decked out in a tweed three-piece suit, the pattern a little heavy on the yellow. He sports a pair of wire-rimmed glasses and a bald pate.

The villagers regard the new arrivals with silent interest. The vicar glances towards the window, but his view is blocked by the wooden blinds. It's as if they're waiting for someone to arrive.

'Ever feel like you've stepped into an episode of Midsummer Murders,' Nish says under his breath.

'They're playing Cluedo,' Effie says.

'What?' Nish looks at the villagers with fresh eyes and now he sees it. Reverend Green is perhaps the least obvious, but Miss Scarlet, Colonel Mustard, Mrs White and—

'And what can I get for you?' says Professor Plum from behind the bar.

'I'll have a lemonade, please,' Effie says.

'Make that two lemonades.'

'You do know it's Christmas, right? It's on the house. Don't want something more warming? Nice mulled wine, maybe?' Professor Plum says as if confused by the concept of soft drinks.

'Long journey ahead,' Nish says.

'It's going to take a long time to get a mechanic out here on a night like this,' Professor Plum says. 'Might as well make yourselves comfortable.'

Steve and Jess must have told him about the breakdown when they arrived.

'You think we can ask Father Christmas for a ride?' Nish says.

The joke earns him a stony look. 'Be careful what you wish for,' Professor Plum says as he produces two ferociously fizzing half-pint glasses.

Drinks in hand, Nish and Effie join Steve and Jess hovering beside the long table.

'Room for one more player, babe,' Jess says to Steve in a sultry voice.

Steve growls like a dog guarding his territory.

The pub door swings open and the bus driver steps in from the cold, face bright red from exertion and cold, clothes damp from the fall in the snow. There's a howl of wind as the door shuts.

The villagers turn towards the new arrival with expectant looks. The pub falls silent, except for the ubiquitous Christmas music. Chris Rea croons about being stuck in tailbacks, but at least he's moving.

'Where are the others?' Professor Plum says.

'There's only one more,' the bus driver says, meek and apologetic. She looks like she's wilting under the villagers' attention.

Miss Scarlet and Reverend Green exchange a look. Mrs White leans close and whispers something in the Reverend's ear. His face remains stony and impassive, but he clenches his jaw as if mustering steely determination.

'One?' says Professor Plum. 'I thought you were a rail replacement bus? How can there only be five passengers?'

Nish senses something change in Effie's body language, just out of his field of vision.

'And where is this fifth passenger?' Colonel Mustard says, asserting his authority.

'Outside,' the bus driver says, looking at her feet. 'Something spooked him and he was off like a steam train. I went after him, but it was no good, I couldn't keep up. Wouldn't have thought it for the state of him.'

'He'll freeze to death,' Effie says. 'We should form a search party or something.'

The suggestion causes some disturbance amongst the villagers. They talk amongst themselves in hushed tones.

'I'm not going out there again,' Steve says to Jess, just loud enough for everyone to hear.

'You lost him, you should go find him,' says Professor Plum. He gives the driver an icy stare.

'I'll catch my death,' she says, shivering to underline her point. 'Far better if it were someone who knows the area. Someone who can work out where he might have gone.'

'We can't go,' Mrs White says, indicating herself and the

Reverend. 'Wouldn't want to ruin the feast. What about you?' she says to Miss Scarlet. 'You know this place like the back of your hand.'

Miss Scarlet's eyes are wide in shock. Of all the gathered, she's the least well-dressed for an excursion into the bitter cold outside.

'We can do it,' Effie says.

'We can?' Nish says, having been quite comfortable enough to sit this one out.

'Sure,' Effie says, eyes flashing as if trying to convey something to Nish. 'Everyone's settled in, but it won't be any hassle for us.'

There's outcry from the villagers, all at once. 'You couldn't possibly.' 'Catch your death of cold.' 'You're our guests.'

'That's very kind of you, but it's not fair to send you back out into the snow,' says Colonel Mustard. 'Make yourselves comfortable. The bus driver and I will sort out this predicament, isn't that right? Wouldn't want GWR to hang you out to dry with charges of incompetence – criminal neglect – *manslaughter* – now would you?'

There's something about the Colonel's booming voice, clear enunciation, absolute confidence in his responsibility to organise and direct makes Nish almost certain he's a teacher. Even if he's retired, teachers never really stop. It's as much a state of mind as a vocation.

'I suppose so,' the bus driver concedes, wilting under the pressure.

Mrs White checks her watch, an ornate silver band on her wrist entirely in keeping with the fusty faded glamour of her costume. 'Be careful, you don't have long,' she says as Colonel Mustard stands.

'We won't be long. I doubt he's got far.'

Colonel Mustard shrugs on a large khaki coat, double-breasted and fitted. Say what you like about the villagers' sincerity, their eye for detail is impressive. The only thing missing from his costume is a rifle, Nish thinks. There's one incongruous detail, however: he wears a pair of athletic-looking trail shoes, rather than the more obvious choice of Doc Martins or knee-high jackboots. The heavy snow must have dictated some of his sartorial choices.

'Once more into the breach, eh?' He says, slapping a chummy hand on the bus driver's shoulder.

'"I am just going outside and may be some time,"' says the

bus driver with an air of resignation. 'That's what he said, wasn't it? Scott, that man who ate the huskies.'

'It was Oates and he hadn't eaten any huskies. Those were the last words of someone who had realised he'd become a terrible burden on his colleagues.'

Yes, thinks Nish, definitely a teacher. And quite possibly one who lamented the end of corporal punishment.

The bus driver exhales slowly, like a party balloon left too long. 'Barkeep, keep a mulled wine warm for me when I get back. I'll need something to regain the feeling in my extremities.'

Professor Plum scowls and is on the cusp of responding—

Until the Colonel addresses him directly: 'We'll be back soon enough, with company. Keep our guests… entertained.'

The Colonel swings open the door. The wooden arch and porch frame a perfect white snowscape. The light spilling from the pub illuminates eddies and whorls of heavy snow. A chill wind blows in. And then the explorers are gone out into the night.

4

'Might as well make yourselves at home,' Professor Plum says, stepping out from behind the bar to take the Colonel's seat next to Mrs White.

'Mind if I stick my phone on charge?' Jess says.

'Be my guest.'

And so the visitors proceed to seek out plug sockets. They each produce chargers from handbags and jacket pockets, and scatter their devices around the pub. Nish can't shake the concern that someone's going to steal his phone. Years of London life have made him deeply suspicious of anyone getting close to his personal belongings.

Steve and Jess drag out seats, leaving a spare place between themselves and Mrs White.

'Aren't you expecting more people?' Nish says, indicating the place settings.

Mrs White gives the deserted pub a forlorn look. 'We were hoping for more.'

'We knew this would happen sooner or later,' the Reverend says. His voice is deep and rasping. It sounds like a spade being dragged over gravel.

'There's still time,' Miss Scarlet says, quietly pleading.

'Stay close with me,' the Reverend says, clenching his lantern jaw.

Mrs White reaches for the Reverend's hand on the table, but he picks up his glass and drains the last of his drink.

Nish and Effie take seats at the table, facing Steve and Jess. Steve is half-way through his pint, tidemarks of foam cataloguing each hearty swig.

'What's with the outfits?' Steve says, pointing at the villagers.

'Babe,' Jess hisses, as if she's told him more than once that it's rude to demand answers of strangers.

'What, no, they definitely don't normally wear that stuff. So, what's with 'em?'

'It's the annual murder mystery night,' says Reverend Green, tugging at his dog collar where it cuts into his thick-muscled neck.

'I told you, babe. Oh I do love a good murder.'

Steve eyes up the Reverend, a few years younger, a few inches taller, and stronger by half. Steve's been to the gym, he's done his burpees and his curls and his deadlifts. Each morning he scrutinises himself in the harsh bathroom spotlights, assessing the bits that go in and the bits that go out. He's making gains for sure, but his definition is more NTSC than 4K. His soft edges are stubbornly hard to shift. But he doesn't feel threatened or envious of the preening young lads down the gym, the ones with abs like ice cube trays, lats so wide they crab-walk through doorways, and biceps that demand specialist tailoring. They're just vain pretty boys. Steve's an elder statesman in the parliament of pain. A dad-bod amongst the teenagers. What he lacks in definition, he makes up for in natural dominance.

But this Reverend, he's the real deal. Strong and functional. Masculine with an easy unpretentious edge. Steve's natural instinct is to assert his authority. He reminds himself of the mantra he utters in the mirror each morning. 'You're the alpha in any situation.'

'Well whodunnit then?' Steve says.

'It'll be Miss Scarlet in the lounge with the lead piping, same as every year,' says Mrs White.

A flash of shock passes over Miss Scarlet's face and she seems to shrink into her chair like a shamed schoolgirl.

The Reverend gives Mrs White an icy look.

'Oops sorry,' Mrs White says. 'Spoiler.'

'Sounds like one hell of a party.' Steve downs the rest of his pint as an uncomfortable silence settles around the table. A log cracks in the fire and East 17's Stay Another Day begins to play faintly through the pub's sound system. 'Don't suppose your Christmas spirit would stretch to another one of these, eh?'

Professor Plum looks over at Steve and holds his eye for a moment. He's about to reply when a rasping buzzer goes off in another room. Miss Scarlet, checks her watch, stands, tugs her skirt down, and makes her way to the kitchen. As the door swings open, the rich aroma of roast meat thickens.

'Ooh, that smells lush,' Jess says.

'Our village tradition,' says Mrs White. The tension melts like brandy butter. It happens so quickly it's almost as if Nish imagined it. 'Every Christmas Eve, we get together in The Slaughter House—'

'The where?' Effie says, eyes wide.

'The pub's name, innit?' Steve says. 'Didn't you see the sign?'

Professor Plum looks Steve up and down and finds something there that he likes. He gives a thin-lipped smile and stands, collect's Steve's empty glass and makes his way to the bar.

'I guess I didn't,' Effie says.

'Every Christmas Eve, the whole village gets together. We have a murder mystery, a meal, a few drinks… Of course, this year we've got fewer players than we'd like.' Mrs White glances round the table. 'But you'll go some way towards making up numbers.'

There's a moment of silence.

'How long do you think the recovery vehicle will be?' Nish asks.

Jess gives Nish a pitying look. Even with the best of luck, it will be hours before they're back on the road. 'Of course we will,' she says, volunteering the visitors as players for the villagers' game. 'It'll help kill the time.'

Mrs White offers a warm, wide smile. 'Oh, I'm so pleased. It's so nice to have some fresh blood.'

'But we can't pay you,' Nish says. 'None of us have any cash.'

'Your company's payment enough,' Mrs White says, laughing with a jollity that borders on the manic. 'And besides, it's Christmas and there's plenty of room at the inn.'

'Thank you. That's very generous of you,' Jess says to Mrs White. Then, more quietly, to Nish: 'Don't look a gift horse in the mouth, eh?'

Something about the combination of generosity and eccentricity is setting Nish on edge. He glances at Effie and sees an expression of suppressed alarm. At least he's not alone.

'Come now,' Mrs White says brightly. 'You must tell me about your glamorous lives in London.'

Professor Plum places a fresh pint in front of Steve, suddy

foam tracing down the side of the glass. And so, the four of them launch into a long and, truth be told, quite tedious conversation about London life. Steve, it transpires, works in sales in a fintech business based in Dalston. Jess, meanwhile, works in human resources for an obscure department of an obscure multinational company with a mission to spread delight that somewhat belies its presence in administrative services and hygiene.

'And tell me, do you all work from home now?' Mrs White says at one point. 'I should imagine I would quite miss the office. But if you can just do your work sat up in bed, well, I'd wonder you all aren't the size of houses.'

Effie stands and checks her phone.

'Anything?' Nish asks.

'Nothing,' Effie says.

The kitchen door opens and Miss Scarlet calls through. 'We're ready. Give us a hand.'

There's some general fussing as the visitors are implored to remain seated while the villagers bring the food through.

'She's one of them,' Effie says to Nish, under her breath.

'Who?' Nish whispers back.

Steve's voice booms across the pub, the sound of a man making conscientious small-talk. 'Guess some of the villagers stayed home this year.'

'Can't blame them in this weather,' Jess says.

'Do you think they've found the drunk guy yet?' Nish says.

Steve shrugs. 'Bloody stupid thing to do. Won't have got far in these conditions.'

Nish wants to ask Effie who she was talking about, but the kitchen door swings open again and the villagers come through bearing trays of food. There's a goose, its skin golden and crisp, fat still sizzling in a roasting tray full of stuffing balls. Then there's a dish of pigs in blankets and devils on horseback, tight-packed morsels wrapped in crisped bacon. And a tower of roast potatoes, sunshine yellow with brittle edges and a light dusting of coarse black pepper. Sprouts come through, too, in a serving dish that billows with steam, fine sliced and speckled with lardons. Thin fingers of parsnips and carrots are interlaced, glazed and sticky. A bruise-purple bowl of red cabbage glistening with swollen sultanas and heady with port. A bubbling and blistered cauliflower cheese, unctuous and oozing. A vast pitcher of thick gravy, a rainbow coating of oil sparkling in the pub lights. And finally, steaming florets of purple-sprouting broccoli scattered with flaked almonds.

'Well, I hope you're hungry,' Professor Plum says, putting two freshly opened bottles of wine on the table. 'Red or white?'

He passes round the table, filling glasses liberally, until he gets to Effie.

'Not for me, thanks,' she says.

'C'mon, it's Christmas.'

'No, really, it's fine.'

'You gonna wash this down with lemonade?'

'Look, I'm not—'

'Just a little something to charge your glass.'

'I don't drink.' Effie says, firm and definitive.

Professor Plum stands back at this. He licks his dry lips and looks Effie up and down. 'I see. I'm a small business owner, but I don't suppose that means anything to you, does it? You know what dry January is? It's a death sentence for places like this. Barely any point in opening at all. If we don't have a good December, we might not open again. But I don't suppose that matters at all to you.'

'You haven't charged anyone for a single drink… and now all this,' Effie indicates the table generously loaded with enough food for a gathering twice the size. 'What gives?'

Professor Plum bristles with barely restrained anger. He speaks slowly, carefully punctuating his response with gaps as if he's navigating a precarious route between righteous anger and outright hostility. 'I have never, in all my life, had my hospitality thrown back at me by such an ungrateful—'

'I'm vegan,' Nish blurts.

'You're what?' Professor Plum's face has turned puce.

'I— I'm vegan.'

'Vegan,' the landlord repeats. He turns to the Reverend. 'You hear that? A vegan.'

'As I live and breathe,' Reverend Green's voice is a blade against a whetstone. He shakes his head, a vein pulsing at his temple. His eyes are hard like blackened diamonds and he prickles with the energy of a prize fighter waiting for the bell. 'A vegan.'

Mrs White emits a forced laugh, utterly incongruous with the foul atmosphere that has settled over the long table. 'Ah, don't mind him, he's the village butcher. Lovely sausages, you should— Well, of course not. Imagine that, a teetotaller at the pub and a vegan at the feast? Will you London folk ever stop surprising us?'

'People ask me what I think about veganuary,' the Reverend says.

Nish briefly considers reminding the butcher that no-one has asked such a thing. Nish might have been a fool to make up a dietary restriction on the spot to try to save Effie, but he's no desire to draw out this torture for the sake of pedantic point-scoring.

'And I'm fine with it, honestly,' says the Reverend who is also a butcher. 'I mean, philosophically, I take it as a sign that society's becoming more puritanical. People are just looking for ways to punish themselves for past excesses. But you know what, so long as they have their excesses, it's all good to me. Sure, have your turducken one month and lentil gruel the next... But so long as you're having a three-bird-roast, it works out alright for me. I can take the month off. But when you people cut meat out entirely for no good reason, well, then I struggle not to take it personally.' He rests hands the size of hams on the table, knuckles chapped and cracked, and looks directly at Nish with dark malevolence. 'Why are you vegan?'

'The animals,' Nish says. 'I can't bear the cruelty.'

'Are you saying I'm cruel?'

'No,' Nish says. But now he's thinking about it, the answer is very much yes. Menace and violence hang in the air around the butcher-dressed-as-a-vicar like the aroma of Lynx Africa on a teenaged boy. Nish wishes he hadn't put himself in the man's way. 'No, not at all. I just like animals, that's all.'

'I like animals,' Reverend Green says. 'Little furry ones. Little feathered ones. Curly-tailed ones too. With their little bleats and cheeps and oinks and their little doe eyes. They're all delicious.'

Miss Scarlet playfully punches the Reverend on the arm. 'Stop playing around or the food'll get cold.'

The Reverend cracks a smile laced with menace as he brandishes a carving knife and two-pronged meat fork. 'Well, all the more for the rest of us.'

As he stands at the head of the table to carve the meat, demanding the remaining carnivores' plates be passed down for loading with slices of goose, Effie quietly and apologetically declares herself to also be a vegan.

'Two vegans?' Mrs White declares with exactly the kind of comic shriek that Mrs Bracknell might screech 'A handbag' in a particularly exuberant production of *The Importance of Being Earnest*.

There is some discussion between the two vegans and Mrs White about what they can eat.

'What about goose fat? Not even a little bit? Oh dear, well no potatoes for you, then. The parsnips and carrots are honey-roast,' Mrs White says apologetically. 'How are you about bees?'

'Bees?' Effie says.

'Yes, they're animals. They weren't harmed, but…'

'They didn't give their honey willingly,' Nish says, finding the words that Mrs White seemed unable to say.

Effie looks at Nish, down at the dish of roast root vegetables, back at Mrs White. She contemplates the crispy caramelised edges, the aroma warm and sweet like a summer's breeze. 'The poor souls. I find it unconscionable.'

'Me too,' says Nish. In for a penny, in for a pound. 'If anything, it's exploitation of labour.'

'What are you people, Marxists?' Professor Plum says, pouring gravy over his meat.

Mrs White plants her hands on her hips and chews her lip as she contemplates the conundrum. 'Well, I suppose you'll be sharing the broccoli. Good job I didn't glaze it with butter this year or you'd have been on bar nuts.'

The Reverend hands plates piled with sliced and steaming meat down the table.

Steve gives his an appreciative sniff before leaning over to help himself to generous portions of all the trimmings – barring broccoli. He pops a parcel of bacon into his mouth and chews thoughtfully. 'So, vegans, huh? You don't eat honey. Where do you stand on truffles?'

'Truffles?'

'Find 'em with pigs, don't they? That "exploitation" of their labour too?'

'Of course,' Effie says. 'Do the pigs have a choice in the matter?'

'If they're any good, they won't end up like this.' Steve skewers a bacon-wrapped sausage on his fork, holds it briefly aloft, before shovelling it into his mouth.

'Could you kill an animal?' the Reverend says, grasping the carving knife.

'No,' Nish says, pleased to find himself on certain ground. 'That's kind of the point of being vegan.'

'Not even if it attacked you?'

'I've never been attacked by an animal. I guess I'd run away?'

'Can you run fast?' Professor Plum asks.

Nish laughs. 'If I was being chased by an animal, pretty fast I'd reckon.'

Professor Plum folds his arms and looks Nish up and down. 'Hmm, skinny lad like him, might be fast too, you know.'

'What if it was a pack of predators?' The Reverend watches Nish and Effie with a predatory intensity. 'Fast ones. Not going to outrun them are you?'

'Vicious, too,' Miss Scarlet adds. 'They'd work together. Surround you. Start closing in.'

'Until first blood,' Mrs White says, pouring thick gravy on to Jess's plate. 'After that, they go crazy. All teeth and foaming mouths. Maybe they'd go straight for the kill, be merciful and quick. But sometimes beasts like to play.'

'Kill or be killed,' the Reverend picks up the thread again. 'What would you do?'

The pub falls silent. The wind howls outside. In the void, Nish realises he's not worried about a pack of dogs or wolves or whatever. That's hypothetical fantasy. No, he's worried about being stranded in a village in the middle of nowhere with a bunch of psychotic murder mystery cosplayers. The inn no longer feels like a sanctuary in the storm.

'What time is it?' Professor Plum says.

Mrs White glances at her silver watch. 'Late.'

'They best be back soon before the game begins. I'll just go double-check the children are safe.'

Nish is grateful that the subject of conversation has changed, but there's something off that makes him watch Professor Plum a bit more closely than he would otherwise. There are hints of childhood in the pub – the stockings, the festoons of paper chains, the presents under the tree – but it's a childhood long past. Professor Plum kicks at something hidden behind the bar. The Professor looks dissatisfied and ducks out of sight. There's the sound of something heavy and metallic being rolled across the floor, and then being set firmly in place on a flat side. Nish pictures a keg, full of beer—

'Is it just me?' Effie says, her voice hushed.

'Sorry, I didn't catch that.'

'I don't like this,' Effie says. 'I've got a bad feeling about all this.'

Nish feels the same. It's all been a bit too Royston Vasey for his liking. But all the same, he's promised Effie that he's going to keep an eye on her and letting her know he's worried isn't going to help. They're here now, stranded in the snow. Blissful acceptance is the only viable option – until a way to get the hell out of dodge presents itself. Then the villagers will see just how fast he can run.

'It'll be fine,' Nish says, mustering all the conviction he can manage. 'Lockdown turned people a bit feral, that's all. I've seen this before and it's fine. An uncle on my father's side went full conspiracy theorist after he spent the pandemic on Facebook. He's harmless enough, just don't get him on to the topic of low-traffic neighbourhoods. We'll be out of here soon.'

'More wine for you two?' Professor Plum says, standing behind Steve and Jess. He's already pouring before either of them have had a chance to reply.

'Wonderful,' Steve says around a half-chewed mouthful.

Jess laughs self-consciously. 'I should slow down, really.'

'It's Christmas,' the Professor booms, finishing pouring Steve a very large glass of red. 'Don't want any of this going to waste now do you?'

Effie watches Professor Plum return to his seat and place the opened bottles back on the table beside his own virtually untouched glass. She leans closer to Nish, holds her glass to her mouth to hide the movement of her lips, and asks the question he's been trying not to think about. 'Why are there children in the cellar?'

5

'You know some people don't think that Die Hard's a Christmas film?' Steve says, making small-talk as he loads his fork.

'Well of course it's not,' Mrs White says. 'All that shooting and swearing.'

'Only an idiot would think it wasn't.' Miss Scarlet accompanies her words with a scornful laugh, aimed at Mrs White. 'No offence, of course. The landlord here watches it every year. He insists it's not Christmas Day until Hans Gruber has hit the ground outside Nakatomi Plaza.'

'How's that going down?' Mrs White says to Steve, changing subject abruptly.

'Mmit'sh mmdelishus,' Steve says, his jaw working overtime on a particularly large forkful of roast potato and goose.

'You'd like some more? There's plenty to go around.'

'I'll have no room for the big meal tomorrow,' Steve protests, his eye straying towards the succulent brown meat of a fat drumstick. 'Got to save something for Christmas, eh?'

Mrs White gives Steve a doting look. 'My nana used to say "You never know what meal's going to be your last", god rest her soul.'

'Wise woman. What the hell, maybe I will – just a little. How'd she go?'

'Coronary.'

'Terrible,' Steve says, shaking his head. 'Think anyone'll want that crispy skin?'

'They've all had their chance.' Mrs White offers Steve the

kind of smile a doting mother might reserve for a favourite child. 'Help our guest out, would you?' She hands Steve's plate to Miss Scarlet.

Miss Scarlet offers a lascivious smile and bats her eyelids. 'I like a man with an appetite.'

Steve watches with hungry eyes as Miss Scarlet stands. Her red dress accentuates her hourglass figure and the warm lighting of the pub casts deep shadows as she leans over the table. He notices her fine-boned hands, her nails painted a Porsche red, as she reaches for the carving knife. She grazes the handle with her fingers before grasping it, firm and confident. Steve's mind is running like a hare when she looks up and meets his eyes, a sultry smile tugging at her lips. 'Now you just tell me exactly what you want.'

Is it hot in here, Steve thinks? He attempts to wet his dry throat with a swig of wine, even though he knows that'll just make this particular thirst worse.

❄ ❄ ❄

Meanwhile, at the other end of the table, Professor Plum and Reverend Green are captivated by Jess, who is gamely picking at her food. A small wall of roast potatoes, parsnips and carrots have been moved to one side of her plate forming an exclusion zone of carbs.

'… and the thing is that this is the company that's looked after him all through the pandemic, you see? I mean, his manager had started a process – an improvement plan, we call it, but really it's just a bunch of hurdles to trigger a disciplinary – but that was before. He was the first to go on furlough and you'd think he'd be grateful. But no, he comes back and the problems are even worse because now – get this – he's got childcare issues. Of course we're proud to be a parent-friendly employer, which is great PR and all, but it gave us a bit of a problem. See, his kid's proper poorly – some bone disease or other – and it would look bad to just fire his father without something really clear-cut. Well, we thought that was us snookered. But then, in December, we found that he'd been using his work credit card to pay for medical care for tiny Tim. And, well, that's gross negligence, isn't it? Got him off payroll in time for Christmas and good luck to him trying to pay for a tribunal. Merry bloody Christmas, we thought! Course, this is all confidential.'

'What a liberty, after all you've done for him,' Professor Plum says. 'Young people these days are so bloody entitled. Think they're owed a job.'

'Makes me glad I'm a sole trader,' says Reverend Green. 'It would break my heart to have someone do me dirty like that. I need people to be straight with me, you know. So, it's just me, and that suits me just fine. Although I wouldn't mind someone to do my accounts, mind.'

'That's the thing with running a small business – you have to be a Jack of all trades.' The Professor picks up the bottle of red and tops up Jess's glass. He holds the bottle up to the light to assess how much remains before upending the remainder, filling her glass nearly to the brim.

'I don't usually have red,' Jess giggles. 'Only when it's really cold, like now. Gives me terrible red-wine lip. Have I…?' She points at her blackened lips.

'Not that I'd notice,' says Reverend Green.

And that's when she notices that he has the most captivating green-grey eyes. Their colour seems to shift in the light, like the inside of a shell. His high cheekbones cast deep, rugged shadows and a dusting of stubble darkens his lantern jaw. He's a hulk of a man, broad shouldered, with thick arms pulling his cassock tight at the bicep, and hands that make whatever he touches look like a child's toy. But his eyes are soft, and intelligent, and compassionate. He's not her usual type, but variety's the spice of life as Steve would say…

'Good appetite on your fella,' says Professor Plum.

'He can certainly put it away. Sometimes think he's got hollow legs.'

'Get you some more?' The Professor glances at Jess's plate, the meat all gone but everything else almost untouched.

'I couldn't,' she says. 'Don't want to end up all big and bloated.'

'Nonsense,' Professor Plum replies in jovial spirit. 'You need some meat on you to stay warm in this winter. You like the devil on horsebacks, don't you? Let me get you some more.'

'Can I have some more sprouts while you're up? I mean, the bacon bits, maybe less the sprouts.' The Professor heads to the other end of the table, leaving her with Reverend Green. 'Well, I guess no one keeps their diet in December.'

'I prefer to have something I can hold on to,' he says. His voice is low and deep, almost a purr. These are words for her ears only.

Jess raises the glass to her lips and watches him over the rim. A little smile plays on his lips, which she notices are plump and biteable. He glances boyishly at her and she feels her cheeks flush.

❄ ❄ ❄

Meanwhile, Nish and Effie have been left to make their own entertainment.

'How's your broccoli?' Nish says.

'How are you not worried?' Effie whispers back.

Nish pushes down his own unease. 'It's not what I'd planned, but things could be worse. At least we're not stuck in the bus.'

'If you wanted to win the trust of a busload of strangers, wouldn't you ply them with drink, food, and—'

'Flirtatious conversation? Maybe the villagers don't want to be lonesome this Christmas.' It's no good getting stuck on this topic, he thinks. No matter how they feel, they're stuck here now. Might as well play nice. 'So, how's your broccoli?'

'Been a while since I've had a vegetable I don't needed to chew.' Effie presses her fork lightly to a floret. It disintegrates like a dandelion in a strong wind.

'And is this the kind of stuff you'd put on if you had some sinister ulterior motive?' Nish whispers, hoping this would be enough to stop Effie worrying. 'What sort of food do they put on at your retreat?'

'Honestly, who knows? First time I've been on one.'

'How long have you been… off it?'

'Thirty-nine days.' Effie utters an unfeeling laugh. 'Forty in a couple of hours. I sort of thought it would get better, you know. The first week would be hard, but the second would be better. That over time it would just get easier and easier until it wasn't a thing. But, you know what, it doesn't work like that. And now, here I am, stranded on Christmas Eve in a pub of all places.'

'Got to admit fate's got a wicked sense of humour,' Nish says. 'What was it that made you quit booze? I mean, I don't mean to pry. Absolutely tell me to butt out if it's none of my business.'

Effie mouths the start to several aborted sentences. She picks up her fork and starts dismembering another floret. Nish thinks he's overstepped, but then she starts talking. 'I kind of wish I could say I'd noticed something was up, you know, lots of little things adding up to one moment of revelation. I don't know, maybe there were, but I missed them. I wish it had been less...'

'Painful?'

'Humiliating.' Effie sucks in a deep breath before continuing. 'I woke up one morning and I'd torn my life apart. My room was trashed, my housemates had given me a week to move out, my phone was full of messages from friends telling me I was beyond forgiveness. Later that day I was given a formal warning at work. It was like everything crumbled all at once. And you know the worst bit?'

Nish doesn't know what to say. He'd imagined her waking up with a killer hangover, or looking at a bank statement, and thinking it was time to call it quits.

'I didn't remember anything. I phoned my oldest friend and asked her what had happened. She was so horrified that I didn't even remember whatever it was I'd done that she just told me I needed help and hung up. She hasn't answered my calls since. So, here I am, trying to claw myself out of rock bottom.'

'Man, I'm sorry. It'll get easier, though, over time.'

There's such a depth of sadness and pain in Effie's eyes, even as she smiles at him. Nish knows he's offered nothing more than cold comfort.

'They say you never get over addiction. You're always in recovery, only one bad day away from falling off and having to start over again. You just learn to substitute other things for the gaps that booze leaves in your life. Right now, I associate alcohol with marking the end of a week, meeting friends, a reward for achieving something, a treat when I feel down, a comfort for a bad day, unwinding in the evening, a trip to the cinema, a meal out... It hadn't just been woven into my life, it was the fabric of my life. It had become part of everything and now there's just a vacuum where drink used to be. But I keep reminding myself of that feeling of waking up and everything having fallen apart. That's really what I should associate alcohol with.'

'That's really hard,' Nish says. His instinct is to reach out, touch her hand, and let her know she's not alone. But he's already pushed her too far. He wants to be more respectful of her boundaries, only go so far as she wants to meet him. 'You're doing the right thing. I really admire your strength – and I'm sorry, when I asked, I didn't think it would be quite such a prying question.'

'Bit more than you bargained for, huh?' Effie reaches for her lemonade glass, but it's empty barring a few slowly melting ice cubes. She drinks the cold sugary water nonetheless, but can't stop her eyes straying towards the bar. 'So where should you be this evening?'

'Home,' Nish says. 'Funny how I still call it that, even though I've lived in London for more than a decade. But I should be there, peeling spuds in my mum's tiny kitchen while she fusses over place settings and dad pretends he needs to do his tax return or something. We have the whole family round Christmas Day – like, extended family, too. Second-cousin-twice-removed style extended. You wouldn't believe how many people mum can fit into their tiny house.'

'You have brothers or sisters?'

'If only. Nope, I'm an only child responsible for all my parents' hopes and dreams.' Nish thinks of his colleagues, who often don't understand quite what this means in an Indian household. 'Maybe it wouldn't be so bad, but my cousins are all doctors or lawyers or accountants and they're all married and bringing new nephews and nieces to the meal. And there I am, my parents' centrepiece, trying to get influencers to post content about some goat-faced toy, no prospects of promotion, no car, no wife, no kids, paying through the nose to live in some shared house. I never feel worse about myself than on Christmas Day when everyone's left and we've had a good chance to measure up all my failings.'

'Christmas, eh?'

'It's the most wonderful time of the year.'

There's the snap of crackers further down the table. A swell of laughter.

Recognition dawns on Effie's face. 'Hold on, wait a minute – that goat-faced toy. Do you mean Grumpy Krampus?'

'Yeah. I've been talking to influencers about him since June.'

'The Grumpy Krampus challenge?'

'That's the one.'

'My god, that thing gives me nightmares.' Effie laughs, a sparkle in her eyes like a sunbeam over a stormy sea.

Steve reads out a cracker joke, boorish and loud. 'What do you get if you cross a snowman with a vampire? Frostbite.' Mrs

White smirks, but Miss Scarlet appears to find it wildly amusing. She throws her head back, her luxurious blonde hair bounces in waves, and puts a hand to her chest almost as if to draw attention to her heaving bosom.

Jess massages moisturiser into the chapped skin on Reverend Green's hands. Professor Plum uncorks another bottle of red to fill her empty glass.

Just an absolutely normal Christmas Eve at The Slaughter House, Nish thinks. He pushes his growing sense of unease down. Nothing good will come from worrying about it unnecessarily.

Effie catches him watching the others. He hopes he's kept a poker face.

'What's their story, do you think?' Effie whispers.

'Steve and Jess?' Nish says, deflecting the question. 'I don't know, maybe a last chance to rekindle a relationship? A big Christmas away, pull out all the stops, see if they can find the magic that was once there. Way things are going, don't fancy their chances.'

Effie tucks a strand of hair behind her ear and leans closer to Nish. He can smell the spice and honey of her perfume. 'Nah, you know what I think? He's a recent divorce – there's a tan line where his wedding ring would have been. He's hooked up with the one-who-got-away after stalking her on Facebook. Maybe they've been together for longer, but this is their first Christmas as an official couple. He's got a kid and they're visiting his ex to call in with that ridiculous teddy bear and she's going to be oh-so-grateful because it's more junk in the tiny house she can only just afford on her wage and he's not been paying maintenance. But the kid will be enthralled, because here's a short sharp dose of fun-dad, while mum's all stressed about bills, run ragged keeping the place clean, and angry because she just *knew* something was up with that old friend from university…'

Nish laughs. 'Got them all wrapped up, huh Sherlock?'

'Elementary, my dear Watson,' she says. 'Of course, they could just be swingers. But here's the real question: what's with the villagers?'

Nish's mind whirs as he prepares to deflect the question. 'Must be kind of lonely and isolated, living in a village like this. They're just glad for the company.'

'They've cooked this enormous feast. They've set a table for twice our number. They've been more than generous with the drinks. But look at their plates, look at their glasses.'

For the first time, Nish notices the detail that's been in front of him this whole time. The villagers have served themselves next to nothing and have barely picked at the little food on their plates. Glasses of wine sit in front of each of them, still fully charged, no more than a few sips taken.

'Why aren't they eating or drinking?' she says, her voice low and deadly serious.

Nish is struggling for a reassuring response when there's an urgent hammering at the front door. *Bang bang bang*. The door rattles in its frame.

Professor Plum looks at his wristwatch and stands. 'Who is it?' he bellows at the door.

'Let us in,' replies a muffled voice.

Professor Plum retrieves a ring of old-fashioned keys from his pocket, a furrowed frown on his face. He unlocks the door, unclips two latches, and swings it wide. A flurry of snowflakes swirl in and settle on the welcome mat. Colonel Mustard and the bus driver bundle into the warm pub, cold radiating from them. Their faces are red from the freezing conditions, clumps of ice cling to their shoes and stretch up to the shins of their trousers.

'Cutting it fine,' Professor Plum says, shutting, locking, and bolting the door. 'Thought we'd be getting started without you this year.'

'Did you find him?' Miss Scarlet says, gripping her cutlery with white knuckles.

'Does it look like we found him?' the bus driver snaps.

'This is hardly her fault,' Colonel Mustard says, just loud enough for Nish to hear.

The bus driver looks to be about to respond, but the Colonel turns away and addresses the larger group.

'There was no sign of the missing traveller. He's still out there somewhere. We have to assume that he's found somewhere to shelter, but he won't have got far.' The Colonel licks his lips, turns to the villagers sitting near the fire. 'We can't assume that he's going to be joining the game.'

The Reverend, Miss Scarlet and Mrs White glance at each other before leaning in to whisper conspiratorially.

'He can't stay out in this weather,' Nish says. 'He'll catch his death.'

'We could go and look for him,' Effie says.

'A second search party might be a good idea,' Nish says.

They might just end up retracing the Colonel's footsteps, but they can't just sit here with someone out in the cold.

'Actually, it's a bad idea,' says Professor Plum.

'A very bad idea,' confirms Colonel Mustard. 'What happens if you get lost in this blizzard, huh? Well, we'd have to send out a search party for the search party. And what if that party gets lost? Well, then we'd end up in a thoroughly preposterous situation.'

'No, no, it's much better if you stay here,' Professor Plum insists.

'The glowing warmth of the pub will act as a beacon on this foul night,' the Colonel says, visibly pleased with his verbal flourish. 'When he comes to his senses, he'll be drawn to it.'

'Like a moth to a flame,' Professor Plum says.

Colonel Mustard appears less pleased with this simile.

'Shouldn't we unlock the door?' Jess says. There's a thickness to her voice, a slight slur, as the wine takes effect. 'In case he finds his way here?'

'Oh no, I shouldn't think that's a good idea.' Colonel Mustard rubs his hands together vigorously to shake off the cold. 'Wind'll blow this door open and we'll all be ruddy freezing. No, let him knock if he wants in. Now, tell me you lot saved some grub because I'm ruddy starving.'

Mrs White implores the two men to stand close to the fire and help themselves to the leftovers. Despite Steve's best efforts, the table is still loaded with food like a Hogwarts feast. Miss Scarlet loads a plate with choice pieces, leaning very close to Reverend Green as she does so, before handing it to Colonel Mustard. The bus driver reaches over and wrenches a whole drumstick from the goose carcass with the kind of table manners that would usually strike Nish as unconscionable amongst strangers – and oafishly rude amongst the closest of friends. The bus driver bites into the meat, a glitter of grease around her chops chewing in closed-eye contentedness.

'Got something stronger?' The Colonel says to Professor Plum, who has just presented a glass of red wine. 'I'd kill for a bit of fire in my belly. Nice glass of brandy, eh, landlord?'

'Right you are,' Professor Plum says. He puts the glass of wine in front of Jess where it won't go to waste.

'The good stuff, mind. Not the lighter fuel.'

'When's this recovery vehicle due?' Jess says, raising her voice to be heard over the chatter.

'Recovery vehicle?' the bus driver says, pausing mid-chew.

'For the minibus. The one you were driving.'

'Ah,' she says, as if driving a bus-replacement service had fallen completely out of her head. 'Yes, of course. Don't you worry about that.'

Jess purses her lips, glances at her watch, and crosses her arms. It occurs to Nish then that she might also be beginning to feel uneasy about the situation. 'It's nearly midnight,' she says.

'Cheer up, babe,' Steve says. 'There are worse places to be stranded.'

Miss Scarlet tops up Steve's glass, which had been precariously close to being only halfway full. Miss Scarlet says something that Nish doesn't quite catch, drawing Steve's eyes back to her. She reaches out, plucks a sausage from its bacon sheath and slides it into her mouth, all the while watching Steve with the intensity of a cobra hypnotising its prey. The sausage disappears between her lips and all thoughts of ever needing to leave Little Slaughter flee from Steve's head.

Effie leans close to Nish, her hair brushing his skin. 'No one's made a phone call all evening,' she says.

Nish glances to the fireplace, where the bus driver and Colonel Mustard are talking quietly and intensely. Perhaps they're working out how many rooms they need if the travellers are stranded overnight. But he's reminded more of a football manager passing on instructions, keen to make sure their body language gives no clues to the opposition.

'I don't see what's to gain by lying about it,' Nish says. For a moment he contemplates pushing on with the jolly, care-free act. 'But you're right, there's something strange—'

There's a sound on the roof, as if something large and heavy has landed on it. Silence follows, broken only by the soft thump of snow sliding from the building and into the drift below.

There's the snap of a cracker. The bus driver unfurls a joke and reads out loud to the silent gathering. 'What do you call a blind reindeer?'

The sound comes again, loud and dangerous. Nish looks at Effie. She's on high alert, her eyes wide open. There's a creak from one of the beams and he has the sense of something substantial putting the ancient building under stress.

'They're here!' Professor Plum hisses.

6

'What's that noise?' Jess says. 'Is there something on the roof?'

Mrs White shushes her with the strictness of a school ma'am.

'What's going on?' Nish stage-whispers.

The villagers pay no attention. Instead, Professor Plum steps lightly to the bar. He ducks down and there's the sound of something opening, metal on wood. Moments later, he reappears clutching a double-barrelled shotgun broken open. He loads a pair of brassy shells and snaps the gun back together. He quickly fills the pockets of his game-show jacket with handfuls of rounds so that they bulge to reveal a cache of brass caps and red plastic tubing.

'Bloody hell,' Steve says. 'That's a bit strong, isn't it?'

Nish has seen guns before in real life. A kid in the year above once turned up at school with a replica pistol. The police were called and lessons were over for the day by break time. And then there's the guns paraded on display at airports and outside embassies in London. But this is different, as if the safety rails of normal life have suddenly been removed. His mouth is dry and it takes some effort to draw his eyes away from the polished walnut stock and blackly glinting barrels. It's only when he does so that he notices that the shotgun is not the only weapon in the pub.

Mrs White rests a cricket bat on her shoulder as if she's about to be called out for the village team.

Miss Scarlet brandishes an axe in both hands, the blunt side of its blade and end of its handle painted a fire-engine red that exactly matches the rest of her outfit. What Nish knows about women's fashion could fit on a single page, if the paper was small enough and font large enough and you didn't mind a bit of white space. Yet, despite the shock of the moment, there's something admirable about Miss Scarlet's commitment to colour coordination.

Colonel Mustard has grabbed a candlestick from somewhere, its brassy metal flickers dully in the light of the fire. The choice of weapon combined with the Cluedo costume is almost too absurd – almost too perfect – to be as alarming as it should be. Upon finding himself in a pub with a bunch of armed strangers, Nish's instinct should turn to self-preservation, but right now he's leaning towards hysterical laughter.

Fortunately, the sight of the Reverend Green is enough to remove any hint of levity from the situation. He clasps a carving knife in one massive hand and a meat cleaver in the other. The man bristles with the kind of malevolent energy that would usually make Nish switch sides of the street, or replan a journey, or head for the nearest tube, or leave a borough entirely.

'I don't like this,' Effie says, standing close to him.

'Feels like this murder mystery evening is going a bit Orient Express.'

'They know what's out there – and it scares them.'

The noise comes again. Nish can hear it moving across the roof above them. Attuned to the sound, everyone moves their head to trace its progress. The heavy scraping sound becomes more distinct, like slow deliberate footsteps. It carries to somewhere around the second row of beer pumps. There's a resonant bang – as if a piston has just hit the roof tiles. There's a sound a bit like broken crockery dropping, followed by the dull thud of something heavy landing in the snow.

Silence follows, broken only by the Jackson 5's version of Santa Claus is Comin' to Town. Professor Plum kills the music, leaving only the soft crackle of the fire and the low howl of the wind across the eaves.

'Is it gone?' Jess whispers, just loud enough for everyone to hear.

'It'll be back.' Reverend Green's voice is deep and low. It reminds Jess of Vin Diesel in that sci-fi film that Steve liked. The one where he wore goggles because he'd had something done to his eyes and there were monsters in the dark. Well, so long as they're in the light, they're fine. She doesn't feel safe here, but senses sanctuary and protection emanating from the man in the cassock. She's not the only one to have this thought. Miss Scarlet also stands closer to him, seeking shelter beside his girth.

'Could someone tell me what the bloody hell is going on?' Steve says, standing tall and puffing his chest out. It's not escaped his notice that at the slightest sniff of danger the womenfolk have gravitated towards that young buck. Not just the blonde, who he swears was coming on to him only a few minutes ago, but also Jess. Bloody Jess! The first hint of a troubled brooding sort with a lantern jaw and she's away. It's a timely reminder that he needs to assert his alpha status. Although that would be a lot easier if he was armed. Being empty-handed while something malevolent stalks around outside is distinctly beta.

'Keep it down, man,' says Colonel Mustard. The old man exudes authority. Steve finds himself meekly complying.

Mrs White fetches a fire poker and places it in Steve's hand and gives him a condescending pat on the shoulder, as if to say: 'See, you can play with the grownups too.'

'Ten of us,' Reverend Green mutters under his breath to Miss Scarlet.

'I don't like those odds,' she says.

'Could work for us, if…'

The Reverend glances round and catches Nish standing close, watching them with interest. He flexes his jaw, ushers Miss Scarlet a bit further from prying ears with a meat cleaver to the small of her back.

'What's that all about?' Nish says to Effie.

'What's out there?' Effie says, loud enough to be heard but not so loud to invite a chorus of shushing. Nevertheless, the villagers glance in her direction, but feel no compulsion to answer. 'Unless someone tells me, I swear to god I'm going to open that door and see for myself.'

Silence falls over the pub. Colonel Mustard adjusts his wireframe glasses, perhaps seeing Effie with fresh eyes. An explanation is still not forthcoming, however.

'Fine,' she says. 'I guess I'll see for myself.'

Effie steps towards the door, reaching for the latch. Her hand's an inch from the bolt when Professor Plum breaks the tense silence.

'You won't make it out,' he says. 'Not without the key. All you'll do is get their attention, and then we'll be in for the night.'

'"Their"?' Nish says. 'As in multiple? There's more than one of – whatever that was on the roof?'

Colonel Mustard glances at Nish, pats the candlestick against his hand. The Colonel says nothing, contenting himself to watch and see how the visitors respond.

'How many of them?' Effie says. She stands near the door, holding close her only sources of power – the noise of the latch and her determination to get an answer. Her eyes bore holes into Colonel Mustard, willing him to share something more than cryptic allusions.

'Eight,' the Colonel says at long last. 'There are always eight, and they won't stop until they've had one of us each.'

'Had?' says Jess. 'As in…?'

'Killed,' says the Reverend, his voice like the first shovel of dirt hitting the polished wood of a coffin.

As Nish is digesting this information, he watches Miss Scarlet walk over to a shallow wooden cupboard fixed on the wall at head height. She opens it to reveal a battered dartboard, flanked on either side by chalkboards for keeping score. On the left-hand side there are chalked entries, one for each year, stretching back to 2010. There are two columns: Home and Away. Under each year is a tally of eight checks. In the early years, the checks are all in the Home column, but as the years pass they even out and then switch to the Away column. Home has kept a clean sheet since 2016.

'May the odds ever be in your favour,' Miss Scarlet says humourlessly.

'What's that?' the bus driver says.

'Same thing she says every year,' Professor Plum says. He holds the gun to his shoulder and peers down the barrel. He swings round, momentarily pointing the muzzle at each of the gathered in turn before targeting a horseshoe hanging from the wall at the far end of the pub. For a moment Nish expects the Professor to fire a testing shot indoors. He half-remembers from playing Call of Duty that shotguns just spray shot. You don't need to a particularly good aim, you just need to be close. He makes a mental note to stay down-wind of the Professor.

'That's *The Hunger Games*, isn't it?' Jess says. 'Why's she quoting *The Hunger Games*?'

'What's that, one of your books?' Steve says, seemingly trailing behind everyone else.

'That film with Jennifer Lawrence. You liked it enough when we saw it.'

'Oh aye,' Steve says, his voice taking a husky tone at the memory.

'If this happens every year, why are you here?' Effie says.

Professor Plum blurts out a laugh. Colonel Mustard pushes his glasses up his nose. Mrs White averts her eyes. Miss Scarlet's mouth hangs open in shock. The Reverend raises a sardonic eyebrow.

'You could be getting some winter sun,' Nish says.

'Dubai's lovely this time of year,' Jess says. 'All that sand and shopping.'

Mrs White is the first to speak. She sounds furious. 'How could we—'

'It's alright, they don't know,' Colonel Mustard says softly, putting a hand on her shoulder. 'We can't just abandon the children like that. It would be unconscionable.'

'We're not suggesting you leave them behind,' Nish says. 'You'd take them with you.'

Miss Scarlet has recovered her composure enough to speak. 'That's not how—'

'We don't have time,' the Colonel says. 'They can learn as they play along, or not at all.'

The villagers set about finding weapons for the visitors. The Professor produces a stumpy edging shovel, the metal of its blade dulled by use, which he holds out to be taken.

Steve is first in line, tossing the fire poker to one side. He grips the shaft of the shovel with one hand, the handle with the other, and tests the weighting and balance. He thrusts into the air twice, each time breathing out sharp and loud. It must be the booze and bellyful of food, because he's feeling a little winded after this exertion. He sees the Reverend watching him with cold interest, blades clasped in his enormous hands and cassock pulled tight by thick muscle. Steve sucks his gut in, breathes in slowly, slowly exhales. He can feel his heart pumping, the first prickles of sweat. Now he's armed, he's ready to assert his alpha status. These poor fools don't know it yet.

More improvised weapons are handed out. Jess finds herself equipped with a small cast iron frying pan, which she finds has a pleasing heft and builds an irresistible momentum when she swings it. The bus driver is equipped with a croquet mallet, chipped and worn on the putting edge. Effie receives a silver-handled cane, light and fast, even if it looks a little like she's going to perform a number from Cabaret. Finally, Nish is handed a catering knife the length of his forearm, with a green plastic handle.

'It's only been used to chop vegetables,' Mrs White says, as she hands it to him.

'It's like that bit in *The Lion, The Witch and the Wardrobe* where Santa gives the kids weapons,' Effie says.

'Father Christmas,' Nish says.

Effie looks about to ask a question, but Colonel Mustard speaks first. 'Keep your voices down,' he snaps.

'How come he gets a knife?' Steve says, using the spade as an extension of his arm to point at Nish.

'You had your pick of weapon,' Mrs White replies, with the same patient tone she might use with a truculent child.

'Yeah, but I didn't know there'd be a bloody knife.' Steve says. Out of the corner of his eye he sees a glint of sharp metal catching the light as Reverend Green traces shapes in the air with his twin blades. 'Here, mate, do us a swap?'

Nish weighs the blade in his hand, glances at the spade. It looks heavy and slow and unwieldy. He doesn't want to be stranded in a strange village, stalked by eight – well – whatever's out there waiting for them. But he fancies his chances better armed with this over-sized vegetable peeler than an undersized spade. 'That's too heavy for me. I think I'll keep this, thanks.'

'Don't be ridiculous,' Steve protests.

'Nah. My mind's made up.'

'The man's a bloody vegan,' Steve says to Mrs White, giving up on attempting to convince Nish. 'What's he going to do with that, huh? Cut zeds in the air like Zorro? Use bad language? Just stand there quivering because he doesn't want to hurt anyone's feelings? Come on. Make him swap. At least with a spade he can dig his own grave.'

'Steve,' Jess tuts. 'No one's burying anyone.'

But Nish has had enough. 'So maybe I worry about animal welfare. But what makes you think I'd extend that mercy to humans, huh? Ever wonder if vegans think of humans as animals? Can vegans be cannibals, huh? Check your priors, mate. Maybe you don't want to go underestimating a vegan. Not when he's got a big knife and is having a pisser of a day.'

'Big man,' Steve says, a cruel smile spread thin on his face.

'Who said that they're humans?' Reverend Green says with a cold disinterest that belies how closely he's been watching this little performance. His eyes sparkle with mischief, as if he's actually rather enjoying how things have been panning out so far.

Jess inches closer to the Reverend. Again, she finds herself thinking of Vin Diesel in Pitch Black – *that's* the film she was thinking of. All muscle and gravel, a killer, a predator, a criminal… and a saviour. He's not her usual type, she tells herself again, he doesn't feel safe. Not in the conventional sense. But sometimes danger is the best protection from danger.

'Come again?' Steve growls, his eyes flicking to the Reverend. If there's one man in this place who has earned his ire more than that bloody vegan, or the idiot bus driver who stranded them here, it's that damned sexy priest. The kind of Father who likes it when you call him daddy, he thinks. He's met sickos like this one before. All strong and silent until there's a ball-gag and a leather paddle.

'What's out there ain't human,' Professor Plum says, his voice hushed and hoarse.

'Then what are they?' Effie says.

She never receives an answer.

No sooner than the words are out of her mouth than there's an enormous thud at the door. The wood shakes in its frame and a picture hanging on the wall slips, slanting at an angle. Effie shrieks and dashes towards the others, putting a table and some chairs between her and whatever's at the door. She holds the cane with both hands, like a very short, very thin staff. Her heart is in her throat and the adrenaline that surges through her body makes her hands shake.

Nish and Effie exchange a brief look. The weapons they grip with blanching knuckles are their best forms of defence. But they're woefully inadequate considering the threatening overtures that have replaced the Christmas music.

They all wait in silence, heaving heavy lungfuls of air, brandishing blades and barrels and a candlestick at the door.

Has it gone?

The moment the thought crosses Nish's mind, there's another thud, equally hard and forceful as the first. And then another and another and another. In the cacophony, he realises that the pounding is not just at the front door, but there's also thumping resonating through from the kitchen where there must be a back door, and somewhere else at the far end of the bar where there's presumably another doorway. Several *somethings* are testing every entrance to the building.

The noise is deafening. He watches in horror as a crack appears in the wall's plaster. One, then two, then a flurry, of pictures and horse brasses fall to the floor with a clatter and a smashing of glass. A paper chain gently unhooks itself from the ancient wooden beams and drifts down with an ethereal grace.

And then, all of a sudden, the noise stops.

The pub is quiet, except for the sound of the fire and their own breathing.

Which is when the lights go out.

7

It takes Nish a moment and a few blinks to adjust to the darkness. His heart thumps like it's trying to break out of his chest, his eyes flash wildly searching for danger, and he wields the catering knife with both hands clasped around the handle. The only light in the pub comes from the fire in the hearth. Faint shadows dance across the walls in the periphery of his vision, phantom traces of possible danger.

'Are you alright?' Effie says beside him. He can sense the tension radiating off her, he knows she's as scared as he is, but somehow her voice is steady and hushed.

'I don't know if alright is how I'd describe the way I'm feeling right now,' he says. The words gradually ease some of the tension in his jaw. He realises he's been grimacing, waiting for the worst to happen.

'This better or worse than your normal Christmas?'

'About the same,' Nish says. 'At least no one's asked me when I'm going to meet a nice woman and settle down. So, maybe a fraction better than normal. You?'

'I guess I was always down the pub on Christmas Eve, so, yeah, standard.'

The jokes help ease some of the tension. He loosens his grip on the knife, feeling the ache in his fingers as his circulation returns.

A light snaps on near the fireplace. The bus driver has a torch, which she shines under her face as if she's about to tell a campfire ghost story. 'Lost power, have we?'

'That's new,' says a voice. The driver's torch beam flicks towards the source and illuminates Colonel Mustard. He squints, his wire-framed glasses flashing in the light. 'Ruddy hell, get that out of my eyes.'

'Oh, sorry.'

The beam is lowered and the Colonel cleans his glasses on his waistcoat.

'There, that's better. I was saying, they always go for the doors – must think we're ruddy idiots if they expect us to leave the door unlocked for them. But the lights? Well now, that's new.'

'What does it mean?' Miss Scarlet says. The beam flicks over to her like a searchlight, lingering on her chest a moment before the driver realises. She politely diverts the light to the wall behind Miss Scarlet, illuminating the dartboard. After a rocky start to the games, the Home team has kept a clean sheet the last few years.

'Means things're different this year.' The Reverend is cast in the light, his shadow massive and imposing, the wide blade of his cleaver flashing bright. 'All bets are off.'

'This is all well and good,' Steve says. As the light swings towards him he raises his hand to shade his eyes. 'But catch us up. What the bleeding hell is out there? And what normally happens? This cryptic nonsense is all well and good for you, but it's no bloody use to us.'

There's silence in the pub. The spotlight wavers, edging past Steve's hand to catch him in the eyes. He squints and ducks out the way as everyone waits for someone to take it upon themselves to speak.

'That's the point, isn't it?' Effie says. The light swings towards her. Even though the beam catches her full in the face, she directs herself towards Colonel Mustard in the shadows near the fireplace. 'Eight of them, each needing one of us. Same as every year. The evidence is plain for us to see on that dartboard over there. But there's ten of us, so only two can make it through the night. Is that how this goes? So, why would you want to help us, when we're easy pickings? When you could keep us confused and armed with the least effective weapons you can find to give yourselves the best possible chance?' She holds up the cane, thin and weedy, and quite plainly no match for whatever's waiting outside.

The revelation washes over Nish like a physical sensation. It's as if an extra layer of reality has been overlaid on the scene and he can suddenly see connections that should have been obvious. The short spade, the frying pan, the metal-capped cane, and the vegetable knife – these are terrible defences against something that can shake the bones of this building. If the villagers knew that the pub would be terrorised the same night every year, why would this represent the best armoury they could rustle up? It wouldn't, of course... Unless they wanted to increase their own chances of survival by adding a bunch of bewildered cannon fodder clutching poorly chosen tools to the battlefield.

'This true?' Steve demands, grabbing Mrs White, who had the misfortune to be the villager standing nearest to him. The flashlight darts to follow the action, framing Steve as he holds the shaft of the spade to her neck, threatening to crush her airway. Mrs White puts up a fight, swinging her cricket bat behind her, connecting a couple of times with Steve's shins. But he's stronger, bigger, and has no qualms about squeezing his grip tighter to show that he means business. 'Drop it,' he snarls in her ear.

There's the sound of willow dropping to the wooden floor.

'Steve, isn't this a bit...' Jess says, seeing the whites of Steve's eyes flashing with an unfamiliar manic energy. She was scared before, but seeing him like this only makes it worse.

'Is it true?' Steve shouts.

'Come on, calm down or you're barred from my pub,' says Professor Plum.

Despite the glare of the torchlight in his eyes, Steve can see enough to know that the Professor is currently regarding him down the sights of his shotgun. 'Expect me to calm down trapped in here with you pointing both barrels at me?'

'Just let her go and we can talk.' Professor Plum's voice is reasonable and calm, the siren lure of sanity in a mad situation. 'I can appreciate that this has been a very stressful day. There's no need for any of this.'

'Start talking and no one gets hurt,' Steve bellows in return. 'Let's start with you telling us what the hell is out there. I'm deadly serious. If you don't give me answers, she goes to sleep in five... four... three...'

'You'll release my wife now,' a gravelly voice whispers in Steve's ear.

Steve feels cold metal against his throat. He wants to swallow, but can't for fear of the sharpness of the Reverend's blade. Despite being such a big man he can move silent as a cat.

Steve contemplates his next move for a moment, but he

recognises when he's beaten. It's over. He releases Mrs White and raises his hands in the air, still holding the spade. Steve wears the grim grin of a poker player who's just had his bluff called.

Mrs White turns to look Steve in the eye and gives him a disappointed tut. 'We feed you, let you drink us dry, and *this* is how you repay us?' She shakes her head and offers another tut before picking up her cricket bat.

'Bigger fish to fry right now,' Effie whispers in Nish's ear. 'But "wife"? Colour me surprised.'

'Yeah, I thought he was with Miss Scarlet,' Nish says.

'I never said he wasn't,' Effie says.

Before Nish can begin to contemplate the logistics of maintaining a complicated relationship in a small rural community, his attention is drawn back to the rather less complicated power dynamic playing out under the searchlight.

The Reverend kicks the inside of Steve's knee. Not hard, but firm and forceful enough that he's compelled to kneel. All the while, the butcher keeps a blade pressed against Steve's jugular. The Colonel, who still has his barrels trained on Steve, takes a step closer.

'Steve,' Jess gasps, a hand flying to her mouth. She steps back in the darkness, as if putting distance between herself and the scene playing out in front of her could make it stop.

'Listen here boy,' the Reverend growls, even though Steve is a good few years his senior. 'I'm going to set down some ground rules. You play nicely, we'll get along just fine. You break the rules, we're going to be serving long pig come the new year. You understand?'

'I'm listening,' Steve says through gritted teeth. He wishes for all it's worth that he wasn't being emasculated in front of Jess, not now of all times. But he's trying to remind himself that pride is irrelevant compared with mortal danger.

'I have zero tolerance for acting up. Try anything like that again and I will personally throw you out into—'

A thin, reedy, high-pitched noise comes from the far end of the bar. Silence falls once more as the group turns as one in the direction of the sound.

The bus driver throws a beam of light into the corner, casting mad shadows against the far wall.

'Turn that thing off,' the Colonel hisses.

The light goes out and they're thrown back into darkness. Dim shadows of chairs and garlands of hops and the gathered crowd ripple over the walls and surfaces of the pub in the light cast by the fire. No one dare move, not even Steve who might have used the distraction to stand and put some distance between himself and the butcher's blade.

The sound continues – high-pitch and grating, like long fingernails being run down a blackboard – edging slowly closer. It could be a bare branch rubbing against the window in the wind, the rationalising part of Nish's brain insists. It's fine. It's absolutely not a monster in the night, staking out its prey, grazing the windows with razor sharp nails. Because that would be absurd, wouldn't it? That kind of thing only happens in schlocky horror movies. And monsters aren't even cool now – it's all found footage and body horror.

But try as hard as he might to rationalise it, he can't deny that the scraping noise is edging closer. It might have started on the far window, barely visible in the gloom of the pub, but now whatever is brushing against the window is beside the front door.

He braces himself for another battering at the woodwork, for more falling pictures and ornaments, maybe even the sound of crumbling plaster scattering on the wood floor. But only silence follows.

Nish swallows. His throat's dry. He has to fight back against the urge to cough. He glances over at Effie. Reflected firelight glitters in her eyes, held wide as she watches the door, waiting for the next violent onslaught.

'I think it's playing with us,' Nish says under his breath.

'Thanks, that's a really comforting thought,' Effie says.

The wind picks up, howls around the edges of the building, filling the silence with a low mournful moan. Is this how they're going to spend the time between now and dawn, he thinks? Trapped in the dark arguing and threatening each other, terrorised by mysterious noises from outside?

Almost as if on cue, the high-pitched scraping noise starts up again. But this time it's a loud chorus that seems to be resonating from every window. For Nish, it's almost unbearable – both because it's terrifying, but also because the sound is so grating. It's fraying his nerves.

'Make it stop!' Jess screams, holding her hands to her ears.

'Get away—' a male voice shouts.

The shuttered window behind Jess bursts inwards in an explosion of broken glass and splintered wood, caught dimly in the firelight. Something metallic flashes for a fraction of a moment, just long enough that Nish can only get the most fleeting impression. It's as if a silver bough has smashed through the window in a storm. Glinting branches fan out either side of Jess. For a moment she is silhouetted dimly against the subtle glow of the snow outside, the effect making her appear like an angel with wings made of quicksilver bones.

Then they fold in on her and she screams.

Nish blinks and ducks away from the broken window. In the millisecond he's not watching Jess is gone.

Her scream comes again from outside, then stops.

8

'Jess,' Steve bellows into the void. 'Jess, babe?'

Beyond the jagged edges of glass and splinters of wood, the winter night is velvety dark and silent. A flurry of snowflakes spills through the shattered window into the pub. Steve rushes forwards, plants his hands on the windowsill and howls his partner's name once more.

'Steve! Get away from there!' Effie shouts. Nish has seen enough horror movies to know that she's right. Framed in the broken window, he's easy pickings. It would only take a fraction of a second for whatever's out there to chalk up a second kill.

But Steve's not listening. He's staring wildly into the dark night, rooted to the spot.

To Nish's surprise, it's the butcher who intervenes. The Reverend places a calloused hand on Steve's shoulder, leaving his cleaver unguarded. 'She's gone,' he says, his deep voice soft and compassionate, the malevolence and rage melted away.

'She can't be,' Steve says, his voice soft and boyish.

'She is. I'm sorry,' the Reverend leaves a pause for a fraction of a second. 'You'll do no good standing by that window.'

Steve allows himself to be steered back into the depths of the pub. The shock of loss has left him wide eyed and startled. There's the silvery trace of a tear on his cheek.

Professor Plum raises an eyebrow at the Reverend, as if to suggest Steve could have been left to fate. Whatever his reasoning, the big man remains unreadable.

With Steve safely away from the open window, the Reverend starts to manhandle one of the slot machines, leaning his body against the cabinet. 'Give us a hand,' he growls at Nish.

'Me?'

'Yes, you.'

'Why not…' Nish glances around at the other men in the room. Colonel Mustard is the archetype of a sturdy fellow, but he's in his sixties, more suited to directing action from a wing-backed armchair than risking a hernia. Professor Plum is younger, though. But there's no way he's going to set down his shotgun, lest someone else pick it up. It occurs to Nish that the shotgun is the only weapon that doesn't require physical force to be of use. Sure, the recoil might put his shoulder out, but provided he's not a completely hopeless aim that's very much a secondary problem. And then there's Steve, a man who in the blink of an eye has turned from machismo to a shell-shocked husk of his former self.

Nish doesn't think of himself as particularly strong. He's lithe and wiry, build for speed rather than strength. And by speed, well, he's run for the bus a few times. Occasionally he takes the stairs rather than the escalator in the tube. Not for any particular reason of fitness or vanity, more for simple expedience when there's a long queue and he'll be at street level faster if he exerts himself a little.

But still, he plants his hands on the side of the cabinet. It's an awkward shape with no real purchase – and heavy and precarious like a bookcase that's still stacked with tomes. There's some grunting and shifting from the Reverend and the cabinet moves, inch by inch, across the floor.

For all Nish is straining – for all the effort he's putting in – the Reverend is doing most of the heavy lifting. Quite literally. Nish is simply helping guide the machine, at best preventing it from falling over.

The cold air that blows through the shattered window is sharp and bitter. On the side closest to the window Nish can feel the prickle of ice on his skin. On the other side warmth radiates from the pub's fire. As he's shouldering the burden, he can see picnic benches in the beer garden, thickly coated with snow, the picket fence, half-buried in a drift. The scene beyond dissolves into darkness, obscured by the fat flakes still falling. He can make out the silhouette of the large yew trees in the churchyard, the hint of the bell tower beyond, but not much more. There are no streetlights, and so the only source of light is the ethereal luminescence of the snow itself.

And there, tracing across the beer garden, Nish can see evidence of the creatures that stalk the night. There are tracks, where the snow has been compacted and scuffed, appearing as darker-than-dark wells in the otherwise pristine coating. It's too dark to make out the outline of the feet, but he has the impression of something purposeful and powerful that has been tracing a path around the outside of the building. This shouldn't be a surprise, all things considered. No, but the size of the footprints is. They're the size of pans. Whatever made those prints is large, and heavy, and strong. No matter how heavy this fruit machine might feel, it's not going to slow whatever's out there.

There's no sign of Jess, he thinks. But with a sick feeling in his stomach Nish realises that's not quite true. Amongst the disturbed snow, there's a dark pool which he had first thought was shadow. Now he realises that the snow is discoloured. Nish doesn't need to look any closer to know it's blood.

The slot machine rocks into place and the view through the window is blocked out.

'Couldn't have done it without you,' the Reverend says. He pats Nish's shoulder with such force his knees buckle. The Reverend picks up his blades and turns to Mrs White to speak to her in low tones. In the flickering light, Nish can just about see her massaging her neck.

'Did you see anything?' Effie says to Nish, putting her hand on his arm.

'Nothing.' Nish thinks about that dark blot of discoloured snow. Effie is emanating a tense urgency and he senses that this might not be the news she needs right now. 'But there were footprints. Big footprints.'

'What is it?'

'I don't know. I don't think I want to know.'

Effie is silent for a moment, her hand still clutching his arm. 'I really want a drink.'

'No, you don't. You want to keep your head clear. You *need* to keep your head clear to make it through this.'

'You're right. You're right. You're right.' Effie sounds unconvinced, but each repetition is fractionally faster as she tries to fix her resolve. 'You're right. Thank you. I – I needed you to tell me that.'

'She's gone,' Steve says, mournful and distraught. The bus driver keeps the spotlight trained elsewhere, letting Steve grieve into the darkness. But as he continues to speak into the awkward silence that follows, each word becomes louder and angrier. 'My Jess is gone. Now will someone tell me what is going on? And what the bloody hell is that *thing*?'

There is a beat or two before anyone speaks, and when they do Nish is surprised to hear Miss Scarlet's voice. 'We owe you that, at least.'

'Don't be bloody soft,' Professor Plum says.

'Why not?' The spotlight flashes back to Miss Scarlet. 'Things are different this year. We're going to have to work together.'

'I've never heard anything so ridiculous,' the Professor huffs, flinching slightly as the light hits his eyes.

'Let the girl speak.' The light flashes round and the Reverend is illuminated.

'You would say that.' The search beam darts left then right before settling on Mrs White. If nothing else, the stage-lighting of the speakers has served to exacerbate the physical distance between the Reverend and his wife, in contrast to his proximity to Miss Scarlet.

'Told you,' Effie whispers. Gallows humour is all she has left to hold off her desire to just give up, to take the easy option and seek oblivion in a bottle.

'Please.' Steve's voice cracks.

In the standoffish silence that follows there's a battle of wills: to tell or not to tell. In the end, Professor Plum lets the barrel of his shotgun slump to the floor with a metallic thump. The bus driver's light arrives moments later, tracing a course up the barrel, up the Professor's sheeny purple jacket, to the sullen expression he wears on his face. 'Fine, but I don't see what good it does.'

'I remember the first time like it was yesterday,' Miss Scarlet begins as if transported in a dream. 'It was a warm and wet year – the kind of Christmas where it doesn't feel like winter. The TV was full of people talking about climate change. The river had flooded and the ground was so drenched it was like a wet sponge. The village green was brown with mud—'

'You probably wondered why this village is named Little Slaughter?' Colonel Mustard says, unable to resist the call to deliver a lesson. 'Slaughter comes from an old English word for muddy. We're known for being a muddy village.'

'It was very muddy,' Miss Scarlet says.

'Like the Somme,' the Colonel adds. 'If you know your history.'

'The whole village lived in wellies that winter. You could

hear footsteps a mile off because of the sucking sound of the mud. *Schlup, schlup, schlup*—'

'More like *pffarp, pffarp, pffarp*,' the Colonel interjects.

'Yes, you're right, it was more… gassy.' Miss Scarlet blows three wet raspberries as if to illustrate the point. 'More like that.'

'Okay, footsteps sounded like farts, we get it,' Effie says. The flashlight whips to illuminate her. The fright of seeing Jess snatched into the night has given her a sickly pallor. 'Just tell us what we're up against.'

'I was just getting to that,' Miss Scarlet says, a little peevish. 'The village mummers were performing on the village green—'

Colonel Mustard clears his throat. 'Mumming is an old English folk tradition, where a group of men perform a short comic play – a battle between Robin Hood and the Turkish Knight. The play was an old tradition for the menfolk of Little Slaughter, but a play has never been performed since that bleak night.'

'It was dark and too wet for a fire, so they were lit by the lights of a tractor. They were being introduced by Santa Claus—'

'*Old* Santa Claus,' Colonel Mustard elaborates. 'All dressed in green, none of this American nonsense.'

'Poor Jethro, he'd really got into character—'

'He was incredibly drunk,' the Colonel says.

'They all were.'

'It was for the best.'

'The play had just begun and Darren was bellowing out his lines for all he was worth,' Miss Scarlet continues. 'The whole village had gathered round. Mulled wine had been flowing and all the adults were full of the Christmas spirit. I'd always loved the mummers' play. For me, that had always been what made Christmas Eve. But it had only just started and everyone was gathered and so when we heard footsteps approaching—'

'*Pffarp, pffarp, pffarp,*' Colonel Mustard adds wetly.

'And everyone was looking round in case someone was missing. But they weren't – the whole village was gathered for the play. And so people start wondering who it could be that's coming across the green in the dark. But it wasn't just one set of footsteps…'

The villagers provide a chorus of fart noises in the dark. Colonel Mustard sets a bombastic rhythm. The Reverend joins in with a deep bass, followed by Mrs White (gingerly touching her sore neck as she does so). Professor Plum adds to the rasping chorus, despite his earlier objection to the story being told. Even the bus driver joins in, producing the most ridiculous high-pitched raspberries. The spotlight whips around, revealing the villagers' grotesque gargoyle faces, tongues out and cheeks swollen.

Miss Scarlet continues: 'And then old screaming Mary—'

'She was known through the village to suffer such awful night terrors.' It occurs to Nish that the Colonel is one of those gentlemen of a certain age who is pathologically incapable of keeping his thoughts to himself.

'—let out this bloodcurdling scream. And first everyone thought it was part of the play. You know, those lads liked to do something a bit different each year, keep the villagers on their feet. The surprise was part of the pleasure. But this year, whatever they had planned was nothing compared to the surprise that was coming for them.

'First I knew about it was when people started pushing and jostling. Wasn't a massive crowd – this has never been a big village – but people were falling over themselves in the mud to get away from whatever they'd seen.

'I remember seeing our poor old vicar – he was a terribly serious man, never really approved of the mummers' play, but came along because his stern eye and the odd dropped hint of eternal damnation was good advertising for midnight mass – his face and cassock coated in mud. His eyes were wide with terror and he was bellowing something, but then he slipped and fell in the mud again. And behind him I saw what was coming.'

The villagers' farting chorus starts up again, this time synchronised and ominous like an imperial death march.

'They were deer.' The flashlight projects Miss Scarlet's shadow on to the pub wall. She raises her hands to her head to turn her shadow into the form of the monsters outside. 'They had antlers like branches, but they glinted silver in the light of the tractor like blades. And they were bigger than any deer I'd ever seen – bigger than any horse—'

'Like a moose?' Effie says.

'They were deer,' Miss Scarlet insists.

'Moose are a type of deer. They get really big,' Nish says. 'I saw a video of one on YouTube and—'

'They were *British* deer. A moose would be like this,' Miss Scarlet spreads her hands wide, so that her shadow antlers become wide slabs. 'Their antlers are much more like this.' She shifts her angle slightly, and the shadow antlers become long, slender and branched. 'Their faces were all mean, too. Big eyes and fangs.'

'Fangs?' Nish says.

'Muntjac have fangs,' Colonel Mustard says. 'But those are, of course, very small deer. These are very large deer.'

'And it was like my feet were rooted to the spot,' Miss Scarlet continues. 'Not with fear, although I was very scared. The mud was like quicksand and had covered my feet. I couldn't move without falling over. So I had to watch as they came into the light and the first one approached Jethro in his traditional green outfit. Now, he was frozen to the spot with fear. I could see it in his eyes. But this deer came up real close and sniffed him up and down and looked him right in the eye almost as if it recognised him or something. But it didn't like what it saw.' She moves her hands and in the shadow her antlers come together before flicking wide apart, almost as if she's miming a breaststroke. 'Ripped him clean in half.'

'Lengthwise,' the Colonel adds, as if this was an important detail.

'Poor Jethro's not even hit the ground before the others start.' Miss Scarlet sniffs back a tear and drops her hands, the lighting shifts and she's no longer casting a long shadow. She's just a young woman reliving a childhood trauma. 'It was over in a minute, maybe less, but it felt like time had collapsed in on itself. When I think back to it, I can see those brave, beautiful, funny men in their outfits – god, how they loved to dress up – how they went to town – Christmas Eve was their time to shine… All gone. All gone.' Her body shudders as the tears come forth.

'I found her rooted to the spot,' Colonel Mustard picks up the story, wrapping a comforting arm round Miss Scarlet. 'Untouched, but drenched in the blood of our menfolk. Looked like Carrie, didn't you, love? A right state. But the deer got their number easy that first night. Eight mummers. Eight kills by the light of the tractor. No sooner than the eighth body hit the ground, they were off.

'You hope something like that only happens once, but us country folk are superstitious. We know a bad omen when we see one. And so it's been each year since. The people you see before you tonight are all that's left of our little village.'

The beam of light drops to the floor and Nish has the strange sensation of a curtain falling. There's a beat of silence and then – clapping. It starts with Mrs White, but then the Reverend slams his ham-sized hands together with rich meaty resonance. The Professor joins in. Again, the bus driver picks up the cue, the beam of light flashing around wildly as it gets caught in the applause.

'Oh, that was marvellous,' Professor Plum says. 'I'm sorry I was so down on the story at first. You really brought it to life.'

'You think?' Miss Scarlet uncovers her face, and there's a beaming smile where Nish might have expected to see tears and snot. 'You liked it?'

'It was like the old tradition,' the Professor wipes away a tear. 'Ah, the boys would have been so proud. I do wish they could have seen it.'

Effie sidles closer to Nish. 'What,' she whispers, 'the *hell*?'

'Yeah, full Wicker Man,' he whispers back. 'Don't know about you, but I really miss London right about now.'

The one person who has watched this whole performance in impassive silence now speaks. 'How do I kill them?' Steve says.

It's the kind of hackneyed line Nish has heard action hero after action hero utter, but never like this. Never with this much conviction. Steve has the resolve of a man who has lost everything, in whose final act he wants nothing more than to see the world that has wronged him burn.

Nish and Effie exchange a look – she sees it too. Nish knows that any sensible plan will take the shape of hunkering down, keeping a low profile, and waiting until this all blows over. Steve, however, seems to think he's a Spartan ready to fight in the shade.

'You don't,' the Reverend growls. 'We've tried. Didn't work.'

'Then what are the bloody weapons for?'

The Reverend gives Steve a hard look, his earlier empathy melted away. 'Slow them down, give yourself a chance.'

'They make you feel less impotent, old chap.' The Colonel speaks with the same mix of weary resignation and dark humour as if he were preparing troops to surge from the trenches and cross a battlefield. So much for that Christmas truce Nish's history teacher used to bang on about to try to capture the attention of teenaged boys he thought were more interested in football.

Steve clenches his jaw and raises his chin to look the Reverend direct in the eye. 'There's got to be a way.'

The wind picks up and whistles against the shards of the broken window. The temperature in the pub has dropped a degree or two as the heat leaches out. Outside, Nish can hear the soft white noise of snow continuing to fall, like static on an old TV set. And something else, a deep resonant lowing. He tries to picture these deer the size of horses, apex predators with silver antlers. The best he can manage is a plus-sized Bambi, sparkling like a novelty bauble.

'What happens if they don't get their eight kills?' Effie says.

'They always get their eight,' Professor Plum says, stroking the barrel of his shotgun. 'Same every year. They come, they make their score, and they're gone by daybreak.'

'But if they didn't find us,' Effie says. 'If we hid down there in the cellar with the children, they might just pass?'

'Keep yer voice down,' the Colonel snaps, his voice rasping.

'I'm just saying, if we hid in the—'

'Enough! They might be listening.'

The wind whistles again.

'Do the deer understand English, then?' Nish says. The absurd question hangs in the air like a party balloon at a funeral.

'We don't know they don't,' comes the Colonel's reply. 'No one goes down there, not tonight. Not while those things are out after blood. You hear me?'

The message is clear: don't bring the children into this.

'You might want to wish everyone you love a merry Christmas, because most of us aren't making it through this night,' the Colonel continues. 'I'm sorry, that's just the way it is. We've had a good run, but every game's got to come to an end sometime.' He speaks these last to Miss Scarlet, and Nish senses a bond something like father and daughter. It's strange, seeing these people in heightened and intimate moments of their lives, while knowing nothing about them, not even their names.

The Londoners feel around in the dark for their phones, still plugged into various sockets around the pub.

'No signal,' Effie says, her phone glowing bright in the gloom.

Nish looks at his. 'Same. You, Steve?'

Steve looks at his screen. His wallpaper is a photo of him and Jess at a masked ball, all feathers and sequins. He doesn't need to answer. He is a man whose world has collapsed around him.

Whatever happens, no one's coming to help.

There's the squeak of chalk on board. The spotlight flicks over to catch Miss Scarlet adding a check under the 'Away' column for this year.

She turns and says: 'First blood.'

9

The fire crackles as Professor Plum puts on another couple of fresh logs. A flurry of embers rise into the air and escape up the chimney.

The group has gathered closer. The temperature in the pub has dropped since the window was broken – since Jess was pulled screaming into the night – and Nish rubs his hands for warmth. Effie hugs herself, her hands tucked under her armpits. Miss Scarlet has wrapped a blanket round her shoulders. Mrs White stands brittle with cold, waiting patiently for the fire or her own willpower to bring warmth. The bus driver, the Professor and the Colonel have all been standing close to the fire since the siege began, but even they have begun to feel the gradual cooling.

As the Professor stands, the first tentative flames licking the sides of the new logs, the mournful lowing of a beast carries through from outside. The group exchange worried looks.

'What are they waiting for?' Nish says. 'They know where we are.'

'They're waiting for us to make a mistake,' Mrs White says, her teeth chattering.

'Boredom or frustration is the real killer,' the Colonel says. 'How many people have run into the fate they feared most because they couldn't bear waiting for the inevitable?'

'Too true, too true.' Professor Plum has a kind of wistful look, as if he's remembering another night much like this one.

Reverend Green has been sent into the heart of the building to investigate the lighting. Occasional sounds filter through to the bar – resonant thumps, brittle snaps, the closing of doors – but so far they're still in the dark.

He emerges at long last, with a torch and a sullen look accentuated by the darkness.

'Any luck?' the bus driver says cheerfully, shining a spotlight on the Reverend.

'What does it look like?' the Reverend growls.

The pub is lit by the flashing beams of two torches and the flickering light of the fire. The electric lights remain off. The fridges and pumps at the bar are unlit. The fruit machines – one of which now blocks the broken window – loom like standing stones in the darkness. The endless Christmas music has been stilled, there's not even the hint of an ironic Silent Night. The tinsel and baubles reflect light from the fire, creating a shimmering outline of the Christmas tree. Everywhere Nish looks, there's incontrovertible evidence that the Reverend did not have any luck.

'Well, I'm sure you tried.' The bus driver flashes a rictus grin in the torchlight.

'There's a fire in the village,' the Reverend says, addressing Colonel Mustard.

'A fire?' the Colonel says.

'You went upstairs?' Professor Plum says as if his inner sanctum has been violated.

'Think it's the substation. Looks like about the right direction for it.' The Reverend delivers this news with the same gravitas he might deliver news of a death in the family.

'Tell me you didn't touch anything.'

'Then they've cut power to the whole village,' Colonel Mustard says. He furrows his brow, strokes his chin and looks into the fire. The hungry flames have enveloped the new logs and burn vigorously.

'I don't think you understand,' the Professor continues, outraged. 'When you live at your work – and your work is a profoundly public space – it makes you appreciate the privacy of your own sanctum.'

'Nowhere else looks to have power. Streetlights are off.'

'This is new,' Colonel Mustard turns to look back at the Reverend. 'They're learning.'

'Or they got lucky,' Mrs White says. She's edged closer to the fire and has stopped shivering.

Nish glances at Effie. He wants to know what she's thinking, to feel some comfort from solidarity at the absurd situation. But she's looking off into the depths of the pub. For a moment he thinks she's spotted something that shouldn't be there, maybe a deer that's found a way into the building, or some imminent horror. But then he realises. She's looking at the bottles of spirits that hang behind the bar, facing her own battle with oblivion.

'Hey,' he says, softly touching her hand. 'You okay?'

She licks her dry lips and forces her eyes away. 'Not really.'

'You'll make it through. I'll see to that.'

'You heard them. There's nine of us and they need seven more.' She swallows and gives him a look of such intense fear. 'You don't need to be a genius to know those are bad odds.'

'Ten of us,' he says. He can't believe he's making this argument, but there's no room for sentiment in the face of such deadly logic. 'Don't forget the drunk guy. He's still out there.'

'If they've not got him already. Then it would be six remaining,' Miss Scarlet says with a smile. 'You might not like those odds, but you don't have to be a genius to see that's better.' Then, quietly, as if letting them in on a trade secret: 'But I'm not chalking him until we've seen a body. You want a tip? Only count the kills you see.'

'Oh god,' Effie groans. 'I can't do this.'

Realising what she's about to do, Nish grabs a handful of fabric at her sleeve. She stops a step away, Nish braces himself against her momentum. 'You can.'

'Honestly, you don't even know me. I can't. You know why I turned to drink in the first place? To escape. Because it made me feel good when everything else was so crappy. It took me away from all the other disappointments and horrors of my life.' Effie laughs humourlessly, her eyes pleading in the firelight. 'If this is it – if this is how I die – what's the point of quitting? If ever I've needed a drink, it's now.'

'It's an open bar,' says the bus driver with festive cheer.

'That's quitting. Having a drink is giving up on life, you see that right?' Nish can feel panic rising. He knows what's at stake. He doesn't know if he can talk her round, but he knows that if he sounds as afraid or desperate as he feels, he'll fail. He clings on to her sleeve, feeling the tension return as she's drawn towards the bar. 'I believe in you.'

She turns towards him. He can still feel the gravity of her pull, he's still holding her back, but it slackens a little.

'That's like believing in Santa Claus. I'll only let you down.

You'll find out the thing you believed in wasn't real in the first place.'

Effie puts her hand on Nish's, not unkindly, but gently starts prising his fingers from the fabric of her sleeve. He's gulping for words – something, *anything*, that will make her see sense – when a long, sad animal call comes through the window.

One of the creatures is outside, drawn back to the broken window by the sound of their voices.

They stand in silence, frozen with fear in case the beast tries to break through. The tension falls out of Effie, she keeps her hand on Nish's and takes a quiet step back to the group. Her skin is cold and Nish closes his other hand over hers, telling himself he's sharing his warmth, but really seeking comfort while his heart races and his stomach lurches.

Steve is panting, heaving in short and fast breaths. In the flickering light, Nish sees him loosen a fist into a claw. His eyes are fixed on something in the dark and it takes Nish a moment to trace a line to the barrel of Professor Plum's shotgun. With dread inevitability he realises what's going through Steve's mind.

There's the sound of metal brushing against brickwork from outside. A loud snorting exhalation that reminds Nish of a horse. In the distance, there's another lowing call. And then, the sound of footsteps – hoof-steps, really – in the snow, gradually fading into the distance.

The sound of a nearby beast is replaced by a silence thick like heavy snow. The first sign that it might be safe is when the Reverend glances at Miss Scarlet. She heaves a deep breath, her skin pink from the warmth of the fire. Mrs White glares up at the butcher until he notices. He reaches out to touch her shoulder, but Mrs White turns and he takes a step back from the fireplace.

Seeing the cue, the remaining group let their guard down. Which is when Steve sees his moment. In a blur of movement, he snatches the barrel of the shotgun and wrenches it out of the Professor's hands.

Nish and Effie duck into a corner of the inglenook fireplace, surrounding themselves on two sides with brickwork. They huddle together, Nish using his body to cover Effie as best he can, while Steve hoists the stock to his shoulder and strides towards the door. He moves with the kind of rapid certainty of a man who has had an opportunity to plot his action and knows that if he falters, he will fail.

The Reverend is caught off-guard, but it takes him only a fraction of a moment to understand what's happened. He takes two powerful strides, vaults over the still-laid table, sending a shatter of glasses and crockery to the floor, before body-slamming Steve into the wall. He fastens one meaty hand around the shotgun barrel and forces it towards the ceiling.

'You want to get us all killed?' The Reverend barks like a drill sergeant, his face little more than an inch from Steve's. Steve is a big man, but the Reverend is bigger, the cassock straining against his broad back.

'I'm going to kill them,' Steve shouts back.

'Told you, you can't.'

For a moment, Nish thinks, they are like two animals fighting for dominance. Out in the wild, one would kill the other, or the loser would be ejected from the pack.

'My poor Jess,' Steve sobs. His resolve melts away, like ice in boiling water.

'You want to die, do us all a favour and just walk out there,' the Reverend says, his voice like a whetting blade. 'You want to stand a chance, listen to what I say. The only chance any of us has is if we work together. You try to fight one of them, you'll lose. And you'll lead them to the rest of us.'

Steve loosens his grip on the shotgun. The Reverend takes it from him, rests the barrels over his broad shoulder.

'Try that again and I'll kill you myself,' he says, just loud enough for his voice to carry to the rest of the pub. The warning is clear and applies to all of them.

The Reverend is navigating Steve back towards the fireplace, one hand clamped on his shoulder, when there's an enormous thud at the door. Effie and Nish are already as sheltered and small as they can make themselves, pressed into a corner with their backs against the wall, but they still flinch. Nish can feel the impact reverberate through the brickwork. He hears the tinkle of broken glass loosened from the broken window and another decoration falling from the wall.

The thud comes again, from a different part of the building this time. Even so, the dull reverberation of impact echoes around the bar.

'We need to get upstairs,' Nish says.

'Upstairs?' Professor Plum says. 'What makes you think you've got a right to go upstairs?'

There comes the sound of scraping at the windows. Another loose piece of glass falls to the ground. Something hard scratches against the back of the dead slot machine. There's the unmistakeable sound of rocking.

'They're trying to find a way in. We need to get off the ground floor.' Nish addresses the Colonel, much to Professor Plum's chagrin.

'He's right,' Mrs White says, matter of fact. 'We're easy pickings here.'

Miss Scarlet nods.

'Very well,' announces Colonel Mustard. 'Upstairs it is.'

Professor Plum is about to argue back, although even he must realise that the argument would be futile, but then his eyes settled on the shotgun in the Reverend's hand. 'Thank you for retrieving that for me,' he says, holding out his hand for its return.

Instead, the Reverend hands the gun to the Colonel. 'Careless is what that was. You're on candlestick and you'll be grateful for it.'

The Colonel seems pleased with this turn of events. He casually reaches a hand into Professor Plum's pocket and retrieves a fistful of cartridges. He shovels the copper-capped red plastic tubes into his own pocket and hoists the gun barrel over his shoulder. 'Follow me,' he announces.

The Professor watches his shotgun lead the way towards his sacred space. The others follow, walking gingerly through the bar, guided by two torchlights. He looks at the candlestick on the table, a heavy silver object with a thick square base that can be used as a mace. It's useless, in so much as any of the weapons the villagers carry stand much chance against the beasts outside. He contemplates leaving it.

The fruit machine in the window starts rocking back and forth. The cabinet teeters before falling back, crunching into the wall.

Professor Plum hears a snort as the creature exhales. It knows what it's doing. It could topple that machine at any point – probably will with the next push – but it's just playing with them.

He pictures facing one of those creatures unarmed. Even a useless weapon is better than no weapon. He grabs the candlestick and dashes to follow the others.

Behind him there's the sound of an impact, followed by the crash of furniture and a spill of coins scattering on the wooden floor. Jackpot.

❆ ❆ ❆

The flat upstairs is a mix of small rooms and strange angles. While the bar has been renovated to become wide and open-plan, the same modernisation has not been applied to the landlord's living quarters.

A narrow and steep flight of carpeted stairs leads to a heavy fire door that has been propped open with a fire extinguisher in what would certainly be a breach of health and safety regulations. Although, should an inspection occur tonight, even the most diligent bureaucrat would have to admit that an open fire door was not the largest risk to workers' or customers' welfare, what with the rampaging herd of murder-deer.

Rooms lead off the narrow dog-legged hallway. Nish glimpses a galley kitchen equipped with an ancient cooker that has an eye-level grill. He remembers his grandmother had one of those, when she was living on her own in an increasingly dilapidated flat. There's a perfunctory bathroom, a glint of white tile and blackened grouting, a lid-up toilet, and a narrow bath. A bedroom, the headboard against the narrow angle of the ceiling.

Nish follows through to the lounge, where the group has gathered. A torch has been angled into a mirror in such a way that there's a reasonable spill of light. The room is crowded and there's the hubbub of separate conversations. It's as if the Professor is hosting a party in his bachelor pad. There's a fusty wing-backed armchair in one corner facing a squat cathode-ray TV, a bookcase full of DVDs – golden oldies on the top shelf, retro action films below that, followed by a complete collection of the Carry On films, and a smorgasbord of arthouse European erotica on the bottom shelf. A small wooden side-table is covered by a cream doily and houses at least two more remote controls than there are electronic devices in the room.

One side of the room has a sloping roof, intersected by three gable-end windows.

'Cosy pad,' Nish says to Effie.

'Character features,' she says looking around. 'Central location. Fully equipped. How much do you reckon?'

'In London? Fifteen hundred.'

'A month?'

'A week.'

'Minimum.'

She still looks shaken. There's a haunted look in her eyes, maybe from how close she came to throwing it all away. But humour makes things easier.

Someone barges Nish from behind him and the Professor squeezes through. He pushes himself to the head of the group, standing in an alcove in front of the middle window, the candlestick he brandishes glinting in the light.

'I suppose it's too late to ask you all to take your shoes off,' he says. 'Although I would be grateful if you could try not to tread muck into the carpets. Meantime, don't touch anything, don't move anything, and absolutely do not make yourselves at home.'

In the silence that follows, the wind howls and rattles the ancient sash windows. Outside, the snow has stopped. The snowscape glows in the dark, the hard edges of the village sharpened in the clear air. It's some comfort to know that the weather might be improving, although it's going to take more than a night to melt this ice. More like a week, during which the pristine white coating will become treacherous brown slush. But before the night is out, Nish thinks, the snow will be stained red with blood.

'So what happens now?' Steve says.

'We wait,' the Reverend says. His head is cocked to an angle by the low ceiling.

'Just – whatever you do – don't attract their attention,' the Professor waves the candlestick around to emphasise his point. It throws sparks of light around the room like a glitter ball.

Effie puts her hand in Nish's, pulls him gently back towards the door to the hallway.

Nish gives her a look of gentle enquiry.

'I've got a bad feeling about this,' she whispers.

No sooner have they taken a couple of steps back than there's an enormous thud. It's different from the sounds of impact earlier that battered the very foundations of the building. This is the sound of impact on the roof. Nish thinks of the sounds earlier, of something moving across the tiles overhead. Are they really any safer up here?

There's no time for warning. The question has barely made it through Nish's brain before the answer crashes in through the window.

10

Glass shatters and wood splinters. The Professor is framed in the window, arms akimbo. A metal blade protrudes from his sternum, glistening with red and silver in the reflected torchlight. The Professor looks down, his mouth gaping open in shock at his own predicament. He is lifted off his feet, suspended on the metal that pierces him – and as the angle shifts, Nish sees that it's not a blade. There are metal branches peeling back, dextrous like fingers, fluid like quicksilver. The sight of the DVD shelf earlier must have put the thought into his mind because he finds himself thinking of the T-1000 in Terminator 2. The branches continue to peel back until they resemble a pair of hands pressing against the Professor's chest. He emits a pained gargle, blood spills from his mouth.

There's no time for more thought, though, because the Professor is snatched back through the window with the sound of more breaking glass and a horrific sinewy tearing noise. In the gaping silence that follows, Nish hears the echoing crump of two substantial somethings landing in fresh snow.

He thinks of Miss Scarlet's story. *Ripped him clean in half.*

Steve screams, high-pitched and shrill. Perhaps he's thinking about Jess's fate?

Perhaps not. Steve is the first to see the creature that stands silhouetted in the window. A vast shaggy mane flowing in the wind, big muscular shoulders like a plough horse, and great boughs of silver antlers fanning out behind its head. It snorts. Plumes of frosted breath billow into the bitter night air.

The stag watches them for a moment. No one moves. What are you meant to do when you encounter a bear on a trail? Is coming face-to-face with one of these beasts like that? Do you need to play dead until it gets bored and goes away? Or do you run like your life depends on it? Why has no one told Nish what to do if he found himself face-to-face with Bambi's bloodthirsty mutant brother?

The beast raises its head and a melancholy lowing resonates through the room. It's deep and powerful and Nish can feel the pressure reverberate in his chest. There's a majestic beauty in this creature, he thinks. It's extraordinary that something like this exists, gilded and magnificent. But, all things considered, he'd rather be seeing it on YouTube from the comfort of his house-share rather than so close that he can catch the whiff of hay and dung that lingers on its fur.

'Run!' The Reverend barks, ushering the group back towards the hallway. 'For god's sake, move now!'

It's not a moment too soon. Somehow the beast's antlers ripple and clasp the aperture of the broken window. Plaster begins to crumble and there's the crack of brick and woodwork as the stag disappears behind a cloud of dust. A pair of fusty curtains turn sideways, detaching from a wall that is no longer there. Effie grabs Nish's hand and leads him into the hallway.

The sounds of demolition continue to come from the room behind. The beast is tearing a hole in the building to let itself in.

There's shouting and barging and it's barely possible to navigate through the pitch-black rooms at speed. Nish barks his shin and collides painfully with a doorframe. They're halfway down the narrow stairs when they hear the first shotgun blast. He turns to look, but someone bumps into him and he stumbles down the last few steps.

'Shut the door!' Mrs White shouts. 'Shut the damned fire door!'

There's a clank of metal as Steve knocks the fire extinguisher out of the way and a beat or two before they hear the firm snap of the door shutting.

It feels both as if barely a moment has passed since they were in the pub and an age. The fruit machine has fallen away from the window, crushing one of the tables and at least one chair. Broken crockery and cold food has spilled over the floor. The village green and church beyond is picture-postcard through the smashed window now that the snow has stopped falling. The pristine coating is iridescent, but churned tracks weave across the village green marking the path taken by the creatures on their hunt for blood. Beyond the green, the yew trees in the churchyard are tall black columns. And something is moving, emerging from the darkness. Nish watches as a stag detaches itself from the negative space of the yew trees, strolling towards the village. It cuts a beautiful silhouette, but if it sees them, it will suddenly become deadly.

'Give me a hand,' the Reverend says to Steve, low and quiet.

The two men gather around the fruit machine and with some effort bring it back to stand in front of the window, once more blotting out the snow scene. There's a heavy thud as it falls back into place. They wait with dread certainty for the inevitable thud of impact against the sides of the building.

But instead the silence is filled by the sound of demolition from upstairs as the rampaging stag continues its assault on the Professor's old digs.

Miss Scarlet goes to the dartboard and marks up the score. Home has lost its clean slate for the first time in a run of years. 'Two down,' she says, as if anyone could forget.

'It still hurts to lose one of your own,' Mrs White says.

'He was a good man,' Miss Scarlet adds. 'He let me pick the shifts I wanted and welcomed me into this pub like it was my home.'

'It was never your home,' Colonel Mustard says.

'I know.' Miss Scarlet gives him a fond smile. 'But, I guess there's a vacancy for a new landlord.'

'Too soon,' the Colonel chides.

'He should have known better,' says the Reverend. 'How hard is it to stay away from the windows?'

'We should have a toast to his memory,' Mrs White says. 'That's what he'd want.'

There's a general agreement amongst the villagers. Miss Scarlet goes to the bar to fix some drinks.

Effie moves closer to the fire, hugging herself close. The gaping hole in the side of the pub has sucked the warm air out of the room, replaced it with a sharp iciness. The fire burns brightly, the logs added so recently have now blackened and begun to crack with fissures of burning embers. There's a stack of chopped wood in a corner of the fireplace, a jumble of wedges that reaches to shoulder height. Nish takes a couple of pieces and adds them to the fire. Sparks lift into the air, followed by flickers of flame grasping the new fuel.

'Thank you,' Nish says. 'For seeing something was wrong, for making me step back.'

'And look how we're now safe.' Effie hugs herself for warmth.

From upstairs there comes a sound of something solid being struck repeatedly and rapidly, followed by the dull rumble of rubble falling. There's another lowing call and then the unmistakeable sound of hooves on the roof as another of the creatures joins the wrecking crew.

'They can't make it through, can they?' Nish says.

'Does it sound like they're giving up?' There's a thud of impact from somewhere in the heart of the building as something that may well be of vital importance to structural integrity comes under attack. 'You saw that thing, right?'

'Yeah, you're not going mad. I saw it alright.'

She frowns. 'I never said I was. But if you want to survive being attacked by monsters, you need to know what you're up against. Stands to reason, right? Find yourself in an Alien film, keep away from the air ducts, never ever stick your head over an egg, and get yourself a flamethrower. Up against the Predator? Roll in mud – or snow, you know, if it's the season – so it can't see you with thermal imaging. Dracula got his sights on you? Grab yourself some garlic, holy water, a stake and a daylight lamp.'

'Watch a lot of monster movies, huh?' Nish says.

'Monsters are rational actors,' she says with a strange intensity. 'They want something.'

'Okay?'

'The aliens want to set up new colonies and reproduce. The Predator is some bored intergalactic rich boy on safari looking for bragging rights. Dracula's just horny. If we know what they want, maybe we can make them stop.'

'Got it all figured out haven't you?'

'I've just had more time to think about this than most people. I knew a guy once who had this whole theory about the rules of time travel. Rationalising monster movies was the only way I could shut him up.' There's something in Effie's body language, a distant look in her eyes, that hints at sadness.

'Getting awful cosy by the fireside aren't we?' Miss Scarlet says, presenting a tray of shots. 'Brandy. For the fallen.'

Nish knows Effie's been wavering so steps in: 'I don't—'

'Chances are you're not going to make it through the night, honey. Might as well have some fun while you still can.' Miss Scarlet thrusts out the tray. It's clear they're not going to be left alone to carry on their discussion until she's satisfied.

'Fine,' Effie says through gritted teeth.

They both take a shot glass each. Miss Scarlet gives them a tight smile and lingers for just long enough that Nish thinks she's going to watch them drink. He raises his glass in salute.

'Got a spare, I'd kill for another,' Steve says, appearing at her shoulder.

'I wouldn't normally, but special occasion,' she giggles. Miss Scarlet turns and leads Steve back to the bar.

Effie stares at the glass in her hand. The refracted firelight makes the amber liquid glow with inviting warmth. It's just the one… It would be so easy… Her mouth is so dry and her nerves so torn by the last few hours. She knows it would steady her. She can almost feel the numbing effect of the alcohol coursing through her blood.

'You don't need it,' Nish says.

'What difference does it make?'

'You had an idea, remember? Rational monsters. It's the only way we get out of here alive.' Perhaps, Nish thinks, the only way to deal with trauma like this is to lean into it. 'You can do this.'

'I can't,' she says.

'Then I'll do it for you.' Nish takes the glass from her hand and tosses it into the fire, followed by his own. There's a sputter of blue flame and the crack of glass, and the drink is gone.

'Thanks,' she says, her voice flat. He sees a sharp fury in her eyes. Has he over-stepped the mark? Is she angry with him, or with herself?

'Rational monsters,' he prompts. The only way is forwards. 'You were saying that they must want something, right? What do you think they want?'

She shakes her head as if to loosen the thoughts that have lodged themselves. 'Right, rational… They want eight—'

There comes the sound of wood rending from upstairs. The pounding of destruction has been steady and percussive – not quite background noise, but something that has taken a remarkably short amount of time to get used to. Like living near a construction site in London. Every now and then, there's a jarring sound of something dramatic, but otherwise it's just another city sound that blends into the background. This, however, sounds close. As if filtered through thinner walls – or not filtered through walls at all.

'They can't…' Reverend Green says, his eyes jerking towards the doorway that leads to the Professor's stairway.

To date the butcher has dealt with the evening's proceedings with the kind of worn stoicism of a man who has done this all before. There's been a strange comfort in this familiarity. A kind of sense that if the world is losing its head, at least here's someone calm and balanced enough to be the group's Lode Star. Except now he looks shocked – genuinely taken aback by the idea that the monsters upstairs could do the unthinkable.

There's a heavy thud, the sound of splintering wood, and the sound of something flying violently down a flight of stairs. He can't see it, but Nish knows that the heavy fire door has been tossed aside like kindling. There comes an animal sound, low and loud. No longer a mournful cry, more a bellow of victory.

'They're coming down the stairs,' Mrs White shouts, the panic straining her voice.

'But they can't,' the Reverend protests. 'How can they…?'

Animal noises echo through the pub, along with the sound of more destruction. Plaster and brickwork tumble down the stairs, colliding with the remains of the wooden door. There comes the sound of creaking floorboards, as if a massive weight is being applied to woodwork for the first time.

'We need to get out of here,' Miss Scarlet says.

'Where do you think we're going to go?' Mrs White pleads?

'We can't stay in here if they're coming down the stairs!'

'We can't go outside,' Mrs White protests.

'You want to be next on the scoreboard?' Miss Scarlet says, treading a fine line between warning and threat.

'There's, what, two of them in here? There's six of them outside!' Mrs White is standing face-to-face with Miss Scarlet now. The two women square up to each other. 'Tell me again why I should listen to you?'

'You think you can take them?'

There's a skittish scraping of hoof, followed by the sound of blade lashing against something solid. It sounds like a predator feverish with bloodlust.

'Fine,' Mrs White says, standing so close to Miss Scarlet that their noses are nearly touching. 'If we're going outside, I say we should just leave you here to slow them down.'

Miss Scarlet flinches as if the words are a physical blow. She shifts her grip on the axe handle and Nish thinks she might be about to swing out when the Reverend pulls the women apart. 'You kill each other, you kill us all.'

'What does that mean?' Nish says to Effie.

'Eight kills,' she whispers back. 'If a deer doesn't do the killing, it doesn't count.'

Nish heaves out a slow breath. 'Hell of a way to call a truce.'

And that's when it happens. There's another creak of complaining woodwork, a skittish volley of hooves scrabbling for purchase, followed by the sound of something heavy falling down the narrow flight of stairs. Something out of sight slams into a solid wall with enough force to reverberate through the structure of the building.

Silence follows.

The bus driver is the first to move, training a torchlight on the doorway, and gingerly approaching. 'I… I think it's dead.'

There's a lowing sound from upstairs. Nish pictures the second stag peering down at its fallen comrade.

Blitzen, you alright mate?

'Don't get too close,' Mrs White says, hands close to her mouth.

'It's not moving,' the driver says, gripping the croquet mallet with both hands, ready to strike at the slightest movement.

'It's stunned,' the Reverend says, his gravel voice an ominous rumble.

'No,' she says, edging closer. 'I— I think it's really dead.'

The bus driver reaches out with the mallet, extending it fully, before bringing the head gently down on to the bunched-up form of the stag. 'Bonk,' she says, high-pitched, as if teasing a child. 'Bonk. Bonk. Bonk.'

'Seriously,' the Reverend says, 'step back.'

'It's fine, really… Its eyes are open but they're all glassy like there's nothing behind them. It's completely—'

There's a snorting, a cross between a racehorse eager and ready to go and the motor of an old car engine backfiring, and the bus driver leaps backwards with a little squeal.

'Said as much,' says the Reverend.

The beast at the foot of the stairs blinks. It twitches its ears, brushing them against the blades of its vast antlers, before it wheels its front legs, pawing into the air. It shifts its wide, muscular shoulders, rocking its body back and forth. And then it shimmies its whole trunk, writing back and forth as if caught in a spasm, until it unfolds its legs and rights itself. With some effort, it stands, shaking its mane and flexing its antlers. Once upright it fixes the bus driver with a hungry stare. It lows softly with a menace that makes the hairs on the back of Nish's neck stand on end.

'It's not dead,' the bus driver says. The statement is entirely redundant – it's bloody obvious to anyone with eyes to see that the creature is not dead.

'We need to get out of here,' Miss Scarlet says.

Her undeniably correct assertion is enough to break the spell.

Nish is up and first to the door, dragging Effie in tow. Everyone else seems to be moving like they're wading through waist-deep water. They are frozen by the stag's gaze as its antlers flex and branch around the silhouette of its head. Nish is in such a hurry that it takes a couple of attempts to throw the latch.

The stag tucks its antlers narrow behind its head and ducks through the doorway. Once through, its metal antlers fan out wide, each tine razor sharp and flashing in the torchlight. As it lows with a bristling menace, there's a blur of fur and blades and bulk as a second stag crashes down the stairs and smashes into the sagging wall.

The bus driver swings the mallet, catching the first stag on the chin with a solid blow. It roars with indignation and – quick as lightning – slashes the weapon with its antlers. The mallet head skitters into a dark corner of the pub, leaving the hapless driver holding a fresh-cut stub that could only ever be useful for kindling or perhaps a door wedge.

Effie watches, her back to Nish. 'Now would be a really good time to get that door open,' she says.

Nish pulls the door handle once, twice more. He tries to turn it, but it won't budge. 'It's no good,' he says. 'It's locked.'

'Locked?' Effie says, turning to see the problem.

Colonel Mustard fires the shotgun at the stag. The noise of the blast is deafening in the confined space. As one, the group duck and hold their hands to their ears. Nish can't hear the shower of plaster falling from the ceiling and walls above the ringing in his ears. Or the roar of the stag, its face bloodied by pellets, eyes ruined. But he watches in dumb horror as it shakes its head, shedding a fine splatter of blood.

Taking two barrels of the shotgun in the face has not dissuaded the stag from its murderous mission. If anything, the indignity and loss of sight has infuriated it even more. It roars again, barely audible over the ringing tinnitus.

Behind the first stag, the second stands and unfurls its glimmering antlers.

'The keys,' Miss Scarlet shouts. She's close, but unable to judge her volume in the aftermath of the shot. 'The Professor had them.'

The Professor, who is lying outside in two separate bloody piles.

'Then we're locked in,' Nish shouts back.

The second stag nudges the first through the doorframe and bellows. Nish feels the creature's rage as the sound rattles through his ribcage.

They're trapped.

11

The Colonel breaks his shotgun in half and fumbles in his pocket for more cartridges. All the while, he watches the bloodied face of the first deer as it advances blindly towards him, antlers whipping out wildly like snakes on a Medusa's head, cutting through the air with deadly swooshing sounds.

Steve shifts his grip on the stubby shovel, lunges forward and swings the improvised weapon with all the force he can muster at a rising angle. He's lucky. It narrowly avoids a flicking tine before the flat end of the blade makes contact with the deer's muzzle.

The creature rears up in shock. The shovel resonates in Steve's hands. He drops the weapon, just as the stag roars at him, spraying mucus and blood.

Steve takes a step back, bumping into Miss Scarlet. Wordlessly, he grabs the fire axe out of her hands.

'You want some figgy pudding, mate?' Steve bellows.

'Huh?'

The deer takes a step forwards, flexing its antlers. *We won't go until we get some.*

'Steve,' Nish shouts. 'The door!'

The deer lashes out an antler. The air sings. Steve and Miss Scarlet retreat towards the fireplace.

'Bit busy, fella.'

'The door's locked. We're trapped – unless you can force it open.'

Miss Scarlet throws a fire poker at the advancing creature. There's a flash of silver as a whipping antler deflects the projectile and sends it flying to embed into the far wall with a thud. The quivering metal shaft grazes the top of a Toby jug as if it were an arrow shot by William Tell.

'Can't the big guy in a dress do it?' Steve says, never taking his eyes off the advancing beast.

'You've got the axe!'

Steve looks at the axe in his hands. Properly looks at it. Because it's only then that its true purpose strikes him. This isn't an axe for splitting logs. No, that's probably out back, buried in a stump. This is a short-handled blade for emergencies, intended to hack away at obstacles in case of a fire. Obstacles such as a locked door. The penny drops.

There comes the sound of wood rending and the tumble of more slabs of plaster and ruined brickwork, followed by a scream. The second stag has forced its way into the lounge bar. The shotgun fires again, but it doesn't sound as loud as the first time. A hole opens in the ceiling and there's the sound of lead pellets ricocheting off swishing antlers.

Steve can feel the heat of the fireplace close behind him. He can hear Miss Scarlet breathing at his shoulder, hot and fast. There's a narrow path through to the locked door. It involves dashing over the crushed furniture, past the dead fruit machine, and banking into the porch. But the stag is hot on their scent – or sound – he's not sure which – and it's fast.

They need a distraction—

But the Reverend is already a step ahead. There's the sound of crockery shattering on the floorboards as he upends a table into the path of the second stag and swings his meat cleaver into the exposed flank of the first creature.

The beast rears up in pain or anger, turning round to face the source of this new assault. Its antlers crash into the ceiling, spreading dust and plaster, and drive into an oak beam. It bellows and pauses, tugging, but the blade is stuck.

Miss Scarlet seizes the moment. She dashes, ducking low and nimble, her skirt hitched up to run more easily. Steve follows, clutching the axe close to his chest. By contrast, he feels sweaty and slow, the feast sloshing around in his belly.

Nish backs away from the door and ushers Steve through. He holds the over-sized vegetable knife like a sword. Effie, standing at his shoulder, grips her cane upside down, ready to use the metal head as a small ineffectual mace should the need emerge.

Steve begins hacking away with the axe, the wood splinters as the blade bites deeper with each swing.

'Nothing seems to stop them,' Effie says to Nish. 'Getting shot in the face from point blank has just pissed it off.'

He watches as the blinded stag frees its stuck antler. It shuffles clumsily round in the confined space to face the Reverend, who grips a blade in each hand, poised and ready for action. Mrs White, meanwhile, swings a vicious arc with the cricket bat and there's the thunk of willow on leather – the sound of hot dry summer afternoons in a Middle England village – as she connects a solid blow on the second stag.

If the beasts turn on Nish and Effie, they stand no chance with these weapons. The realisation dawns on Nish afresh. All it would take is to get within whip-crack range of those antlers and they'll be sliced like charcuterie. The helplessness of the situation washes over him.

'This happens every year and yet these are the best weapons they can find?' Nish protests.

'There's something that's been bugging me…' Effie says.

'How come there's only one gun?'

'No,' she says. 'I mean, sure. But Cluedo—'

'Here's Johnny!' Steve bellows, giving it his best Jack Nicholson impression. He's hacked a splintered hole near the lock. He kicks at the door once, twice, and it gives. It swings wide and fast to reveal the dark snowscape outside.

'It's open. Come on!' Miss Scarlet shouts at the Reverend.

'You go,' the Reverend says, ducking and deflecting a stray antler with the flat of his cleaver. 'We'll slow them down.'

'We'll what?' Mrs White says, throwing a barstool at the second stag. Shock is etched on her face. The stool is snatched out of the air in a flash of metal.

'It's the only way,' her husband shouts back.

'But that's suicide,' Miss Scarlet says, her voice choking with emotion.

'For god's sake, go!' The Reverend bellows. 'We'll meet you at the church.'

As if sensing the stakes of the decisions in the room, both stags bellow in unison, their mouths hanging wide to reveal rows of sharpened incisors. Nish is no naturalist, but those aren't the teeth of ruminants content with a diet of grass, tender stems and acorns.

Miss Scarlet casts a final forlorn look at the butcher as he prepares to swing his blades once more. Reluctantly, she turns and follows the others out into the frozen night. The sound of metal-on-metal rings in her ears.

Steve was the first through the doorway and is furthest ahead. He grips the axe in one hand and pinwheels his arms as he clears the beer garden perimeter and starts out across the void of the village green. He's followed by the bus driver, who picks a surprisingly sprightly path, knees high to avoid the drag of the snow that sucks at her feet. The torchlight dances across the path cut by Steve.

Nish and Effie follow behind, racing at first, but slowing to a more careful pace as they struggle to stay upright. Fresh snow is the easiest underfoot, but it saps energy with each crisp *crump*. The stags' churned trails are deceptive. The massive creatures have compressed the snow to ice, leaving slippery traps for unsuspecting victims.

The trails are also a reminder of the danger that lurks out here. Predators hunting their prey.

As he slows, Nish looks around. He's no idea what time it is, but at this time of year daylight doesn't break until eight – and that's on a clear day. There are no stars in the sky, but there is a silver patchwork to the scudding clouds that obscure the moon.

A plane of midnight blue snow spreads out before them, glowing ever so slightly. Ahead looms a pitch-black cut-out of the church and the imposing yew trees. To one side, in the distance, there's the black scatter of low buildings of the village beyond. And somewhere roaming through the darkness are the six deer not currently tied up in battle at The Slaughter House.

They've had two kills so far. Maybe there's two more chalked up already, the villagers' attempt to slow the deer down having paid a high price for only a few seconds. And the drunk, what of him? If they've had five, then only three remain… But either way, the six figures, exposed and picking their way through the snow would be irresistible.

'I – am – not – prepared – for – this,' Nish gasps to Effie, frozen breath billowing around him.

'Worst – Christmas – ever,' she pants back.

'Shh, your voice carries,' Miss Scarlet hisses as she passes them. Her skirt is hitched up and she is power walking, rather than running. Her stocky shoes *crump* in the snow. Colonel Mustard follows after her a couple of steps behind, shotgun over his shoulder, looking for all the world like he's out for a brisk constitutional.

Left in the villagers' wake, Nish and Effie start to walk –

and progress becomes easier. Not easy – but less of their energy is wasted in trying to stay upright.

There's the sound of retching ahead and they find Steve bent over in the snow.

'You alright,' Nish whispers.

'*Bleugh*,' Steve groans loudly. There's the sound of wet matter slapping into the snow and the smell of rancid meat mixed with stale red wine.

'It's too soon for food poisoning,' Effie says.

'You think they…' Nish glances around. Miss Scarlet, the Colonel and the bus driver continue away from them, towards the looming church.

'Did they poison the food – or drink – maybe?'

The thought is horrifying. Nish and Effie ate little, drank only lemonade, but that's no reason for them to have escaped a dose of rat poison or whatever was at hand. Nish thinks about how the villagers sat with small plates of food in front of them, barely touched… But they did eat – they did drink. He remembers Colonel Mustard picking at food and demanding a brandy when the search party returned.

'I'm fine, honestly.' Steve stands and wipes his face with his sleeve, there's a sheen to his skin that might be the beginnings of a fever – or sweat from his recent exertions. 'Just losing some ballast, that's all.'

'Really?'

'That's the thing about Christmas dinner, isn't it?' Steve grins sheepishly. 'You just eat until you can't move.'

'Nothing quite like a walk to work it off. We need to move now,' Nish says. 'Don't want to miss midnight mass.'

The sounds of demolition coming from The Slaughter House ring out over the village green. There's no sign of the deer inside – or the two villagers left behind in the building. It won't be long before the stags force themselves out of the pub. The survivors need to get to shelter.

They pick their way onwards, following the tracks left by the three survivors ahead. The leading party has vanished – there's no sign of the dancing flashlight ahead.

As they approach the church, more details become visible in the gloom. There's a drystone wall, around waist height, that surrounds the graveyard, iced with a fat layer of snow. A tall, wide wooden archway marks the main entrance, leading to a path lined by big yew trees. Clumps of white have settled precariously on outcrops from the trees, at constant risk of being dislodged in the stiff breeze. The church's crenelated bell tower rears up behind the trees, a monolith of grey stone with snow-dusted ridges.

The remaining villagers must be inside already. Nish has lost their tracks in the dark, but the snow is freshly churned and slippery with compacted ice. A stag has passed recently, searching for blood. The disturbed snow leads up through the churchyard gate, up the path, to—

'Wait,' Steve whispers, holding his arm out like a barrier. He licks his finger and holds it to the air. The axe has gone, probably left in the snow beside a rapidly freezing pool of vomit. 'I've got a mate who took me hunting once.'

He indicates that they should duck down using brisk hand gestures. Nish imagines Steve has watched some military thrillers in his time, maybe grainy footage of an SAS raid, or read some Andy McNab. Nish and Effie crouch to the level of the dry-stone and follow Steve's lead, peering round the wall.

'I can't—' Nish begins, but stops when Steve holds up his hand.

There's a crack, like a branch snapping, and a yew tree shudders as a cap of snow tumbles from its branches, light and powdery. And then Nish sees it. A shimmer of light catches on the forks of the deer's antlers as it raises its head. He can't make out much in the gloom, but the stag's muzzle is wet and dark. It chews lazily. And he can see shoes – the rest of the body remains out of sight. The deer is feasting on a corpse. The survivors are at least one more person down.

12

They duck back behind the wall.

'Must've got them, poor buggers.' Steve speaks with the weary resignation of a war veteran who has seen too much death in his lifetime.

'They'll have run right into it.' Nish's words turn to clouds of ice. With his back to the wall, Nish picks out the dim light of The Slaughter House. He thinks about the scoreboard. How many kills are chalked up now?

'Oh, there you are,' says a cheery voice to Nish's right, making him jump. He turns and sees the bus driver, and behind Miss Scarlet waves brightly. Colonel Mustard holds his shotgun at the ready, surveying the broad white expanse.

'You're alive!' Nish says, more surprised than relieved.

'There's one of them in there,' Steve says.

'We tried to warn you,' Miss Scarlet says. 'But you didn't see us.'

'You could have signalled with your torch.' The words come out sharper than Nish had intended, but the sight of the Maglight clutched in the bus driver's hand stirs up a wave of anger. How could the villagers be so stupid? The three of them could have just walked straight into that stag.

'There's gratitude for you,' huffs the Colonel.

But Nish is too busy with his own self-recriminations. How could he be so stupid as to follow those tracks and think it would lead to anything other than a murderous deer?

'I guess we found your drunk,' Miss Scarlet says.

'Ooh, he'll be like a chocolate liqueur.' The darkness makes the bus driver's ghoulish grin somehow even worse. 'I do so love a whiskey barrel.'

'If we can't get into the church, then where do we go?' Effie directs the question at Miss Scarlet.

'We've still got to get in or the others won't be able to find us.' She glances at the pub in the distance, vulnerable and unable to acknowledge the sacrifice that may have been made in their name. 'We can still get in. There's a stile the other side of the churchyard.'

'What if that thing sees us?' Effie says.

'You got a better idea?'

The village is dark and distant, little more than a cluster of buildings unlikely to be more secure than the pub. They are separated by a vast expanse of open land. To attempt to make the crossing would require them to be exposed and vulnerable. The church has two significant advantages, by Nish's calculations. Firstly it's close. Secondly, its jagged rooftop makes it look a bit like a castle. Plus sacred ground has got to count for something, right? So make that three advantages. Enough to pin some hope on.

And so they walk, crouched low, tracing the line of the wall. As they follow the curve, the snow underfoot becomes shallower and easier to traverse. And, perhaps it's helpful to leave less obvious footprints? Even so, Nish is conscious of the soft crunch of frozen ground underfoot.

He thinks about what Effie said earlier, about rational monsters. So what does he know – or what can he remember from half-watched nature programmes – about deer? That they have highly sensitive hearing and an acute sense of smell. Steve's licked-finger test of the wind direction no longer seems absurd. In fact, it seems like it kept them alive when they could so easily have become deer chow. Perhaps he's underestimated the man?

Being constantly alert for sounds of danger makes progress slow and laborious, but eventually they reach a stile in the wall. It's a step up, just narrow enough to stop sheep or cattle – or whatever other creatures might have been grazing on common land back when the church was built – set into a gap in the wall.

Steve tentatively peeks his head over the wall. Nish catches a nervous look on Effie's face. She glances at him. They're waiting for the same thing: the thunder of hooves bearing down on them.

'And that church door's open?' Steve says.

'Yes,' says Miss Scarlet with a fraction less certainty than would be ideal, given the current circumstances.

'You sure? Because I don't have an axe this time.'

'It's open alright,' Colonel Mustard says. 'Does this look like the kind of village that has a problem with petty thieves?'

'Famous last words, eh?' Steve grins. 'Local guides first.'

Miss Scarlet's eyes widen in shock, but she steels herself and slips through the gap in the wall. Colonel Mustard harrumphs and squeezes through, his gun barrel trained in the direction of the stag. The bus driver follows close on the Colonel's heels, ginger-stepping. She would be the very essence of stealth were it not for the luminous yellow tabard lined with reflective strips and sequinned Christmas novelty jumper.

Effie is about to follow when Steve puts up a hand. 'Be careful,' he whispers, just loud enough for Nish to catch the warning. 'I don't trust the Colonel – or the broad in red. The other one's just an idiot.'

They're all in agreement. The villagers can't be trusted. There's no firm evidence that the villagers have tried to put their guests in the way of danger to save themselves, but there's an increasing amount of circumstantial evidence. The villagers have the advantage of being on home turf and a record of having survived previous sieges, but for now they don't know the Londoners are suspicious.

Nish follows, with Steve taking defensive glances around from the rear. They duck between gravestones until they reach the solid walls of the church. Back in the snow shadow, they can walk more easily. The line of yew trees runs parallel to the church, slicing the sight-lines available. Each time an angle aligns a long vista towards the village opens. And each time, Nish holds his breath, expecting it to frame a silver-bladed stag.

They bunch up at the porch where Miss Scarlet peers cautiously round the corner. She retracts her head and leans against the cold stone, heaving in heavy breaths.

'Well?' Steve whispers.

Miss Scarlet shakes her head.

'Let me see.' Steve begins making his way towards the head of the line, but stops—

There's a soft snorting noise, gentle and equine. The noise a horse might make with its big rubbery lips. But it's close and almost certainly not a horse. Nish pictures a magnificent stag, antlers glimmering in the night, standing proud in the middle of the yew-lined path. It's not a particularly comforting thought.

Steve presses himself back against the church wall, eyes wide and flicking around as he searches for options.

Their best defence is a shotgun. That will only slow it down for a second or two – and will signal their location to the rest of the herd.

Nish knows that they're all thinking the same thing: If that creature comes round the corner, who will it go for first? What am I willing to do to make it through the night? The brutal truth is that if it comes round the corner, there's only one line of escape. The stag will be fast and steady, even in the snow. But the survivors don't need to be fast to escape, they just need to not be the slowest.

He thinks of Steve vomiting into the snow.

He wasn't poisoned, but was he plied with food and wine to slow him down?

There's the sound of movement, the light crunching of gravel and ice underfoot. It's slow and gentle, as if the monster is cautiously approaching. Miss Scarlet places one foot against the church wall, crouches herself so she's like a coiled spring ready to bound away, a sprinter primed for the starting pistol. They all take her lead, tensed and ready to move.

The crunching continues and they wait, and wait, and wait… until Miss Scarlet shakes out some of the tension and peers round the wall. She watches for a second or two, which stretches out to become an eternity.

'Well?' the bus driver says when Miss Scarlet turns back.

'It's moving away,' she says. 'We – we can make it.'

Miss Scarlet is the first to go, this time without any prompts from the other survivors. She slips round the side of the church and is gone from sight. The Colonel is next, followed by the bus driver. Then Steve, who peers round the wall and gives a thumbs up behind his back before crouching SAS-style out of sight.

'I don't like this,' Effie says.

'Worst stag do ever.'

'I keep thinking there's something we're missing.' Her eyes dart around for danger as she speaks. 'Something that's going to make this whole thing make some kind of sense.'

'I know,' Nish says. 'But life doesn't always have neat solutions. Sometimes you get stranded in a village on Christmas Eve and picked off one-by-one by killer deer for no reason other than bad luck.'

Nish peeks round the corner. In the distance he can make out the wicked glint of steel antlers and a shadowy bulk that gently undulates as it picks its way towards the perimeter of the churchyard, one graceful foot at a time. He sneaks round the corner, followed by Effie, to join the others standing in the sheltered porch of the church.

The big oak door is open. Not just unlocked, but swung open to reveal the dark void beyond.

'Not locked then, huh?' Nish says.

'It was already open,' Miss Scarlet says. She leans round the corner to watch the beast departing.

'You think…?' Effie says, nodding in the direction of where they all know a body lies.

'Poor sod probably took shelter in here – then came out when he'd sobered up and…' the bus driver says with the kind of respect reserved for the recently departed.

Even with the cold and the threat of prowling deer outside, no one seems keen to enter the dark of the church. There's a safety to it, but also an ominous threat. However much it might represent sanctuary, it wasn't enough to save the drunk.

'Someone's coming!' Miss Scarlet hisses with excitement.

'What?' the Colonel says.

'Someone's running across the green. They made it out of the pub!'

'Who?' the Colonel adjusts his wireframe glasses.

'I can't see…' The bristling enthusiasm drops from her body language as the realisation dawns. 'But they're heading straight for the stag.'

13

'Can't they see it?' Steve says. 'They're running right into danger.'

'Which one is it?' the bus driver says.

Nish strains his eyes to see. In the dark everything that's not snow is little more than a black outline. The figure, stumbling and flailing over the ice, is too distant to be distinct. Is that a cassock or a skirt? Even their relative size is impossible to judge as the vast snow-covered expanse flattens perspective.

The runner won't know they're headed head-long into a trap, that's for sure. Having recently made the journey himself, Nish can confirm they'll be too focused on staying upright to notice the stag patiently waiting for them to draw close.

'Blast, I should have brought my field goggles,' huffs the Colonel.

'Look – there's another one!' The bus driver is getting quite excited, straining not to shout. 'They both made it!'

There is indeed a second runner, coming round from the rear of the pub. The second figure is more sure-footed, more minimalist in their motions, their silhouette a darker shade of black. Seeing the two together, Nish is sure that the Reverend is bringing up the rear. The big man moves with a muscular momentum, past where the beer garden's picketed fence must be, and out into the wide open space of the green.

The bus driver gasps. 'The deer got out of the pub…'

The pub is a squat snow-covered shape, with the faintest flickering glow from the windows closest to the log fire. There is a black blot on the pristine coating of its roof – the gaping hole where the creatures tore their way into the building. And there, bounding wide of the pub with giddy grace, is one – no, scratch that – are two stags.

As he watches, the first takes a wide course around the beer garden, bounding with the frisky vigour and fey charm of the Babycham mascot. There is something irrepressibly magical about the deer. Nish has to remind himself that he's watching an armoured killing machine the size of a plough horse.

The second stag takes a course directly through the beer garden and crashes straight into something solid that sends it flying face-first into the snow in an ungainly tangle of antlers and legs.

The unharmed stag skids to a halt and watches its blinded fellow struggle to stand. It glances towards the figures flying in the direction of the church and lets out a low resonant tragic note that carries into the night air. It bounds back to the stricken stag and begins nuzzling.

'Got that one right in the eyes,' the Colonel says triumphantly.

'What do you call a blind reindeer?' the bus driver blurts.

Colonel Mustard looks her up and down in the same way a lord of the manor might occasionally notice his serving staff. 'Shush now. Our vegan friends won't find that sort of rough humour very funny.'

The bus driver mouths the word *sorry* at Nish and Effie like a truculent a five-year-old who's opened their presents before Christmas Day.

'You need to do something,' Miss Scarlet says to the Colonel. 'Otherwise he'll— they'll run right into that stag.'

Rudolph, Nish thinks remembering the red-nosed cartoon on the beer pump, is certainly having his revenge tonight.

'If I shoot it, it'll just turn on us,' the Colonel says. 'We'll be barricaded in the church and they'll be exposed outside. We have to let them take their chance.'

'There must be something.' Miss Scarlet is distraught, but she can't turn away from the chase for long.

Across the snow-coated green, both stags are back on the move. One bounds with an easy, fluid grace, its legs rising and falling in pairs. The other trots behind at a more leisurely pace, a slight stiffness to its movement. This is a creature that has taken a shotgun to the face, a butcher's cleaver to the flank, whatever else has been thrown at it as it battled its way through the pub, and now a picnic bench to the shin. Yet still it keeps coming.

Meanwhile, the gap between Mrs White and the Reverend has closed. With the flattened perspective, they have almost become one figure. Her arms still wheel wildly as she moves, every now and then she ducks as she stumbles, but she's still upright. He moves with the sure-footed certainty of a rugby winger attempting to score a try from the half-way line.

'I've got an idea,' the bus driver says, holding up the key fob for the minibus. She presses a button with a look of victory… but, nothing. 'Must be too far away.'

The group watches the bus driver expectantly.

'What?'

'You need to get closer,' Miss Scarlet says.

'Why me? Anyone could do it.'

The bus driver looks around, growing increasingly frantic.

The Colonel gently clears his throat and shifts just enough to scrape his gun barrel on the flagstones underfoot. The black metal glints darkly. If the Colonel were to raise the gun – as he's poised and ready to do in the event of danger – both barrels would be aimed squarely at the bus driver.

'Fine. Some gratitude wouldn't kill you,' she says, pointedly directing the words at the Colonel, before crouching low and ducking out of the porch and into the snow.

Nish cannot help but watch with creeping dread as the bus driver dances, stooped with bent knees and arms spread wide, in the snow-shadow of the yew trees. The colour of her luminous tabard is softened by the gloom of the night, but the reflective strips glimmer dimly as they catch the refracted twilight of the snow.

The stag stands under the gates to the churchyard, waiting for the villagers to run directly on to its antlers. There's a milkiness to the air around its head where a fine mist billows out with each breath. Even though each of these creatures would merrily tear him in half – and despite spending the worst night of his life under their assault – the great beasts inspire a sense of awe Nish hasn't felt in a long time. They are magnificent and wild, the very opposite of the kind of urban wildlife he's used to seeing in London. Flea-bitten foxes slinking between gardens fed on a diet of KFC. Pelicans in St James's Park bored under the leaden skies. Flocks of noisy green parakeets mobbing bird feeders designed for robins and blue tits. They all fade in comparison to these murderous stags, which fill him with childlike wonder.

The bus driver, sheltering behind a yew tree raises a hand and presses the key fob again. Still nothing.

Miss Scarlet shoos with her hands, mouthing the words 'Get closer.' She's a woman at the edge of desperation, praying for a miracle as she watches the deer close in on her lover and her nemesis.

The chasing stag is getting close now. The running figures glance around – they must have heard it approaching – and something changes in their body language. They know danger's on their heels. But still they haven't spotted the danger that's right in front of them.

Then: disaster. The conjoined silhouette of the runners breaks. Mrs White – who has cut a flailing figure this whole time, trying to steady herself with wheeling arms while racing over the ice – falls. It's a proper face-plant as she drops flat to the snow, legs springing up behind her.

Effie gasps audibly. She clamps her hand over her mouth to prevent any further noises escaping, but she can't tear her wide eyes away from the scene.

Meanwhile, the bus driver has moved one yew tree further down the path towards the waiting stag. Once more her arm goes up and Nish hears Miss Scarlet saying 'Come on come on come on' under her breath.

Tweep tweep.

The sound of the minibus unlocking rings out over the silent night, like the warble of a dawn bird. Beyond the churchyard, there's an orange glow that rises and fades in two bursts accompanying the chorus.

All eyes turn to the stag standing in the gateway. There's a dim glimmer of metal as it turns its head in the direction of the minibus. It stands watching for a heartbeat, frozen breath pooling around its muzzle. For a moment, Nish thinks it's going to turn back to watch the chase, but eventually it decides to stalk towards the vehicle to investigate.

'Come on come on come on.' Miss Scarlet whispers her mantra, willing the creature to move faster, to get further away.

The bus driver looks back towards the church porch, giving two thumbs up. Colonel Mustard summons the bus driver back. She peeks out between the branches, checks the coast really is clear, before running giddily up the path.

'We need to get inside and prepare the barricade,' Colonel Mustard says. 'We won't have a moment to lose when they get here. Come on, chop chop.'

Steve, Nish and Effie are ushered into the dark church,

followed by the triumphant driver who is panting heavily from the dash back to safety. 'Get in,' they hear the Colonel hiss from outside. But Miss Scarlet protests. They can't hear her words, but it's clear that she's planning to wait until she knows the Reverend has made it.

Plunged into a deeper darkness, it takes Nish's eyes a few moments to adjust. Inside it's cold in the way that only a high-ceilinged, stone-built, single-glazed church can be. It radiates cold. Perhaps ideal on a hot midsummer's day, but in the bleak midwinter there's a good chance the weather might get them before the deer if they have to spend the rest of the night here.

With his sight temporarily gone, Nish could probably identify the building from scent alone. There's the musty aroma of old tomes printed on whispery Bible paper and the faint farmyard twang of hay. He imagines a nativity scene set up with real haybales. Something designed for the children of this strange village, who are currently cowering in the basement of the pub, same as every year.

Gradually, shade by shade, his eyes adjust and he can make out the arc of a large stained-glass window at the altar-end of the church and nooks of midnight blue where smaller windows let in more chill than light.

There's the scraping of something heavy against flagstones.

'Give us a hand, mate,' Steve says.

Nish follows his voice and joins Steve at the end of a wooden pew. He grips the carved wood and they drag it towards the big door. With Effie's help, they raise the bench and rest it against a wall. Several items tucked into the back pockets of the pew fall to the ground. There's the sound of books with pages like grease paper and embroidered kneeling cushions skidding across the stone floor.

'Do you think that will hold them?' the bus driver says, still panting.

'Come on, for god's sake get in!' The Colonel stands in the doorway, barking orders at Miss Scarlet. He's no longer whispering and his raised voice echoes around the church air.

He reaches out and drags Miss Scarlet in by the arm. 'It's no good you getting yourself killed,' he mutters.

Miss Scarlet backs away from the door, but is unable to take her eyes off the gap. She heaves great breaths and bunches her hands into fists. She's like a gambler at a horserace watching a tense final furlong, desperate for her horse to make it over the line first. She has the manic air of someone on the edge of winning or losing everything.

From outside, come the sounds of a final sprint. Footsteps, heavy and fast, crunching through snow and gravel. And behind – but getting closer all the time – the steady beat of hooves landing in pairs with great grace and terrible power.

Miss Scarlet gasps, holding her hands to her mouth. A hand the size of a ham appears at the door, adorned with set of chapped knuckles.

There's a flutter of cassock and the deep breaths of a man who has had the run of his life. The Reverend throws himself into the church with the last of his energy. 'Close – the – door,' he says, heaving lungfuls of air, bent double.

Outside, hooves canter past. There's a scrabble and scraping with each following footstep as the chasing creatures attempt to make an abrupt turn having over-shot the porch.

'What about—?'

'Gone,' the Reverend says.

For a moment, the Colonel looks like he's about to say something, but he decides against it. He shuts the big wooden door and Steve lets the pew slip down the wall so that it hits the woodwork with a resonant thud.

'Fell, did she?' the Colonel's tone is one of polite enquiry.

'Yes,' the butcher replies blandly.

In the darkness, they work together blindly to wedge the pew across the doorway. It comes to a rest, firm and solid, just before the first powerful thud lands, booming richly around the cavernous building. The door shakes and the pew slips a few inches, but it holds. Another thud follows, but it's weaker than the first, almost half-hearted.

There's a flick and a beam of light as the bus driver turns the Maglight back on. The spotlight picks out each of the group in harsh white light, throwing wild shadows around the church. The driver is lit up from under the chin, carving grotesque shadows into her face. Nish flinches from the light, his eyes having adjusted to the dark. Effie holds her hand in front of her eyes, prepared for the inevitable blinding, her delicate features pensive. Nish has come to recognise this as the look she wears when her brain is whirring. Steve glares back at the driver with something like murderous loathing. Miss Scarlet and the Reverend are caught in a passionate embrace. As they kiss, he presses her close to his body, one hand cupping her head, the other in the small of her back. Her arms barely reach round the girth of his back. There are slashes across his cassock where a sharp blade has passed, tearing fabric and scratching deep into his skin. The blood drawn has not yet dried. The light lingers a little too long to be proper before moving finally to Colonel Mustard, who averts his gaze with barely concealed furious disgust.

'A terrible accident I suppose?' The Colonel says.

There's a sound like two suction cups being separated and a long low sigh of urgent need.

'She didn't make it,' the Reverend says looking down on his lover.

'Really?' Miss Scarlet says with the same kind of delighted surprise she might greet a lavish Christmas present. *For me?* Her hand is tiny and delicate on the Reverend's chest as she looks up into his brooding face with open admiration.

'It's just you and me,' he says.

Nish averts his gaze as the displays of affection resume. He looks towards Effie just as she's turning to look at him. He offers a meek smile, as if to say 'Well, this is awkward.' She gives him a look that indicates that she's got something urgent and important to say.

Whatever it is, though, it's going to have to wait because there's worse news in store.

Somewhere from the deepest shadows of the church, they hear the familiar equine snort of a deer.

14

The bus driver swings the torchlight around, catching the assortment of wide eyes and slack jaws as the group collectively tries to calculate the significance of the noise. The spotlight casts a kaleidoscope of shadows as it shifts over thick stone pillars and the side aisles until it arrives at the altar.

With a dread inevitability, the circle of light illuminates a stag. The flashlight reflects off its antlers like a glitter ball, spraying shards of light into the darkest shadows of the church.

For a moment the stag is frozen in the light. For the first time, Nish has a proper look at one of the monsters that have been terrorising them. It is the same height as the carved wooden pulpit, which a vicar would ascend via a short flight of stairs. It towers over the neat rows of pews. The creature's muscles are sculpted and defined, twitching under its fur. Its coat is a shaggy grey, with brown roots where the fur parts over its breast and down its legs.

The stag's face is ugly. Utterly repulsive. So unnaturally awful that Nish is torn between averting his eyes and being utterly fixated out of sheer fascination. It's like a car crash in venison. For a creature that has cut such a magnificent silhouette – that has looked so dashing, despite its murderous intent – it really does have a face that only a mother could love.

But there's a certain cold logic to the way the normally docile features of a reindeer – for that's perhaps the closest cousin of this beast – have become distorted on the evolutionary journey from herbivore to carnivore. Its eyes, big and black, are set at the front of its face like those of a predator, framed by a heavy brow and tufts of short fluffy mane. Wicked-looking fangs jut downwards from its muzzle, curved and sharp like those of a sabre-tooth tiger. Its nostrils flare wide, glossy with mucus.

Its antlers are the biggest diversion from its cousin. Like a highland stag, the murder-deer's antlers branch into two groupings – a front pair that are short and curve outwards for butting, and a rear pair that fan out to the shoulders, dramatic and wide. But there the similarity ends. Rather than bone and course fur, these antlers are made of a pure metal with the sheen of a finely whetted blade. And they're mobile.

As Nish watches, the antlers spread and tangle, curving and arching into vicious hooks until they become an armoured crown. They shift and distort like a fluid, so subtle that if he'd not seen the way they can tear a man in half, he'd think it a trick of the light.

He is frozen to the spot, mesmerised by the display of efficient, deadly beauty – for the antlers are beautiful, even if the face they're framing is that of a Medusa-moose – until the beast rears up. It paws the air with its front legs and bellows at the group with its maw wide to display a full set of razor-sharp teeth. Its rubbery lips vibrate, spraying strands of saliva and mucus over the floor.

There's the blast of a shotgun from nearby. Nish sees a burst of orange flame flash from the corner of his eyes as he ducks to the ground. Behind the stag, the big stained glass window shatters, fragments of glass winking in the torchlight as they cascade to the floor like a calving iceberg.

The noise of the blast echoes around the cavernous building, almost drowning out the tinkle of the shards hitting the stone floor. Or, at least that's what Nish assumes is happening. He puts his hands to his ears. His eardrum aches from the battering it has received by its proximity to so many shotgun blasts of late. All he can hear is the high whine of tinnitus.

Meanwhile, chaos has erupted in the church. The bus driver's torch beam flicks around wildly, shining light into dark corners in the distance. It catches the close-up horrified faces of the survivors, and the shadowy shape of the stag as it darts out of the spotlight.

Effie grabs Nish by the collar and leads him low and fast between two pews. There's a rush of air as something large and powerful passes close like a freight train. He can't hear, but he can feel the thrum of the flagstones as hooves clatter, heavy and percussive.

She turns to him and says something he can't hear.

'I can't hear you,' he says. 'I was standing too close.'

'I told you to be quiet,' she shouts. He knows she's shouting because he can hear the strain in her voice, even though it's very faint above the persistent ringing in his ears. 'They've got good hearing, remember?'

She shifts her grip to his hand, waits a beat and pulls him after her with all her strength as she bolts out to the side aisle.

There's a crash of wood and metal as something collides with enormous force against the pew they have just vacated. The long bench sails up in the air with an ease that belies its weight. An end just grazes Nish's back as he's dragged behind a solid stone pillar. Had he been a fraction slower, he'd have been crushed.

Sound is slowly returning to his world and Nish hears the thunderous crash of the flying pew colliding with the rows of sturdy benches. There's a splintering that sounds like an old oak being split by lightning.

The bus driver's light shuts off, but not before catching on a narrow stone doorway a couple of metres away. There he can see the first few worn stone steps of a spiral staircase, and a flash of red fabric as Miss Scarlet makes her escape ascending at full sprint. It's too narrow for the stag. The only route to safety is up to the roof.

He's about to run for the doorway, a ghost of which lingers in his vision, when Effie puts her hand on his mouth. The intimate feeling of her soft skin against his lips makes his heart thud in his chest with something other than fear. But he understands her message. *Don't make a sound.*

There's a soft click of hoof on stone and a gentle snort as the church falls silent. He can hear footsteps still racing up the stairwell. How many of them are climbing upwards to the bell tower? How many are still stuck down here with the stag that's stalking so close?

And it is close. The echo of the church makes sound tricky to place, but the musty animal smell fills the air. He pictures it waiting patiently the other side of the stone pillar, sifting through the scents and sounds for a trace of human.

Nish becomes conscious of something resting against his shoe. He holds Effie's hand as he ducks down, hoping that his knees won't crack, and picks it up. It's a soft leather-bound book with gold lettering that flickers in the darkness. He makes out two words: *Good News*. At bloody last, he thinks, as he throws the Bible as far into the church as he can manage.

The pages flutter in the air and it lands with a heavy thunk amidst the wooden jumble of broken pews in the nave.

There's a snort and then a heavy canter as the stag takes the bait.

They don't wait for it to hit the rows of pews before they run. The creatures build momentum quickly, but their turning circle is terrible. It's not going to be easy for a couple of tonnes of deer to suddenly change direction on age-smoothed flagstones. For now, they have an advantage.

Nish mis-judges the angle slightly, running his shoulder into the solid stonework as he follows Effie. From behind there's the crash of something heavy hitting woodwork and the frantic pedalling of hoof on stone as the deer realises its mistake.

He feels his way through the doorway, finding a thick rope attached to the wall to use as a handrail. Nish tries to contain the rising panic. It won't take the beast long to close the gap, and he needs to be sufficiently far up the stone stairs to be out of reach of those whipping antlers. But he also needs to avoid tripping on the stairs or falling back into the danger zone. His only option is to work his way steadily and carefully up the stairs, never mind the urgent hammering of hooves coming closer and closer.

The stonework of the stairs is smooth underfoot, worn treacherous over the centuries. They narrow where they curl round the central pillar. Nish clutches the rope as his foot slips.

There's a spark of light and the sound of metal striking stone. Nish throws himself up the next stair and risks a look behind. The stag stands wedged in the doorway, its broad shoulders blocking its progress. There are little flickers of light as its antlers lash wildly with snake-strike speed, producing bursts of sparks. In a strobe of spark light, Nish sees the stag twist its neck to watch him hungrily with those big black predatory eyes. It opens its maw, champing at the air with its long fangs.

'Are you alright?' Effie says.

'Yeah, just.'

'Come on, you're just teasing it. The others are further up.'

Slowly and carefully, Nish stands, turns his back to the

beast, and climbs the stairs. He's shaking as the adrenaline courses round his system.

The stairs curl round tightly and he can hear voices and footsteps ahead. He can't make out distinct words because of the noise of antler smashing against stone further down the stairwell. The beast sounds less frantic, maybe more annoyed. He pictures it having some kind of tantrum, venting its anger having got so close to a kill. Will it give up and just wait for them? It's trapped in the church. And, he realises, the deal works both ways. The survivors are now trapped in the bell tower.

A flat slab marks a wooden doorway to the bell chamber, but the door is locked. The stairs continue a little further along, tighter and narrower than before. Nish carries on climbing, taking each step carefully until he reaches a low archway and is out into the open.

'So, all made it then?' Colonel Mustard says, the barrel of his gun cracked open to reload.

In the thin moonlight Nish sees the crenelated walls, a flat stone terrace, and a flagpole dutifully flying the St George Cross. The bus driver is bent double, winded from the climb, her torch dark in one hand. Reverend Green and Miss Scarlet stand huddled together, his big hands caressing warmth into her bare shoulders. Steve leans over the parapet to see what's going on below.

Effie gives Nish a meek smile.

'Thanks,' Nish says. 'You saved my life.'

'Don't thank me yet,' she says. 'We're trapped. I mean, we've been trapped all evening. But this is worse. So... yeah, I postponed your death at best.'

It's cold on the roof, exposed to the icy wind. Nish folds his arms and tucks his hands into his armpits. How long would it take to die of exposure out here? Would it be a worse way to go than the death waiting for them in the belly of the church?

Effie goes to join Steve looking over the snow scene below. Nish follows, preferring the company of other Londoners to making small-talk with the bus driver and the villagers.

The cloud cover has started to thin, revealing patches of velvet sky and spinning a milky halo around the moon. In the dim moonlight, the village below looks small and chocolate-box pretty, squat stone houses iced with pristine snow. There's a churn of tracks cutting across the village green, a blue-grey against the glowing white. The bodies are less picturesque.

Silhouettes splayed on the frozen ground, dramatic crimson bursts leaching into the snow.

'I'm sorry for your loss,' Effie says, gently touching Steve's arm.

'She always loved the snow. She wanted to go to Iceland this year, see in the new year from a hot spring. But I said "Nah babe, maybe give the credit card a break, eh?" If we'd have gone, she'd still be with me.' He heaves a shuddering sigh, a cloud of frozen breath erupting around him. 'She knew it was off the moment we stepped in that pub. She realised they were all dressed like Cluedo characters. "I thought there were six suspects in Cluedo," she said. And she was right, wasn't she? I didn't listen, but I should have seen it. The truth was right in front of us from the very start.'

'Seen what?' Nish says.

Down below, there's a long mournful lowing that echoes out over the snowscape. The source of the call is out of sight, but it's a matter of moments before it's answered by similar responses. Then the dark darting shape of a stag comes into sight, bounding across the snow in fey strides, coming to a halt at the churchyard gate and raising its head to the church tower.

'It's seen us,' Effie says.

'Not the only one,' Steve says.

Another two stags have joined the one at the gates. They stand together, watching the survivors watch them from on high. Their antlers sway like reeds in the wind, shimmering in the thin moonlight. Again Nish finds himself marvelling at the creatures. It's a lot easier to be in awe of their majestic nature when you're too far away to see their ugly mutant faces.

'You've let them see you?' Miss Scarlet says, incredulity dripping from her voice even though she's whispering.

'It's not like they're going to get up here,' Steve says.

'And it's not like we're going to get out,' Effie says. 'There's one in the church below. We're trapped.'

Miss Scarlet's jaw hangs open as she tries to think of a sufficiently scornful response. But she comes up dry and settles for staring daggers. The Reverend holds her close, giving the three strangers a silent look of disdain.

'So, anyone got a plan?' the bus driver says with the manic energy of someone trying to deny the inevitable.

'Actually, I think I do,' says Colonel Mustard adjusting the grip on his gun. 'The deer need eight kills tonight and they've had four so far. There are seven survivors on the roof and by my maths...' he steps in front of the Reverend and Miss Scarlet, 'there are three of us who will make it through the night and four of you who sadly won't.'

As if his point needed any further elaboration, Colonel Mustard uses the barrel of his shotgun to indicate Nish, Effie, Steve and the bus driver in turn.

'That's not even funny,' the driver says.

'This is no laughing matter,' the Colonel confirms.

'But— But— You can't.'

'Give me one good reason I shouldn't.' The Colonel's gun remains trained on the bus driver as if there's a level of personal animosity.

Nish tries to think of a reason why the Colonel is singling out—

In the weak moonlight, the sequins on the bus driver's novelty Christmas jumper sparkle. They shape out a bird with a turquoise neck, a golden crown, and a large fanned tail decorated with baubles... No, not baubles, they look more like eyes. Something clicks into place in Nish's head. The clue had been in front of them this whole time. It's a peacock.

Jess had been the closest to seeing it. She'd been right all the time. Cluedo is a game for six players. Mrs Peacock had been hiding in plain sight.

'But Geoff—'

'First rule of Christmas Eve, *Barbara*. No names.'

'You're one of them,' Nish says, feeling the vertigo of shock.

'Welcome to the party, pal,' Steve growls.

'Really?' Effie says.

'There's been a lot going on,' Nish says apologetically.

She whistles out a breath. 'Just you wait till you work out what happened to Mrs White.'

The argument between the villagers has continued to boil over, regardless of Nish's shock at the revelation.

'After all I've done,' Mrs Peacock protests. 'Over all these years. And now you have the cheek to do this?'

'You had one job,' the Reverend says, his voice like a gravedigger's spade dragged over gravel. 'Eight people, same as every year.'

'You don't understand!'

'I understand perfectly well. Now—'

Steve lunges for the barrel, bursting across the space

between the two groups like a spring suddenly uncoiled. Steve is fast, his fingers so, so close to closing over the cold black metal. The whites of Colonel Mustard's eyes are wide in the half-light as he attempts to angle the shotgun towards Steve. But he's not as fast as the butcher.

The Reverend closes one big hand over Steve's throat and pushes him so his back is against the parapet and his feet are scrabbling for purchase.

'You only get to pull that trick once,' the butcher growls.

'Don't kill him!' Miss Scarlet shouts.

'Do you think it counts if I throw him on to one of their antlers?' The Reverend's muscles ripple under his cassock and his jawbone clenches, but he's careful to keep Steve conscious. Steve clutches at the arm that pins him in place, desperate for more air.

'If anyone gets any ideas, don't think I'll hesitate,' Colonel Mustard says to Effie, Nish and Mrs Peacock, lowering the shotgun to aim squarely at their kneecaps.

The Reverend releases his grip and Steve falls to his knees, holding his throat and gasping fresh air. Effie ducks down beside him to check he's okay.

'Now come on, let's get this over and done with because it's bloody freezing out here. Don't know about you, but I've worked up a proper appetite for some figgy pudding.' Colonel Mustard ushers them towards the darkness of the stone doorway that will lead them back down towards the stag trapped below.

15

'I'm not going first,' Mrs Peacock protests.

Steve, rubbing at his throat, croaks: 'Ur-ly… 'ight.'

'I'm sorry, what?'

'He said "Only right",' Nish explains. And now he knows she's one of them, he finds he's furious – at her for this situation, but also at himself for being so slow. 'Meaning it's your fault we're here at all, so it sounds pretty bloody fair to me that you should go down first.'

'No, no, I'll fall… I'll break my neck.'

'Bloody well would as well, wouldn't she?' Miss Scarlet says.

'Fine, then he goes first.' Colonel Mustard aims both barrels at Steve.

'No,' the Reverend growls. 'I know bravery from idiocy when I see it and that man's an idiot. He's got nothing to live for. He'll dive headlong down those stairs if it'll condemn one of us to death.'

'Okay,' the Colonel says. 'Then him.'

'Me?' Nish says, the shotgun's twin sockets eye him vacantly. They echo the beady close-together eyes of the stag waiting for them downstairs. The thought of its murderous antlers lashing around, lighting its hellish face with sparks, turns his blood cold. Or it would do, if his blood weren't already freezing from exposure up here on this rooftop. 'Well— I— I might throw myself down the stairs. Then you'd be screwed, huh?'

'What do you think?' Colonel Mustard says.

'That one's an idiot too,' the Reverend growls. 'But he doesn't want to die.'

'I'll go first,' Effie says, her voice clear and steady. 'Give me the torch.'

Mrs Peacock hands over the Maglight with unseemly speed.

'You don't have to,' Nish says.

Effie's expression is stony serious. 'You think going second's a mercy?'

The flagpole thrums as the wind picks up. A sad lonely chime fit for a death march.

'Interesting,' says the Reverend.

'I'm not going to listen to this nonsense a minute longer. She's first, then him, then you, then him.' Colonel Mustard flashes the gun towards Effie. 'Go on then.' He turns towards Miss Scarlet and the Reverend. 'I'll escort them down. You keep her safe. We'll get you inside and warm soon enough.'

Effie turns on the torch and directs it towards the precipitous stone stairs. A curtain of darkness peels back to reveal the steps below. She takes the first step and heaves out a deep fogging breath.

'I always thought I was good with heights,' she whispers as they descend.

'I don't think I've ever been so scared of a staircase in my life.' Nish grips the rope as he takes the stairs slowly behind her. He uses his other hand to balance against the central pillar and keeps his feet to the outside edges where the steps are widest. But this is also where they dip with centuries of wear, the stone polished smooth and slippery.

What would happen if someone behind fell? Would they take out the others? Would they tumble and roll in a tangle of broken limbs, arriving dead at the feet of the stag? He thinks about Steve, the Colonel's shotgun pressed into his back, making sure he doesn't do anything stupid.

'There's a door down here,' Nish whispers.

'It's locked,' Effie says. 'Tried it earlier.'

'Been locked for years,' Mrs Peacock says from behind. 'One of the bell ringers went mad one year. Them deer took his whole family right in front of his eyes, sent him clean out of his head. Made a terrible racket. The fight we'd have trying to get him out of there each night. We ended up breaking the lock to stop the bells for good. Next year he was the first to go, we made damned sure of that.'

The silence that follows is punctuated only by the shuffling of feet on the stone steps.

'Pity really, ran the local shop,' Mrs Peacock continues. 'But I suppose with supermarket delivery and Swindon's out-of-town shopping centres so close, we'd have lost that shop anyway sooner or later. Some people call it progress, but you know what I call it? The end of a way of life.'

'I suppose you could call it that,' Nish says, contemplating the end of his way of life, creeping closer with every step.

'But at least we've managed to keep our pub. You know how difficult it is to keep one of those running in the countryside? Landlord realised that he had to offer more than just drinks if he was going to stay afloat, so brought in the butcher's wife to manage the kitchen. Turned it into a proper gastropub. City folks love sloshing around the countryside in their hiking gear and coming back hungry for a slap-up meal. Who'd have thought the pub would do so well through lockdown? Although I suppose it'll close now they're both gone.'

'I expect she'll take it on,' Colonel Mustard says from behind, his voice echoing around the stonework.

'You think? Oh, that would be wonderful. Do you think she'll be able to do food? Getting a bit short-handed in the village these days. But those two – her hospitality and his cuts of meat. It's a marriage made in heaven, I tell you. I suppose they'll get married now the wife's gone. Cheaper than a divorce, eh? Do you think they'll have children? A new generation for the village! They'd have such good-looking children, I'm sure.'

'I think it's a bit soon for any of that,' the Colonel grumbles.

'I'm sorry, I'm rambling. Haven't had the chance to chat all evening – I've been in character so much longer than everyone else. I usually love Christmas – chance to make some new friends, get to know people—'

'Before you kill them?' Nish says. The stairs are hard enough work without Mrs Peacock's incessant chat and the prospect of impending doom. Effie's making slow progress ahead of him. He can see that they're approaching the doorway to the bell chamber, halfway down already. He's not sure if it's any consolation that the stairs after this point become a little wider, a little less steep, making the going a little easier. Either way, they're getting closer and closer to the deadly antlers of the murder-deer below.

'There's no need for that tone on Christmas Eve, is there? Honestly, you London folks. Whatever happened to goodwill to all men? I forget that you out-of-towners simply don't get village life. Did you know the council put in plans to build a big new development here? You wouldn't believe it, would you? Hundreds of little boxy houses just plonked into our village. People with no roots here, driving to the city each day so they can afford the mortgage on some overpriced new build. Said it was in the local plan, didn't they?'

'Local plan? More like some scheme cooked up in Whitehall,' the Colonel harrumphs.

'More empty houses, as if that's what this village needs after the last decade. Well, they hadn't reckoned on the collective might of Little Slaughter. We got ourselves organised, didn't we? Set up one of those online petitions. Each time some hikers came to the pub after a yomp in the marshes we'd bend their ears about it. "Like these fields do you? Beautiful in the springtime en't they? Such unspoilt countryside. Real rarity these days. Here, you know what that council of ours is planning to do? No, you don't like that do you? How about you sign this 'ere petition while you wait for your food?" No, they didn't reckon on us.'

'People need somewhere to live,' the Colonel concedes. 'But not here. No, their local plan didn't plan for the locals getting organised.'

Mrs Peacock cackles triumphantly. 'Of course, that was before the radio mast caught fire. We'd have to do it with pen and paper these days.'

'I'm trying not to go too fast, but I don't know how much more of this I can take,' Effie whispers.

'Honestly, I'd welcome the relief of sweet death,' Nish says.

Oblivious to the dissent, Mrs Peacock continues to list the local infrastructure a rapid expansion of Little Slaughter would require, but which was not provided for in the local plan. At no point does she stop to consider whether the expansion of the village might have at least postponed her own death by providing a fresh influx of sacrifices.

Effie's torch beam turns one last corner to reveal the doorway into the church. She stops and Nish almost carries on into her back. There are fresh chips in the stone, a raw chalky white, carved by the stag's lashing antlers. He's known that this gateway to hell would be waiting at the bottom of the stairwell, but anticipation makes seeing it no less heart-stopping.

'I guess this is the end of the road,' Effie says.

'I can go first if you want.'

'... and there's no school here anymore – that shut down years ago – so what are those families going to do? Nearest one's two villages away and the bus only runs Tuesdays and Thursdays, so what're they meant to— We've stopped! Why have we stopped?'

'We're just taking a moment,' Nish says.

'It was nice meeting you,' Effie says, her voice soft and tender. 'I wish it could have been under different circumstances.'

'Me too,' Nish croaks. Despite all the fear, all the adrenaline still buzzing through his system, he feels a deep sadness that catches at his throat and threatens to blur his vision. He reaches out and she takes his hand. Her skin is soft and warm as she twines his fingers with hers.

'Why've you stopped?' the Colonel barks from behind Steve.

'She's stopped,' Steve says, meaning Mrs Peacock.

'They've stopped,' Mrs Peacock says, meaning Nish and Effie. She leans closer, scrutinises the pair in front of her, before a big smile cracks over her face and she clutches her hands to her heart. 'Ah, young love! Christmas is such a romantic time of the year.'

'There's no time for any of that!' Colonel Mustard barks. 'Let's get this over with so I can get back into the warm, if you don't mind.'

'I can't move if she's not moved,' Steve says with the tone of a man who's just felt the muzzle of a shotgun pressed to the small of his back.

'I'm sorry for the inconvenience,' Effie says with one last look at Nish.

Nish wishes he could hold on to that moment. He wishes they could be transported somewhere else. He wishes that he could spin those few seconds of connection out for a lifetime. But it's over in the blink of an eye, just like his life will be.

Nish follows Effie, keeping close to her, watching over her shoulder as the torch beam picks out shapes in the gloom, all the while expecting the snort and canter of impending death. There are worse ways to go, he tells himself. He can't think of any right now, but there's got to be something worse than being skewered by a plus-sized stag.

The church is a wreck of splintered and jumbled wood where pews have been thrown into each other. A few clean edges, as if cut with a band saw, show where woodwork has succumbed to the stag's razor-sharp antlers. Prayer cushions and Bibles are scattered over the floor. Despite all the destruction, an altar beside the staircase remains untouched, covered by a pristine white cloth and hosting a selection of unlit tea lights framed by two chunky metal candlesticks.

Effie sweeps the beam across the church, sending mad shadows jumping as she looks for the stag. The building is silent, except for the whistle of wind that cuts through the lead mesh left by the broken stained-glass window. And a faint thud, slow but regular. The kind of unexplained noise that draws the unsuspecting victim in a horror film.

'What's happening?' Mrs Peacock hisses.

'I can't see it,' Effie says.

'Come on, out with you,' Colonel Mustard says.

Steve stumbles out of the doorway and gives the Colonel a vicious look. The Colonel keeps his gun trained on Steve. He stands on the first step, prepared to duck back in at the first sight of the creature.

Effie scans* around again with the torch. Every glint of silverware fills Nish with the dread of inevitable doom. But each time it's an age-tarnished candlestick or crucifix. Even the lectern, a brass eagle with wings spread wide, shimmering in the torchlight looks like a pair of deadly antlers in his heightened state. There's some comfort in seeing how the others flinch at the same glimmers in the dark – except for Effie, whose hand remains steady as she searches for signs of the stag.

'Well, go on then,' the Colonel says, ushering Effie to step further into the church with the gun barrel. He's quick to turn the muzzle back towards Steve, however, lest he get any ideas.

Effie steps softly over detritus as she picks her way towards the aisle. Nish follows her close enough to hear her slow controlled breathing, watching intently as she shines the light into corners of the building.

'Where is it?' the Colonel demands.

The slow thud gets louder, more resonant, as they approach the aisle. Effie shines the light towards the altar. Nish's mind replays that first sight of the creature, the torchlight reflected in a constellation of broken glass, the night sky framed behind a leaden lattice.

The thud sounds again, close by. Effie whirls round to light up the doorway to the church.

'Well?'

'It's gone.'

Effie's breath freezes in the cool air that blows through the shattered door. There's no sign of the pew that had blocked the doorway, although the fractured jumble of woodwork behind them is perhaps slightly larger now. The wooden panels of the ancient door have been stripped and slashed to nothing, leaving only a splintered stub attached to the hinges. Nish watches it rock back and forth slowly in the wind, each time the door stub thuds against an ancient metal doorstop.

'Where's it gone?' Mrs Peacock says.

As if in answer to her question, there's the clatter of something heavy landing on the angled roof. Nish ducks and the torch beam skitters around the building as Effie does the same, all the while keeping an eye out for hidden danger.

Moments later, the sound comes again, and again, and again. There's the sound of bone hoof scraping on slate tile.

'They're on the roof,' Mrs Peacock says, not yet tired of entirely redundant exclamations.

Nish pictures the deer steadying themselves on the snow-covered pitched roof, dislodging little avalanches as they crane their necks to the tower, where Miss Scarlet and the Reverend wait. Their antlers sheen like forks of lightning in the thin moonlight, flanks twitching, powerful muscles veiled by a thick fur coat. He tries to picture the height of the tower above the summit of the roof. It sure felt like a long way climbing those stairs. He glances up at the roof beams dimly distant above. How could they make it?

'Know your monster,' Effie whispers. 'Deer can jump really high.'

'But that's...'

A sudden loud sound from the roof resonates through the church like a peal of thunder. Silence follows, pregnant with menace. Nish and Effie exchange a look of astonishment and grim wonder at what happens next.

A scream, faint and distant, echoes down the stairwell. They all turn to look at the Colonel, who has blanched. The shotgun shakes in his hands. There follows the sound of footsteps in the stairwell – fast and stumbling, surely a pair – and then the blacksmith sound of furious metal against stonework.

'They couldn't,' Steve says. 'How the bloody hell did they jump up there?'

'The deer want one of the villagers,' Effie says.

'What?' Nish says.

'They're not stupid, those creatures. They could have waited for us to come down and just picked us off one by one. But instead, they've gone to the trouble of getting up to the tower. They're rational monsters – they want *something*.' Effie turns her attention to the door to the stairwell. 'Or someone. Only question is which one?'

The frantic footsteps are getting louder as they get closer.

'There's not a year gone by that I don't wish she'd stayed in her room that night,' Colonel Mustard says. 'If only she'd done as she was told and stayed in bed with her room locked instead of—'

'They're in the tower!' Miss Scarlet yells, piling into the Colonel's back.

A flash of silver catches in the torchlight, followed by a heavy thunk. The Colonel emits an 'Oof' before collapsing to the ground, the shotgun flying out of his hands and skittering across the floor.

There's a commotion in the dark, picked out in fleeting glances in the spotlight as Effie tries to piece together what has happened. She knows one thing for sure: the ghosting impression of metal in the light wasn't a stag. Miss Scarlet stands with one hand to her mouth, eyes wide. The Reverend's bulk bursts through the doorway to the stairwell. Nish stands frozen to the spot. Mrs Peacock crouches down beside the Colonel, who is spreadeagled on the floor. A tarnished silver candlestick rolls back and forth on an uneven flagstone. A brogue-clad foot reaches out to still the silverware and the torch traces up the dark skinny cut jeans, up the untucked Ben Sherman shirt and Ralph Lauren v-neck sweater, to reveal Steve. Steve clutches the shotgun and aims it squarely at the Reverend.

'Now I have a machine gun. Ho-ho-ho.'

'It's a shotgun, you idiot,' the Reverend growls.

'You've killed him!' Mrs Peacock screams, her voice echoing around the church.

'He's dead?' Miss Scarlet joins in, her face contorted into a snarl of horror. 'What have you done? *What have you done?*'

Lest anyone be unclear, the Reverend spells it out: 'Only two of us can make it out alive.'

16

The survivors are all thinking the same thing: If only two of us can make it out of this alive – of whom I am surely one – who is my natural partner in this endeavour?

For some, the answer is easy.

Miss Scarlet and the Reverend Green, so recently freed to openly declare their affection, are Little Slaughter's power couple. Young and athletic. Veteran survivors of Christmas past. The home-team favourites.

Then there's Nish and Effie, two strangers brought together by a missed connection. A rapid bond forged in adverse circumstances. Also young, but wiry, wily and wary in that London way of people who live payday-to-payday in the uneasy truce of over-priced house-shares. They might be in entirely alien territory, but they've spent their lives fighting for the last drop of milk in the fridge, an equal share of the electricity bill, a seat on a rush-hour tube, and now they're preparing to fight for their lives.

And then there's Steve and Mrs Peacock.

The woman who led the rag-tag bunch of strangers to a festive death trap and the man who lost his beloved partner in the first steel-antlered attack. A little thicker round the waist, but older and more experienced, they can teach these young bucks some new tricks. Might enemies turn into allies under the right conditions?

Well, the truth is that they're not all thinking the same thing.

What Steve's thinking could barely be more obvious if it was written in capital letters across his forehead with a

Sharpie. Mrs Peacock is looking very, very nervous. And justifiably so.

'Look, let's not be rash about this,' she says.

'Give me one good reason,' Steve says, his voice laced with poison. He has the shotgun trained on the Reverend as the most likely threat to his trump card, but it's clear he won't hesitate if given an excuse to turn on the woman who brought them here.

'We can still make it.' Mrs Peacock licks her dry lips, eyes darting back and forth for reaction. 'There's still a way.'

'If there's a way to survive, how come the stags took their eight kills each year for the last decade?' Effie says.

Mrs Peacock stammers a response: 'I-if we c-can—'

'No,' snaps the Reverend.

'Keep her in sight,' Steve says, directing his instruction at the Reverend. He has subtly manoeuvred himself in front of Miss Scarlet, his bulk eclipsing her.

'Then put that gun down,' the Reverend growls. 'You city boys don't know how to handle weapons.'

Steve smirks with a Bond-villain energy that makes Nish's stomach somersault. 'Went on a stag do to Prague, mate. Fired an AK-47, think I can handle a little shooter like this.'

The Reverend returns the smirk. 'A fiver says you dislocate your shoulder.'

'If you two are quite finished, can we get back to working out how to survive?' Effie flicks the spotlight on to Mrs Peacock. 'You were saying?'

'If we can get back to the pub,' Mrs Peacock says. 'Get into the cellar—'

'I told you, no.' The Reverend takes a step towards Mrs Peacock but pulls up short as Steve raises the shotgun barrel.

'You said it yourself,' Mrs Peacock says. 'Things are different this year.'

'Think of the children,' he says.

'They've never made it into the cellar,' Mrs Peacock says. 'It's the safest place in the whole village.'

'This is madness.' Miss Scarlet screws up her face in a mix of rage and horror. 'Have you heard yourself? This is madness. I can't believe you'd be so *selfish*.'

A lowing bleeds through from outside, the distinct mournful bellow of a stag calling out to its comrades.

'They know where we are and if one of them arrives while

we're arguing we're done. We can't stay here,' Nish says. 'Can we at least agree on that?'

'The pub's the closest building,' Effie says. 'It's not safe – but it's safer than here.'

'We get to the pub, we regroup,' the Reverend agrees. 'We make a new plan.'

Mrs Peacock opens her mouth. 'But—'

'No cellar, no matter what.'

'There are other buildings in the village,' Miss Scarlet says. 'We pick one, we lie low, we see what happens if daybreak comes.'

The uneasy truce is agreed with silence rather than words.

Steve flicks the gun towards the church doors, indicating that he wants the Reverend to lead the way. The Reverend takes Miss Scarlet's hand and leads her slowly and stealthily towards the smashed doorway. Steve turns the barrels towards Mrs Peacock and repeats the gesture. She swallows dryly, but follows the others with the exaggerated loping gait of a child attempting to be stealthy. Steve follows, swinging his sights over the smashed remains of the church pews, taking one last look in case a patient deer has been lurking in the shadows.

Nish exhales, letting out the tension that had been building in him while the others bickered and postured. 'A family argument. It really is beginning to feel a lot like Christmas – just with more firearms.'

'You're thinking what I'm thinking, right?'

'You want to know what's in the cellar, don't you?'

She smiles and his heart flutters. It's not that he hasn't noticed it before – maybe it's because his senses are heightened by the proximity to danger – maybe it's because in contrast to the death and fear since they arrived in Little Slaughter life feels more vibrant and sacred – but she really is beautiful.

In that moment he thinks about kissing her. The memory of the feel of her soft skin as she pressed her hand over his lips, her hair brushing his cheek, the warmth of her breath, the spiced aroma of her perfume rushes through his mind. If not now, then when? There may never be another moment…

But they're standing over the cooling corpse of Colonel Mustard, the chimes of murderous antler against ancient stone still echoing down the stairwell, and he can feel eyes on him from the doorway.

The moment passes.

'I think it's the key to everything,' she says. 'Know your monster.'

Effie leads the way towards the door where the others are waiting. She flicks the torch off, plunging the church into darkness. They allow their eyes to adjust to the indigo darkness of the night outside. The snow shimmers blue and a weak moonlight shines through a gauze of cloud.

'We're only trying to escape a horde of unkillable man-eating deer, but don't let our survival get in the way of you two mooning at each other,' Steve says.

'Where's your sense of romance?' Mrs Peacock says, her tone gently chiding.

'Lying dead in the snow, thanks to you.'

'If we're going to do this, we need to move now,' the Reverend says, his voice a low rumble.

So, irreconcilable differences parked for the moment, they step back out into the winter landscape. Shards of splintered oak are scattered before them like shrapnel, wedged into the deepest drifts of snow. The stag must have burst through the door with explosive force.

Hiding in the shade of the porch, peering down the yew-lined avenue towards the gateway to the churchyard, Nish notices reminders of death all around. The soft moonlight brings the ice-caked world into clearer focus. The gravestones that peek through the snowdrifts cut ominous shapes, crosses and urns and a scatter of winged angels silhouetted against the pristine white snow. Between the trees, the dark shadow of two feet peeking out mark where the gored corpse of the drunk lies. There's a hunched shape on the village green, not quite blending into the snow, surrounded by a spill of red where Mrs White fell. And there, under the gate, is a stag. It stares straight at them.

Nish's heart skips a beat. First the flutters of love and now the lurching dread of fear. He's going to need to see a cardiologist if he ever makes it through this. The stag has been waiting patiently for them to leave the church. It must have seen them. His eyes flick over the obstacles before them as he tries to pick out an escape route.

He's traced a path that's not too littered with gravestones and trip hazards – although it's impossible to know what's hidden under the thick snow – when Steve catches his eye. He clutches the shotgun with one hand and covers his eyes with the other.

'What are you trying to say?' Miss Scarlet whispers.

Steve gives her an exasperated look before more vigorously covering his eyes.

Miss Scarlet looks at Nish and Effie, as if they might be able to better understand Steve by virtue of being from the same city.

'No idea,' whispers Nish.

Steve points at Nish, as if he's just won a round of charades.

Mrs Peacock barely conceals a snort. 'Like the cracker joke,' she wheezes. 'What do you call a deer with no eyes? *No-eye deer!*'

Steve gives her a look of pure fury. 'It might be blind, but it can still hear you.'

There's a mournful lowing in the distance. The stag's ears twitch and it raises its head, angling its remaining senses towards the herd on the church tower. It lows back in response, slow and dreary. In the moonlight, if he looks closely, Nish can see where the fur on its face is matted with dark blood. There's a milky glimmer where its eye sockets were raw meat not so very long ago. It's healing, he realises. At some point, the creature will regain its sight. Which means they're not just unkillable, but even a point-blank shotgun blast to the face only slows it down for a bit.

The blind stag calls out again with its own haunting note, long and plaintive. Its breath freezes, a fine white haze in the moonlight that dissipates on the breeze.

'We need to go back the way we came,' the Reverend says. He indicates the frozen route in the church's snow shadow.

Nish glances back at the stag standing guard at the gates. It twitches its ears rapidly before lowering its head to scratch with a front hoof. It doesn't know they're watching it and – if anything – it looks like it might be bored with sentry duty.

They leave the porch – the Reverend first, followed by Miss Scarlet, then Mrs Peacock, Steve, Effie and finally Nish – each stepping gentle and tender over the frozen ground under the building's eaves. Gravel and loose-flaked snow crunch softly underfoot. It's impossible to tell just how much noise they're making – whether it might carry on the wind to the stag's super-sensitive ears – but it feels too loud. Nish's footsteps are clumsy, his breath is a roaring gale in his head, and his heart a marching drumbeat. Everything is too loud.

But they are putting distance between themselves and the stag. They stretch out in single file, each taking slow cautious steps, taking turns to glance back in the direction of the gate where the steel-antlered harbinger of death is fading into the distance.

As they reach the fringes of the church the Reverend pauses. They come to a halt, remaining in single file.

'What's up?' Mrs Peacock whispers.

'We're going to need to break cover,' Miss Scarlet says, glancing back up at the church tower.

Looking back, Nish can see the outcrop of one of the wings and the porch. The church walls stretch up, meeting the angled plane of the snow-coated roof before the grey stonework climbs further and disappears behind the overhanging eaves. Ahead of them is the path through the graveyard that will take them back to the stile, after which they will cross the village green, steering wide of the sentry deer. But when they do so, they will be completely exposed to anything looking over the parapet of the church tower.

If the stags are still distracted with frustratedly chipping away at the doorway leading to the winding stairs, they might be safe. But the night air is silent. If the stags were still lashing their antlers, the sound of metal on stone would be covering the sound of their footsteps. Then what are the deer doing? Nish realises there's only one plausible option. They're using the church as a watchtower.

And then something else occurs to him.

'How many of them made it up the tower?' Nish whispers.

'What?' says Miss Scarlet.

'When you were up there, how many did you see?'

'We weren't going to stick around to count them,' Miss Scarlet says.

'I got to the stairs when the third one arrived,' the Reverend says.

'How many do you think could fit on that space?'

'Oh bloody hell,' Effie says.

'Four or five max,' Steve says, tightening his grip on the shotgun.

'Which means there's two, three – maybe four – still unaccounted for,' Nish says. 'It's a trap.'

He desperately wants Effie to contradict him, for her to have seen something else. But his logic is disappointingly sound. There's a moment of indecision as the survivors try to work out their next course of action. If leaving the church grounds is a trap, would they be better staying in the church itself? Was there a third option, somehow yet undiscovered?

'We've been caught in a trap since we left Paddington,' Steve says. 'Nothing's changed. We stick with the plan.'

'I agree,' says Effie. Nish wonders if she's now so caught up in finding out what's in the cellar, she'd veto any option that didn't involve heading back to the pub.

'The man's an idiot,' the Reverend says. 'But he's right on this occasion.'

'Who wants the casting vote?' Nish says.

Steve nudges the shotgun into Mrs Peacock's side. 'Right you are, boss. Nothing's changed.'

And so, with heightened awareness of the trap closing in around them, they proceed in pairs. The Reverend and Miss Scarlet are the first to break cover. She goes first, lithe and sprightly, darting and ducking between gravestones and trees without so much as a glance back until she's through the narrow gap in the wall. He covers her every move, perfectly synchronised, so close to her heels that he's like her shadow. It takes Nish a moment to realise that he's covering her from sight, concealing the bright red dress behind his own monochrome silhouette.

Then it's Steve and Mrs Peacock, who follow the same path. Steve hovers close to Mrs Peacock, his shotgun clutched in both hands, always keeping his eyes on her. Mrs Peacock, however, glances back up at the church tower and immediately flinches and ducks down. She stumbles over something in the snow and ducks behind a snow-capped stone angel. Steve ducks in ahead of her, clutching the gun in readiness.

Effie clutches Nish's hand, holding it tight as they watch on in horror. It's clear from Mrs Peacock's body language that she thinks they've been seen. She presses herself to the stonework. Steve watches the tower behind, holding himself still and silent. There's just enough light to see him swallow. The whites of his bulging eyes glow like the snow.

Eventually – although it's probably only been a matter of seconds – Steve gives Mrs Peacock a signal to indicate that the coast is clear. She doesn't seem to take any solace from this. Steve readies himself to move again, but she continues to press herself against the stone angel, as if she hopes to find safety by absorbing herself into the statue. Seeing that she's frozen, Steve reaches forward, grabs her by the novelty Christmas jumper and drags her across the remaining distance to the narrow stile. He pushes her through without ceremony and ducks through himself immediately after.

'And then there were two,' Effie says.

'This is okay,' Nish says with what he hopes sounds like confidence. 'It's just like playing hide and seek with my nephews.'

'How many nephews do you have?'

'Two. One's five, the other's eight.'

'And they're murder-deer?'

'Well, no, but they throw some pretty wild tantrums.'

'Tell you what,' she says. 'I'll take your nephews over Prancer's 'roid rage buddies any time.'

He smiles. 'Yeah, we make it through this, I'm going to be feeling a lot more tolerant of them.'

'You ready?'

'Not really.'

'Me neither.'

But they can't wait any longer. The others managed to make it through without being spotted, and now it's their turn. Effie ducks low and picks a careful route between the gravestones, pausing for a moment behind each to check her next move. Nish follows her lead, making himself as small as possible as he crunches through the deep snow.

As he waits for her to break cover again, he glances round the stone to see the church tower. It's lit up in the moonlight, the texture of the stone and gold glint of the clock visible for the first time. It's one minute to midnight, although it feels like it should be much later for all that's happened. Up top, the crenelated wall of the tower looks like the battlements of a castle, the George's Cross flutters in the wind. He can see branches of antlers lit electric blue like inverted bolts of lightning and the dark looming bulk of the deer attached to them.

They seem to be just milling idly rather than keeping watch, until one puts its front hooves on the wall and leans over the parapet. Its onyx black eyes shimmer darkly.

He turns to warn Effie, but it's too late. She's moving steady and crouched to cross the final distance to the stile when he hears the loud low rumble from the tower. The stag leans out into the night air, its mouth wide as it fixes its eyes on the patch of snow-covered wall where Effie has just vanished out of sight.

There's another loud lowing in response that echoes across the graveyard from the wooden gateway. He wonders what information the lookout could have conveyed to the blind deer. Enough to let it know where the survivors have been spotted?

Would the creature begin slowly picking its way across the graveyard, steered by scent and sound alone?

The call is answered again, but from a different direction across the village green. And again, and again, and again.

It's time to move, stealth be damned. Nish stands and runs for the gap in the wall, his feet crunching on the snow – compacted and icy tracks left by the others or soft and yielding pristine powder – and squeezes through the stile. He looks along the wall and sees no one—

Effie grabs his arm and pulls him in the opposite direction. 'They went this way,' she says.

They move crouched behind the shelter of the dry-stone wall. Nish glances back over the expanse of the green behind them. There are two dark blots emerging from the low-slung village in the distance, running to the call from the watchtower.

'They didn't fancy waiting, huh?'

'I guess not.'

Ahead, Nish can see Steve's back. Nish keeps to the shadow of the wall, low and determined. The wall curves around and he can't see beyond, but he imagines that Mrs Peacock is a little ahead of Steve. Then, with a larger gap, the village power couple will be trying to put more distance between themselves and the others.

And why wouldn't they? If they could barricade themselves in before any of the others arrived, then they could guarantee their survival.

The settled snow starts to become thicker as the wall curves around to face the wind. As it does, they're forced further from its shelter and so begin to stand straighter as they pick through the deeper powder. Nish has lost feeling in his toes and his jeans are soaking up to the knee. His leg muscles are aching and sore from sprinting, climbing stairs, and stealth-waddling. If he makes it through to the morning, he's barely going to be able to move. But for the time being he tries to bury the pain and discomfort and keep going as if his life depends on it. Which it does.

As they come into the open, Nish can see the route through to the pub. They drop down a bank to the road that leads into the village. Up ahead is the minibus, parked at an awkward angle on the verge. It has a fine coating of snow but seems to have made it through the worst of the night's blizzard thanks to the bare-branched trees that overhang the road.

The path of the road is marked out as a gulley of nearly

pristine snow, which swings around towards the pub. It marks the perimeter of the village green with a thin hedgerow, bare of leaves, through which Nish can see the exposed space beyond and the church.

The tower bristles with antlers as the deer keep watch for their prey. A stag stands guard at the gates, although it's impossible to tell from here whether it's still the blinded one or if it has been replaced with one of the newer arrivals from the village. A creature stands in the middle of the green, lit by bright moonlight – the thin cloud cover has shifted, the sky is now a velvet black with a spray of stars.

The stag's silver antlers drift and warp like seaweed, but the rest of the creature is thoroughly land-bound. Its sturdy and powerful muscles are carved through its thick fur. It stands proud, swivelling its ears and sniffing the air for clues.

Nish and Effie exchange a glance. The pub is so near they can smell the woodsmoke that still drifts from its chimney, but it's still so far. And it offers so little sanctuary if they should get there.

They continue to pick their way, slow and cautious behind the thin cover of the hedgerow, all the while watching the stag closely for signs that their cover has been blown.

Which is why it takes them a moment to catch on when Mrs Peacock makes her move.

17

When things go wrong, they go wrong fast.

'Get back here,' Steve stage whispers. His voice is sharp and loud enough to carry down the silent country road.

The stag standing sentinel on the snow-covered green tilts its ears towards the perimeter of bush. It slowly turns its head, exhaling a fine mist of frozen breath, clearing its lungs to sort through the scents that hang on the cold night air.

Footsteps crunch, loud and fast. Nish, taking his eyes off the stag for a moment, sees Mrs Peacock running. The reflective strip of her day-glow tabard flashes brightly in the moonlight. She has one hand raised high in the air, wielding the key fob like a weapon.

The minibus's indicators glow a vibrant orange. There's a mechanical *thunk* as the doors unlock and the unmistakeable *tweep tweep* of the alarm being disarmed.

In the distance ahead, Miss Scarlet glances back, aware that something is off. Even from here, Nish can see the look of aghast horror wash over her face as she sees the burst of light from the minibus. Perhaps she understands that Mrs Peacock is attempting to stage an escape, leaving them all to the deer. Perhaps her reaction is driven by the more immediately pressing issue that their cover has been blown.

On the snow-coated plain, the stag stands to attention. Its antlers coil out wide as they slide into fiendish hooks. It raises its head to the moon and bellows. The sound is part hunting call, part cry of despair. There is something primitively haunting and melancholy about these shire horse-sized killing machines. If nature were to take revenge on mankind for the devastation it had wrought on the world, Nish thinks, this would be a fitting form. A brief encounter with one of these abominations would be a million times more effective than some trust-fund kids supergluing themselves to an art gallery.

Mrs Peacock's legs move in slow-motion as she closes the distance between her and the driver's door. She runs with wild limbs, feet slipping with each step and arms spread wide to keep her balance.

Steve raises the shotgun, stands with his legs shoulder-width apart, steadies his feet on the frozen ground. Cocks his head and closes one eye.

'*No!*' Effie and Nish shout in horrified unison, their voices echoing into the night air.

A flash of bright flame spurts from the shotgun's muzzle. It leaves a ghosting impression on Nish's vision. The report of the shot echoes sharp and resonant, followed by the cawing of rooks rudely woken and thrown whirling into the night sky. Glass shatters and the minibus's windows fall to the floor in a scatter of blue-green detritus.

For a moment, Mrs Peacock carries forward as if untouched. But then she lands an uneven foot, falls to both knees with her arms raised in the air. An image of the film poster for Platoon flashes through Nish's head. Her day-glow tabard is shredded and already blackening with blood. She slumps face-down into the snow.

Nish and Effie are frozen to the spot. Even though they've only recently seen Steve kill the Colonel, this is somehow different. The Colonel was in self-defence, but Mrs Peacock was personal. Even though she was trying to get away, she didn't pose a threat. Steve could have let her go to take her own chances. Instead, he shot her in the back.

'What did you do?' the Reverend bellows back towards them. His deep voice is strained with distress. 'What the hell did you do?'

'There can be only one,' Effie says. She gives Nish a sad look.

'No. There's got to be another way.'

'I guess I owe you a fiver,' Steve says, his voice drawn with pain. His right arm hangs loose, the tell-tale sign of dislocation. He tries to hold the emptied shotgun with his remaining good hand. He winces, shakes his head, like someone trying to wake themselves up with a splash of cold water.

❄ ❄ ❄

Meanwhile, back on the green, the stag lands its front hooves solid on the ground and snorts out a mist. The shotgun blast startled it, sudden and loud enough to cause it to rear up like a whinnying horse. Now, however, it knows exactly where its prey has been hiding. With a strong kick of its rear legs, it bounds into chase. Its hooves throw up puffs of powdered snow.

From the tower of the church another stag bounds, momentarily framed against the moon that hangs low in the sky as it leaps gracefully to the snow-capped roof. A thick slab of snow slips as it lands, an avalanche racing down the side of the church. For all its grace and poise the creature is caught out by the movement underfoot. It skitters and wheels its hooves, trying to find purchase. But instead it succumbs to gravity and tumbles from the side of the building with a clumsy lack of dignity.

Another stag leans over the parapet and issues an enquiring sound. *Prancer, you alright mate?*

The unfortunate Prancer shambles to his feet, shakes the snow from his fur. The branches of his antlers fluid and lank hanging around his shoulders like wet hair before becoming solid and broad and magnificent and deadly.

Prancer stretches his head up to the sky and replies. *Mind that first step.*

❄ ❄ ❄

Meanwhile, further up the tree-lined road Miss Scarlet pulls insistently at the Reverend's arm.

'We need to move,' she says, gently.

'That stupid city—'

'Now,' she says, firmer.

They both know the truth.

Over a decade of attempting to survive the annual onslaught of the stags, they've learned the rules the hard way. The deer won't stop until they've had their eighth kill. There is no question of surviving until daybreak. There was one year when they managed to draw out the ordeal long enough that the sun should have risen, but time had frozen until the blood of an eighth victim had been spilled. Another year they'd tried to escape, driven as far as they could from the village, only to find themselves on the same stretch of road, driving endlessly past Little Slaughter like a chase scene from an old cartoon where the background had been reused on an endless loop.

The laws of time and space are bent out of shape until the eighth victim – sacrifice – tribute – is claimed. They've never been sure what to call them. But until that final death, the terror will never end.

And because Steve has killed Mrs Peacock – gunned her down just as she was about to find herself trapped in that Tom and Jerry loop – he's condemned one of them to die. The first night that they can reveal their true feelings for each other to the world will also be their last. There's a certain Romeo and Juliet romance to it.

Miss Scarlet leads the way as they run, feet crunching through the fresh snow.

❄ ❄ ❄

Meanwhile, back down the road, near the minibus, the three remaining Londoners stand rooted to the spot as Mrs Peacock turns the snow red.

'Don't just stand there – go,' Steve says.

'What about you?' Nish says.

Steve stands braced, the shotgun gripped in one hand, his other arm hanging limply by his side. His eyes are fixed on the green where danger is approaching at a gamely canter.

'Score's not settled yet.'

What do you say to a man so determined to meet his fate head on? Nish's mind is blank, so he just places his hand on Steve's shoulder. He means to do it gently, but Steve winces and then leans into it, hard. There's a soft crack as his shoulder slips back into its socket.

Steve tentatively rotates his shoulder before gripping the barrel with both hands like a baseball player preparing to strike a home run.

'Thanks mate. You vegan kids are gonna want to get out of here. Daddy's getting himself some venison tonight.'

Nish and Effie run, taking short shuffling strides that kick up a prow of loose snow as they move.

Steve tenses as the beast bounds closer, just a fine gauze of hedgerow and a rapidly diminishing stretch of snow separating them. The shadow of its shoulders riding high with a steady rhythm as it cranes its neck forwards, its snooker-ball eyes fixed on him with the determined malfeasance of an old-school football hooligan at an England friendly.

With one last bound, it springs high over the hedge. Its front hooves tucked primly into its breast, the soft fur of its underbelly, and its powerful outstretched rear legs soar past overhead as Steve rolls out of the way.

❄ ❄ ❄

Meanwhile, up on the church roof there's a smooth flow of movement as each subsequent stag bounds down the steep angles of the ancient building.

They leap from the tower, plant their hooves on the narrow stretch of slate roof cleared by the unfortunate Prancer, antlers trailing behind them like forks of lightning. Then, with a fluidity and grace that defies their murderous intent, spring down to land in the churchyard with a charming little cantering dance. As they wait for the next, their antlers fan out like thorned crowns.

As the last comes down there's a shower of slate. Several roof tiles shatter and dislodge under the assault, disappearing into the thick snow. Vixen looks up towards the roof, as if expecting more destruction to follow.

This way, lows Prancer, taking the lead.

They skip lightly through the cemetery, flicking up dainty flurries of powdery snow as they dance down the aisle of yew trees.

One of them pauses to inspect the corpse, its blood freezing where its chest has been torn open. The man's been dead for hours now, long since discarded and left to the elements. But the scent is strong and powerful to Vixen's hyper-sensitive olfactory system.

I think this one's pickled. Kind of reminds me of the old guy.

Prancer pauses to look back.

Stop that. You don't know where it's been.

Vixen leans down and tentatively licks some snow that has turned crimson with spilled blood.

Oh wow, that's strong.

Strong? Dancer says.
Yeah. Like, you should try it.

Comet takes a step closer, sniffs the air above the corpse, licks the snow.

Oh, man, that's got a kick.
Like a margarita, huh? Dancer says.
A Bloody Mary, amirite? Comet says.

Vixen lets out a flirtatious little snort, before leaning back in to try another lick.

Prancer lets out a great lungful of air, his rubbery lips spraying flecks of saliva into the snow as his breath freezes in the air. *Come on, before—*

Where are they? Demands a new voice, its timbre low and rumbling like thunder on a stormy night. General Blitzen is framed by the churchyard gate. He's big and powerful, a towering beast of muscle and bulk. His antlers shimmer deadly in the moonlight, coiled into a thicket of scimitar blades. His fur is darker than the others, shaggier, almost wolf-like.

Prancer gives a pointed glance back at Dancer, Vixen and Comet. He'll be damned if they make him look like a fool in front of the General again. *That way.*

What are you waiting for then?

Move, Prancer lows, attempting to preserve at least some of the authority that has melted off him at the first sign of a true leader.

The deer begin to move, falling behind General Blitzen.

Dancer skips to close the distance behind Prancer, embarrassed to have been caught engaging in horseplay.

Vixen and Comet exchange a look, a hint of wry humour behind their dark murderous eyes.

Whoever had this one is going to be waaay-sted.

❄ ❄ ❄

Meanwhile, back on the tree-lined path, where the minibus sits abandoned under a holly bush and Mrs Peacock lies face-down in the snow, Steve scrambles to his feet. He whirls around to keep the stag in sight, the empty shotgun clutched fiercely by the still-warm barrel.

The dive into the snow was exhilarating – the burn of the ice against his skin – and, if he's honest, sobering. Despite ejecting the contents of his stomach halfway over the village green some time ago, the free booze from earlier has been fuzzying his head. At times it's been as if he's driving himself from a distance. But the shock of the ice has cut through the alcohol and given him a clarity of thought.

He has the fleeting Sunday-morning feeling he remembers from his youth. The sudden awareness of strange surroundings with no clear memory of how he came to be here. The montage of disconnected scenes that play through his mind. The cold-sweat flush of shame.

There's a crash as something large and heavy hits the undergrowth.

The stag lies on its side, halfway buried in a holly bush. If there's one thing that Steve's learned this night, it's that gigantic murder-deer have a terrible turning circle. They can run through snow faster than Usain Bolt, they have the strength and power to tear through buildings like the Incredible Hulk, but they've got the turning circle of a shipping container.

But perhaps this is a lesson this stag has only just learned itself. It wheels its legs helplessly as it wriggles its body back and forth. It gives him a frankly demented look, its big pink tongue lolling out between its fangs and its huge beady black eyes rolling. Its maw is smeared with dried blood. The creature has already had one kill this night. There's a whiff of spirits behind the beast's farmyard aroma.

Steve pictures the shotgun cartridges stuffed into the Colonel's pockets. The Colonel is lying on the cold church flagstones, his cache of ammo well out of reach. Then he thinks of Professor Plum, who had been the first to wield the shotgun. He too had stuffed his pockets with cartridges, only to be torn in half and thrown off the pub roof.

Why in bloody hell didn't he think of picking up the remaining cartridges? It's rule number one in a first-person shooter: get ammo.

But no.

The writhing beast manages to get some purchase and scrabbles to its feet. It emerges from the bush with a great nest of foliage tangled in its antlers and its fur a mess of twigs, dead leaves, and snow. It shakes itself like a wet dog, scattering a shower of detritus and ice. It loses some of the foliage caught in its antlers, but it still wears a wreath of holly like a crown. The beast staggers a little. Is it drunk? Even so, its coal-black eyes are fixed on Steve.

'Still got a little bit left, mate,' Steve says, tapping his head.

As if understanding, the stag flexes its antlers. They move like snakes on a Medusa's head, fluid and with a collective intelligence straight out of a horror film. The vegetation falls to the ground, shredded with a cool efficiency Steve recognises from that one time he went a bit mad with a work credit card, a wrap of marching powder, and a high-end sushi restaurant.

It's funny. When he was put on formal warning for misconduct, he'd thought it one of the biggest mistakes in his life. He'd worried about losing his pension and how much debt he and Jess were in. But now, looking back, he'd do it all again. And more. Guess he's not going to need to worry about the ever-increasing retirement age, eh? Looks like the joke's on the banks that were so generous with those unsecured loans, huh?

The stag snorts out a mist of frozen breath, a gossamer strand of mucus dangles from its nostril. It stamps one hoof, paws at the snow, and lowers its head ready to charge.

'Olé, Rudolph.'

The beast storms forwards, the thunder of its hooves softened by the snow.

A few years back, before the pandemic, Steve and Jess had rented a villa in the hills outside Seville. A beautiful, whitewashed place with a roof terrace, an infinity pool looking out over the city sprawl below, floor-to-ceiling windows and no curtains.

Steve had taken Jess to see the bullfighting. Never mind the tight-fitting outfits and silly capes, they were there for the ever-present risk that a foot wrong would bring danger and death. The bull always got it, but sometimes it went out in a blaze of glory. It was sexy as hell.

Afterwards, they played the dance of the matador in the baking sun. Didn't sleep for three days. The places he had to rub aftersun. Sometimes you've got to feel close to death to feel alive.

And he feels alive right now, diving to one side as a tonne of prime venison ploughs past. It passes so close he can hear the fine blades of its antlers sing as they cut through the air. He lands hard in the snow, the ice pricking at the back of his neck. There's a blast of farmyard-scented air in the deer's wake. The canter of hooves slow as it overshoots.

He looks up at the sky. With the clouds cleared and so far away from the light pollution of London, he can see the stars.

Not just the usual ones – the Plough, the North Star, Orion's Belt if you're lucky – but the midnight blue sky is speckled with pinpricks of light, like it's been airbrushed.

One winter, he flew Jess to Oslo. The first few nights they went clubbing, losing track of time in the days when the sun never rose. Eat, sleep, rave, repeat. Money spilled through their hands like water, but that was a problem for another day. He wanted Jess to be happy, even though looking at each night's bar tab on his phone in the bathroom each morning after brought him out in a cold sweat. But she was happy. That's all that matters, he realises. She was happy.

Their appetite for partying sated, they drove out to a cabin on an island in one of the fjords. Steve drove for hours, never passing another car in the midday moonlight, even though the roads were pristine – lined with walls of snow, yet not a single snowflake spotted the flawless tarmac ahead.

When they arrived, their cabin was warm and light. Clad in black wood, wrapped in a thick layer of snow like royal icing, and perched on an outcrop. The lounge had a wall of glass that framed a view up a fjord lined with shaggy pine trees. There wasn't another soul for a hundred miles or more. They called it their cabin at the end of the world. They would spend hours with the lights off, watching the haunting flicker of the Northern Lights lick up and down the valley or just marvelling at the sprays and swirls of galaxies a billion miles away.

'Do you think there's life after death?' Jess had said one time.

'Jeez babe, that's a bit heavy isn't it?'

'It's just... I don't know... I'm happy. I can't bear the idea that this might end.'

'If there is, I'll find you.' He had kissed her head, breathed in her scent. 'We ain't come here to worry about death.'

Jess had pressed herself closer to him, put aside her maudlin thoughts. 'Alright... do you think there's life out there?'

'With an infinite number of planets circling around an infinite number of stars and an infinite amount of time? I don't see why we'd be the only ones to crawl out of the primordial soup.'

'Do you think they're watching us?'

'Maybe.'

'Shall we give them a show?'

The memories are vivid as he lies there in the snow. He should be getting up, he should be moving, but nostalgia is a hell of a drug. Better than anything he's tried. It's warm and comforting and so real he could reach out and touch the moment, even as he's reliving it in the third person.

He should be getting up, but he can't. He can't feel his limbs. In fact, he's not cold, even though he's lying here in the snow. He's warm and comfortable, like waking up on a Sunday morning next to Jess. He can't think of anywhere he'd rather be.

A large head looms overhead, blocking his view of the stars. Its rubbery lips drip mucus and its black eyes watch him with a kind of detached interest. The silver crown of metal antlers above drip with fresh red blood.

Another head nudges into view, its face a matted mess of fur and gore, its eyes white and sightless. The first stag nuzzles the blind creature with something approaching tenderness. The blind creature scents the air with flaring nostrils, smelling hot fresh prey. The first stag twines its antlers with those of the blinded beast. Any observer might be forgiven for thinking that these murderous creatures were capable of affection and care. But then any observer would see the wounded deer open its terrible maw wide to display a fine array of razor-sharp teeth moments before it plunges down with a vicious hunger.

Whether Steve saw these last moments of his life or remained cocooned in the comfort of his life flashing before his eyes will forever remain unknown. But his last words, whispered up to the world in a shallow echo of the scene he was reliving, were: 'Babe, I'm coming!'

18

General Blitzen surveys the battlefield before him. He snorts, to express his dissatisfaction, projecting a spray of mucus and a misting of breath into the frozen night air.

The white expanse is dotted with the fallen. Two beside the building in which the enemy first took shelter. One in the middle of the battlefield. One in the walled garden behind. And one behind a thin hedgerow being confronted by Major Dasher and Lieutenant Cupid.

It's no coincidence that pair are working together, he thinks. Yes, they've separated one of the enemy. They're following the strategy laid out by the squadron's leadership. Sure, they're following the protocol in word. But in spirit?

If there wasn't a job to do, he'd bound over and separate them before they start fraternising again.

But the General is on task.

Latest count: five.

Three to go.

They're behind schedule and he's getting impatient with this interminable night.

He glances back at where Lieutenant Prancer is attempting to instil some order and discipline into Officer Cadets Dancer, Vixen and Comet. Good luck with that. He's rarely seen such poorly behaved conscripts, and they've only got worse over the years.

When they lost the Field Marshal, they lost the rigour and authority to bring the young bucks in line. General Blitzen tries, but they have no respect for his authority. If he had his way, he'd set an example of one of them. A court martial. Show them a bit of hard justice. Maybe then they'd fall in line.

Are you quite finished, Lieutenant?

Yes sir. Sorry sir.

If you can't control your unit, I might start asking myself why we need two Lieutenants. Am I understood?

Yes sir... Sorry sir.

That's the problem with Lieutenant Prancer. Simpering and spineless, and not a little bit clumsy. If he'd tried to stand up to the General's authority, put up a fight, maybe then he'd be worth some respect. There's a perverse part of General Blitzen that wishes Lieutenant Prancer would turn the question back on him. *If that's the case, then why do we need two Generals, huh?* It would be completely out of character, but if he did... Well, then he'd see that General Blitzen's temper was true to his name. But he holds back. He always holds back, even though there's a part of him that wants nothing more than to let loose with the anger and hurt he's been bottling up all these years.

The ragtag bunch of Officer Cadets shamble up behind, coming to a halt in a ragged line. There's whispering and giggling at the back.

Ten-shun! General Blitzen bellows.

The line snaps straight, each deer faces forward, antlers thrown back and glistening in the moonlight. Muscles twitch in readiness, frozen breath pools on the night air. The General appraises the gathered unit. They're shabby, ill-disciplined, inexperienced, positively resistant to training, and yet... There's potential. He's hard on them – he has needed to be hard on them ever since that night – but *dammit* he believes in them. Against all the evidence of his own experience. At times – times like now, when they fall in line and recognise his authority – he even *likes* them.

He looks at their keen fresh faces. Some blood will do them some good. The thrill of the hunt. The catharsis of the kill. Discipline only gets you so far. They're on the killing fields and he needs them lively and brutal. They need some fire in their bellies. He directs them each in turn.

You're a bum. Go Prancer! You're a punk. Go Dancer! You're a scumbag. Go Vixen! You're a maggot. Go Comet! Happy Christmas you arse, I pray to God it's our last.

The deer fly past in a thunder of hooves and a kick of powdery snow. It's not his most inspiring speech, but it seems to have done the trick. Have they even noticed that he's cribbed half the lines from some song that was playing from the enemy's fortress earlier? Does it even matter?

Pushing down his own melancholy thoughts, the General Blitzen turns and bounds after Comet. From the far corner of the battlefield, he sees General Dunder cantering onwards, big and powerful.

The family's all here, so let's get this Christmas started.

❄ ❄ ❄

Meanwhile, back on the road…

Above the sound of their own frantic footsteps, the rasping of their own breath, the thunder of their heartbeats, they hear the crash of impact behind. A sort of meaty slap, followed by the casual slowing of hooves. They know Steve's gone.

Five, Miss Scarlet thinks.

Three to go.

They need to move faster.

The road stretches out ahead, the perimeter of the village green marked by thickets of hedgerow and the occasional gnarled tree. Bare branches are silhouetted against the star-strewn sky, orbs of mistletoe hung like baubles. The Slaughter House is out of sight for the time being, but edging closer with every step.

Right now, they're hidden from the herd, but there's an open patch up ahead where the foliage falls away and a fork in the road runs in front of the pub and into the village. There's no hiding from the beasts when they get to that point.

She sees her lover slip, his arms thrown wide to catch his balance. There's a look of panic in his eyes. She reaches out, takes his hand. 'We can make this,' she says.

'Go,' he says.

She gives him a stern look. They've talked about this. The other couple is trailing behind, a fine decoy if ever there were one.

The hedgerow parts and she glances over her shoulder to see a stream of deer tearing across the green, arcing round to intercept the stragglers.

We're going to make it, she thinks.

Reverend Green squeezes her hand. She knows that he knows it too—

But he starts slowing her down, putting himself in front of her, and then she looks ahead and sees it too.

❄ ❄ ❄

The thunder of hooves behind him builds and builds until it's the only thing he can hear.

Nish and Effie run side-by-side, trying their best to be fast and steady on their feet. They had a head start, but that advantage would be blown with the slightest careless move. The deer could close the distance in a matter of seconds.

There's no denying that their cover is blown. He doesn't even need to glance over to see that Effie knows it too. They push on, desperately hoping for a miracle.

But a miracle never comes.

The insistent beat of hooves gets closer and closer until it's on them.

It surrounds them and Nish can feel the ground shaking beneath his feet – and then the deer pass to their right.

Nish sees a flash of fur and the metallic glint of moon-caught antler through the thin winter foliage as the herd surges on, tracing the arc of the village green ahead of them.

Effie slows to a walk, grabbing Nish's hand to make him do the same.

They need to keep moving – the pub is their only potential source of shelter – but all of a sudden, the racket of cantering hooves has come to a halt, leaving the night deadly silent.

❄ ❄ ❄

'Oh god oh god oh god,' Miss Scarlet says under her breath.

'Get behind me,' the Reverend says, putting out one big arm as he steps in front of her.

The stag walks slowly closer, watching them with eyes so big and black he can see the treeline warp around the curve of each orb, a pair of twin moons shining back at him. Its fur is shaggy and rough, a deep grey. It smells of fermented hay, stale urine and death. The antlers are the width of his wrist where they fuse into the creature's skull. They stretch and fork and arc in deadly whorls, tapering to the precision sharpness of his finest paring knife.

The butcher is a tall man, but the creature stoops to look him in the eye. He's always thought of the stags as having an intelligence of a sort – enough to surprise the careful observer every now and then, but primarily successful in their kill counts each year through sheer brute force. But he recognises something cold and calculating in the way the stag appraises him.

It could just kill him.

If it wanted to, it could just skewer them both on its pliable antlers and that would be that.

Instead, it sniffs the air, flicks its ears, moves its head a fraction to one side to look over the Reverend's shoulder.

'Run,' he hisses.

'It's— It's over,' she says.

He risks taking his eyes off the massive stag for one moment to plead with her and then he realises she's right. It's over. They're surrounded by another five stags. His senses have been so consumed by the creature in front of him, he hasn't noticed the closing of their one escape route.

The big beast lows long and soft. It's a dull, flat noise twinged with a sadness that he feels in his heart. But it's somehow more than that. It's an instruction. The new arrivals fan out around them, completely encircling the Reverend and Miss Scarlet. Again, he senses an intelligence, darkly purposeful.

Miss Scarlet takes his hand. Her skin is cold and her knuckles chapped from washing glasses at the pub and exposure to the elements. Life in the countryside is hard and manual, and even the tenderest of blossoms must grow their thorns. He closes his hand over hers, willing the warmth of his hot blood to transfer to her.

'I'm sorry…' she says.

'Don't…'

'I didn't know,' Miss Scarlet sobs. 'If I'd have known… but I didn't.'

The great stag snorts, ejecting plumes of steam and a fine mist of mucus.

Another stag lows gently.

The leader – for that's undoubtedly what it is – stamps a hoof.

The deer close in, separating them.

By the time he's aware of a looming presence behind him and a snort of warm air on the back of his neck, the Reverend is caught. Silver bands snake around him with a delicate precision. They're under his armpits, around his chest, caressing his throat, twisting around his arms, weaving between his legs.

He freezes in place, trying to push down the rising panic. The slightest move will result in laceration. A sneeze would turn him into mincemeat. His breath is slow and ragged. Held at this angle, he can only see what's going on by wheeling his eyes madly.

In front of him, Miss Scarlet is similarly trussed with silver. A single stag nudges its head into her back. There are fine shallow cuts on her exposed skin, fresh and welling with blood.

They stand facing each other for a moment in the still night.

The great stag whinnies.

'I love you,' he says, his voice cracking.

'No,' she says. 'No no no!'

❄ ❄ ❄

There's nothing to be done.

That's the hard truth of the matter. Never mind the fact that the villagers lured them to Little Slaughter as unknowing sacrifices for their annual bloodbath. The two remaining villagers are surrounded. They're as good as dead.

If Nish or Effie attempt to distract the stags, they'll only hasten the inevitable. In fact, the two stags restraining Miss Scarlet and Reverend Green might continue to draw out their suffering while the remaining four take flight in search for the single kill that will end this year's hunt.

Even so, Nish feels a sense of pre-emptive survivor's guilt slowing his legs, forcing him to watch.

Effie grabs his hand, leads him on with a determined urgency. She gives the gathering of deer a wide berth but is quick and quiet as she leads him past them.

She's relentless where he's drawn to keep glancing back.

'Come on,' she whispers, leading him through the snow-caked beer garden. 'Hurry up.'

She's through the smashed front door and running for the bar, where there's the trapdoor to whatever is hidden in the cellar.

Nish hears Miss Scarlet's voice crack as she says 'No no no!' He glances back from the doorway.

When Obi Wan is struck down by Darth Vader's light saber, he vanishes, leaving just a crumpled cloak and a threat to become more powerful than could ever be imagined. And when the deer strike, the Reverend falls to the ground as a crumpled cassock.

But where Obi Wan's death was Universal rated and bloodless, the Reverend becomes a jumble of prime cuts spilling out of a fabric skin. There's something darkly poetic that the village's butcher is reduced to something that looks like a pile of black pudding.

Nish turns and dashes inside just as Miss Scarlet's scream pierces the night, only to be abruptly cut short.

19

'Give me a hand,' Effie says from behind the bar, her voice straining with effort.

Despite the front door being left gaping open all night, the smashed window, and hole torn in the roof, the temperature inside the pub is a notch warmer than outside. The imposing inglenook fireplace glows and flickers with firelight. The moonlight spilling through the broken window reveals two or three small tables thrown at odd angles, one still laden with cold food, and a scatter of intact pub stools. The wooden floor is strewn with broken crockery and destroyed furniture.

Nish stands with his back to the door. It's closed, but it swings loose in the frame from where Steve broke the lock. Only a thin skin of wood separates him from the horde of murder-deer. His eyes are wide, the whites glowing in the gloom, but he can't see anything in front of him. His mind is replaying the last moments of the Reverend's life in 4K HD. It doesn't need to elaborate or add sound effects or fill in blanks. The horror is complete. He touches the doorframe to hold himself steady.

'Nish, a hand if you've got a moment?'

'He just...'

'Come on, stay in the game.' Effie steps away from the heavy keg she's been trying to shift. He looks queasy and shaken. She doesn't know specifically what he's seen, but she can picture the scene, painted in great swashes of crimson. It's inevitable – after the terror of the night, after all they've seen – that there will be some post-traumatic stress. But they're still mid-trauma. Processing what they've been through can wait – it needs to wait. She pictures the stags finishing up with the remains of the villagers and finding him standing limply in the doorway. Easy pickings. They only need one more. 'I can't do this without you.'

Her words filter through Nish's dulled senses. The spectral replay of the Reverend tumbling in pieces fades like smoke blown through the air and he sees her caught in the soft moonlight. This night he's seen the worst, most horrible things he hopes he'll ever have the misfortune to experience. But he's also met her. He's sensed the possibility of a connection far deeper than just a shared instinct to stay alive. If he survives tonight, he knows that years from now he'll wake up in the middle of the night, these scenes still seared on to his brain. He dares to hope that when he does, he'll turn to her and she'll understand.

The flicker of hope, no matter how dim and distant, shines with the brightness of a thousand suns on this dark night.

He stumbles through the pub, his legs weak and unstable, but recovering slowly with each step.

Behind the bar there are rows of wine glasses, pint glasses, and boxes of McCoy's. The trapdoor to the cellar is made of the same thick ancient, varnished wood as the floor and has a thick metal ring embedded in its surface. But there are three big metal beer kegs covering it, keeping the trapdoor firmly closed.

'I think they're full,' Effie says.

'Well, I guess we're going to wake the kids.'

Nish puts his hands on the cold metal rim of the first barrel. Effie does the same. They rock it once, twice, three times until it falls heavily on its side and they can roll it away.

'There are no children in there,' Effie says as they move to the next barrel.

'What?'

The second barrel is on its side and knocking against the first by the time Effie answers.

'You heard Mrs Peacock, right? There have been no children in this village for years. The school shut down.'

Nish thinks back to the slow descent of the church tower, all the while waiting for an imminent death at the bottom of the stairwell. 'I think I was too distracted to listen properly.'

'She was kind of rambling.'

They rock the third barrel out the way and Nish grips the iron ring.

'Whatever's down there,' Effie says, 'I think it's the key to everything.'

The trapdoor is heavy and its hinges squeal as it swings open. There's a precarious moment as Nish steps around the hole in the floor and manoeuvres the heavy wooden door to rest against the metal barrels. The gap reveals a steep set of bare concrete steps that disappear into the dark underbelly of the pub.

Effie eyes the stairwell cautiously. 'There's a moment in every horror film where someone goes into the cellar and you think "No, don't do that, the killer's down there."'

'If you've got a better plan, I'm all ears.' The impenetrable darkness below makes Nish's stomach turn somersaults.

She takes out the Maglight and flicks it. The beam flickers between weak and strong for a moment. Once it has settled on bright, Effie shines the spotlight down the stairs. 'Channelling strong final girl energy right now.'

Effie takes the first step and glances at Nish, more nervous than she's pretending to be.

Nish glances at the window to the outside world. The snow is pristine and glowing in the moonlight, the yew trees and bell tower illuminated in the background. Just add a red-breasted robin and a sprig of holly and the scene would be the distilled essence of a W.H. Smith Christmas card. Yet, just out of frame, a horde of mutant reindeer feast on the bloodied carcasses of their latest victims. It won't be long before they come hunting for their final kill of the night.

A now-familiar melancholy lowing noise echoes through the night.

He hurries after her.

Downstairs, the cellar opens up to become a wide, high-ceilinged space. It smells of stale beer and a persistent ancient damp. The air is the kind of moist cold that chills to the bone. Effie's torch beam cuts through the darkness as it flicks back and forth. The underside of the wooden floorboards reveal narrow gaps where gravy from the spilled food has coagulated in glistening drips. Brick columns rise from the floor to join thick blackened beams, like the ones in the bar above, but bare rather than adorned with hops and horse brass. The floor is a dusty concrete, discoloured by years of spilled ale. To one side there are dully gleaming steel barrels, some linked to the bar pumps above by rubber tubing, others stored in place, waiting to be used. Boxes of crisps and nuts and pork scratchings are piled up in Jenga towers. There are stacks of plastic pint glasses, foil takeaway containers, sporks and napkins. There's even a jumble of 4-pint plastic beer jugs that pubs round the country started using to sell takeaway ale during lockdown.

Effie's beam swings around, the pillars casting exaggerated shadows in a call-back to the dark insides of the church. The memory's a little too close for comfort. Nish is not ready to be confronted with spiralling shadows just yet. Perhaps he never will be again.

The torch beam flickers, switching between very dim and very bright. Effie knocks it with her palm, and it settles for the moment.

'There's nothing down here,' Effie says, disappointed. 'It's just a pub cellar.'

It's undeniable. The cellar has all the appearance of a dumping ground for everything the pub landlord had wanted to keep out of sight. It's a big room and it's not full, but there's nothing here that makes it stand out from any other pub cellar.

In some ways, Effie would have preferred some horrific Blair Witch denouement. To come down here and find themselves face-to-face with the real monster. To find that one of the villagers was some kind of deer shaman controlling the herd. Coming down here to find a rather mundane beer cellar is like going to the boiler room of the Overlook Hotel and finding Jack Torrance methodically working through a tax return. She'd rather anything that would offer some kind of closure than this anti-climax.

'Wait, what's that?' Nish says, glimpsing something shining in the torchlight. He directs Effie's spotlight back to a point on the floor beside the final stair. 'Is that wax?'

'It looks like a candle.'

Indeed, it is a candle. One that has long since been burned down to a flat sweaty pool of dried white wax with a crater containing a blackened wick. And, as the circle of torchlight moves, an altogether larger candle looms out of the dark. It's wrist-thick, foot long, and creamy off-white, its wick proud in a shallow well. There's a box of extra-long matches next to it, and a few burned-out stalks scattered carelessly on the floor.

This would be strange, if somewhat unremarkable when judged against the scale of the evening's events, except that Effie's roving beam reveals a scattered row of similar candles of different heights as the cellar spreads out behind the stairway.

The shadows of the forest of candles and brick pillars spin like a dark kaleidoscope. The cellar becomes a cave, wax stalagmites accumulating over the years. And at the far end, framed by this detritus, is a box made of pine raised on a plinth of beer kegs.

'Now we're talking,' Effie says.

The torchlight flickers as if there's a loose connection.

'On balance, I think I preferred anti-climax.'

'Wouldn't you rather see what this has all been about?'

The torch shuts off, plunging them into darkness.

'Oh, ha ha,' Nish says.

Effie slaps the dead torch against her palm.

'I'm not joking, it just cut out.'

'Well, so much for *seeing* what this has all been about, huh?'

There's the sound of matches rattling in a box, a scrape, and then a flare of light as Nish holds the flame to the nearest candle wick. It sputters, dims, then catches.

'Oh yeah, that'll help the horror film vibes,' Effie says.

'It'll be fine, at least there isn't a goat skull and a penta—'

'What?'

'No, just joking. No pentacles, no skulls.'

'Just a load of candles arranged around a mysterious box,' Effie says. 'Nothing to see here.'

The cellar fills with guttering light as Nish lights each new candle. The air carries the scent of struck matches and wisps of smoke, normally comforting, but in this dark cavernous space, ominous and occult. The candles have been used recently – perhaps not in the last few hours, but certainly in the last few days. Most of them take easily.

'What do you think it is?' Nish says.

'You're thinking what I'm thinking, right?'

'It's about the right size to be a coffin.'

The box is rough-made from pine, held together with steel nails. Some of the planks of wood have fractions of words or logos printed on them, as if they've been reused and repurposed. It's big – maybe seven feet long, three feet wide and deep – and unmistakably funereal.

'But whose coffin?' Effie says, running a finger over a rough edge.

'You think that'll explain everything, don't you?'

She looks at him, soft lit by the candlelight, flames flickering in her dark eyes. 'I've got a hunch. It's pretty wild… But I want to know if I'm right.'

'You do know the story about Pandora, don't you?'

'The Greek myth that's basically a warning to women not to pry into their husband's business?'

'Well, I guess...' Nish says, apologetic. 'I was meaning more about being careful we don't make things worse.'

'What's going to be worse than eight murder-deer?'

Nish tuts. 'Well, that's cursed it.'

'What?'

'"What's going to be worse"? You might as well have said "I'll be right back" and stepped out of sight.'

Effie laughs. 'I thought I was the one who had watched too many horror films.'

When Effie tries to lift the lid, Nish expects it to be nailed shut. After all, if the villagers had taken the trouble to build a shrine in the cellar and cobble together this coffin, they'd surely have nailed the lid shut, right? But no. One edge lifts, the wood flexing and creaking as it does so. Nish helps and together, taking one side each, they shift the lid and slide it to the floor.

They stand over the open casket in silence. The candles bluster in the draft that blows through the building sending shadows rippling up the walls. Even so, in this flickering and dim light, they can see well enough to understand the contents of the box.

'So, that hunch of yours...?'

'Yeah, near enough.'

'Including the chains?'

'Uh-uh, nope. Didn't see that coming.'

Inside the box is a body. Time has decayed and desiccated it so that the flesh has been eaten away, leaving a hollow-eyed skull draped with leathered skin and filaments of white hair all that remains of what must have been a thick, shaggy beard. There are holes of shattered skull the size of pound coins. The man must have been big and broad. He's been contorted to fit into this frame. He was buried in a fur-lined suede two-piece suit, brown with the slightest tinge of mossy green. He has knee-high leather jackboots, glossy black sheen faded to a worn matt that matches the thick-buckled belt that once pulled taught over his stomach.

Thick chains snake around the body, holding it in place. They wrap around the arms and legs, the barrel of the chest, and are joined with a rusted and ancient padlock. Where once they must have been tight and firm, now they are now loose. The figure they hold in place has deflated.

But no matter how shrunken and desiccated the corpse, he's unmistakeable.

'Santa,' Nish whispers with reverence.

'No, it's Police Sergeant Neil Howie,' Effie says, giving him an incredulous look.

'I'm sorry, what? Who...?'

She laughs, not unkindly. 'Sorry, little Wicker Man joke. Yeah, it's totally Santa.'

'What's with the chains?' Nish says. 'It's not like he's going anywhere.'

'You ever see Jeepers Creepers 2?'

Nish is about to reply when there's a distant snort, the sound of a rubber-lipped exhalation that has become so familiar over the past few hours. Nish and Effie exchange a wide-eyed look. Upstairs a floorboard groans under the weight as a deer – a *reindeer* – takes a further tentative step into the pub.

Nish's first thought is of the flickering light that fills the cellar. There are narrow gaps between the floorboards and some of the light must be bleeding through into the pub above. Is the light visible? Can they smell the candles? Have they heard the voices of two remaining survivors?

There are hoof steps above, like hard-knuckled raps at a door. The floorboards creak under hoof, dislodging little puffs of dust and detritus as they shift under the weight of the creatures. There's a gentle, sad lowing noise from above that rumbles and reverberates around the cellar. The candles gutter and dance, even though Nish can't feel a breeze on his skin.

'You did shut the trapdoor didn't you?'

Nish's blood freezes in his veins. Did he? He dashed down after Effie when he heard the deer and—

'Tell me you shut the trapdoor,' Effie whispers.

Nish glances back towards the stairs, where the candles thin out, giving way to boxes and kegs and other more mundane traces of pub life. The far corners flicker and waver in the light from the candles. The trapdoor is open, he knows with dread horror. He was in such a rush to get down, he didn't think to shut it after them. And the warm, flickering light from the candles will be shining out invitingly from behind the bar... and once the deer get to the bar, they'll see the way down.

But they'd never make it down the stairs, right?

And there's something that's been bugging him. When the first pair of stags made their way into the pub through the

Professor's flat, they couldn't have been as large as they loom in his mind. What if they could grow or shrink as needed? Like Alice in Wonderland, but with revenge-seeking livestock. It should be impossible, but he can't dismiss the idea. Not after everything he's seen tonight.

He dashes towards the stairs as quietly as he can, stepping around the candles that flare and flicker in his wake. As he runs, he tries to place the stags based on the noises on the floorboards above.

Nish reaches the column of the stairs and glances up just as a hoof tentatively steps on to the first of the concrete steps. He presses himself close to the staircase and indicates to Effie, only a few steps behind him, to hold back. He looks back up and sees the hoof testing the weight and angle of the stair.

There are two stags that have fallen down narrow staircases so far tonight, although they've recovered from the fall with no real damage to speak of. The stairs to the cellar might be steep, but they're wider than the route down from Professor Peacock's rooms. They are, Nish concedes, no barrier at all to these beasts.

Nish and Effie retreat to the shadows behind the staircase, snuffing out candles as they go, and crouch together in the narrow gap below the stairs. Candles still flicker at the far end of the cellar towards the coffin. They press together, breathing in and out as one, holding hands and waiting for their luck to run out.

The deer know they're down here and there's no way they're giving up now. Their last kill is in sight.

20

The sound of boned hoof on dusty concrete echoes through the cellar as the first stag tests the stairs. There's a gentle lowing, as if of enquiry. *How's it going?* Followed by a wet snort. *Give me a moment!*

The wait is almost unbearable. Nish and Effie have made it through so much this strange night, but there's no denying that their luck has run out. They're trapped in the cellar with Santa's desiccated corpse, his distraught herd of revenge-seeking reindeer are closing in on them, and one way or another the bloodthirsty beasts need just one more kill to end this year's rampage.

Nish wants to say something comforting to Effie. Something to make up for his mind-numbing stupidity at leaving the trapdoor open. Or, if not that, a chance to salvage something good from this foul night. He has a half-formed thought about it being better that they found each other like this than not at all, but he has no words. And besides, isn't that a bit presumptuous? What if she doesn't feel the same way? What if he's been misreading signs? What if, on the cusp of being found and disembowelled by Rudolph and his buddies, he declares unrequited love and she says 'Sorry, Nish, I think of you as more of a friend'? His last few seconds would be filled with regret and excruciating embarrassment. Honestly, death would be a sweet relief. Better to say nothing and shuffle off this mortal coil with some dignity.

Meanwhile, Effie's contemplating her last moments on earth, crouched in this dirty cellar, trapped like a prey animal with her heart hammering in her chest. Her mouth is dry, her lips cracked. She's been too distracted by fear and danger for the past hour or two to notice it, but the thirst is on her something terrible. She's cowering in the basement of a pub thirty-nine days stone-cold sober and moments from death. (How's it not forty yet? It's like time has frozen.) Has it been worth it? The fights, the fallout, the turning her life upside down to try to regain control – and for it to end like this? If there's no hope, then what was the point of it all? If she's going to die, would she rather have drunk herself to oblivion than cower here awaiting her inevitable fate feeling the sharp edge of entirely justified terror?

They both put their maudlin thoughts to one side as the first stag tumbles down the stairs in a racket of hooves. There's a crash of impact as it lands amidst cardboard boxes and Tupperware, followed by animal noises and rubbery snorts. A round plastic lid rolls lazily past and comes to rest beside one of the recently snuffed candles.

They exchange a silent wide-eyed glance.

One of the deer in the pub above lows down into the void. *Mate, you alright?*

The stag huffs. *Oh, sure, yeah, fine. No, seriously, thanks for asking. Nothing a limp carrot and stale mince pie couldn't fix.*

Ah, man, those were the days. What I wouldn't give to see a handful of browning sprouts and a glass of room-temperature milk waiting for the big man.

Hooves shuffle on the concrete floor, loud and close. Nish pictures a stag backing up to make space for the next to leap down the stairs, perhaps turning to see the path of candles that will lead it to the body in the box.

Sure enough, the nearby creature makes a strange whinnying noise. *What's this?*

The sound of steps moving closer is blocked out by the next deer crashing heavily down the stairs.

A hoof comes into sight. Two black front pads of thickened bone, a third to the rear, fringed by a shaggy coat of fur. The beast's plate-sized hooves are powerful yet elegant like a pair of plus-sized high heels. Even this close – even as Nish's nostrils fill with the scent of stale hay, urine and the iron twang of fresh blood – there's something magical about the terrible beasts. Nish feels a strange childish fascination with them, a sense of awe and wonder that fights for dominance with the heart-stopping fear.

Effie squeezes his hand hard.

He squeezes back, never once taking his eyes off the deer's legs as they gradually emerge from behind the stairs.

They have the same alien tight-sprung physicality as a horse, the leg zigzagging between an ankle joint and a knee joint and a hip joint. The stag walks slowly, gingerly stepping, the low ceiling forcing it to walk with its head bent low and its steel antlers folded down its back. There is something dignified and respectful about the way it approaches the coffin, like a mourner at a wake.

Another stag crashes into the cellar. And another, and another. The air fills with animal smells and the fresh scent of death. It's almost overpowering. The beasts continue to hammer into the cellar as the next pair of deer legs appears behind the stairs.

The leading stag stops mid-step, its front hoof held off the ground for a moment as if unsure whether to go on. It reconnects with the floor with gentle grace and heaves out a great melancholy noise that vibrates low and powerful through the thick air. The sound is so immensely and innately sad that Nish feels tears prick at his eyes. He doesn't need to understand the stag's language to know exactly what it's saying.

There's a reply. A snort of enquiry. *What?*

A whinny and rubber-lipped snort in response. *Come see for yourself.*

The second stag shuffles forwards to stand at the shoulder of its colleague. It takes a moment to take in the scene before a pained noise escapes.

And god is it terrible. Not in the cold-sweat-and-ragged-breathing genre of terror that has so far characterised this Christmas Eve. No, it's the black-star terror of words unsaid and things undone. The eternal yawn of absence as a loved one becomes a void. A gap. As they become past tense.

The remaining deer shuffle through after that, stepping daintily around the lit candles. All eight stags huddle close around the coffin, their heads held low and antlers drooping around their shoulders. The ceiling is high, but the beasts seem smaller somehow, as if they have shrunk to fit the available space. Their eyes, glistening darkly in the candlelight, become pits of despair. They keen and low in waves, their noise becoming a rumbling funereal lament.

Nish feels his heart break with a snap like a candy cane. It's so horrible, he expects everything to stop. But it doesn't, and somehow that's worse. To go on living in this dulled world, drained of magic and joy. These aren't even his thoughts, they flow from the same place as the childish magical wonder, entirely drowning out the space where logical concerns about his own bodily safety should be, such as—

'We need to go,' Effie whispers in his ear. Her hair is soft on his face, her breath warm on his skin.

He turns towards her, unable to speak. They hover, faces nearly touching, breathing each other's breath. In the darkness under the stairs her eyes are dark and kind.

Here is hope, they both think.

'We need to go,' Effie repeats, so quiet and so close that the words seem to enter his consciousness less by sound and more by osmosis, or some other chemistry.

Effie carefully unfolds herself from under the stairs, keeping close to the shadows and glancing towards the mourning deer.

Nish does the same. His legs complain and his feet prickle with pins and needles, but he pushes down the pain as he shuffles in the shadows. He follows Effie, slipping alongside the concrete staircase, constantly looking back to make sure that the deer are still absorbed in their vigil.

He can feel the rough edges of the steps against his back as he shuffles into the shadows. He senses Effie start to slowly, carefully climb the stairs in silence. The gentle lowing of the deer continues to cover the sound of his feet on the dusty concrete. As he turns and the staircase blocks out the sight of the stags he dares to feel a sense of relief—

And in that moment there's a loud bang and crunch as he steps on a grab-bag of McCoy's ridge-cut cheese and onion crisps. The foil bag explodes underfoot like a land mine, blasting fried potato shrapnel across the floor.

There's a moment of absolute silence, filled only with horror.

Nish runs clumsily up the stairs in the dark as the cellar fills with the sound of hooves racing towards him.

He emerges into the pub with leaden legs, feet burning as the buzzing cramp from sheltering under the stairs intensifies. He's barely through when the trapdoor slams shut behind him.

'Give me a hand,' Effie says, rolling one of the barrels.

Together they manoeuvre it on top of the trapdoor, but it takes all their combined effort to right the full metal canister on top of the entrance. All the while, the sound of deer hooves swells from the cellar below, ricocheting and echoing through the pub.

They're rolling the second barrel when there's a solid thud against the trapdoor. The upright barrel jolts upwards, a gap appearing in the floor to reveal a set of onyx-black eyes, a blood-stained snout, a pair of yellowed fangs.

Effie jumps on top of the upright barrel. The addition of her weight is enough to push the deer back down for the moment. Nish continues to roll the next barrel single-handed, but then the deer strikes again. There's a flash of antler from the gap that appears leading to the cellar. It punctures a hole in the metal drum, sending a fine jet of foamy beer spurting from the slash.

The deer disappears again as the trapdoor shuts and Nish manages to heave the second barrel upright, helped in no small measure by the amount of beer that has sprayed out of the puncture. Upright, the metal wound foams and bubbles, dripping a constant stream of Carling Black Label.

There's no time to recover, though, as Effie adjusts her balance for the next onslaught and Nish rolls the third barrel. There's the thud of contact again, the barrels rattle, Effie crouches low and adjusts her balance.

The whipping antlers burst a hole through one of the planks in the trapdoor, sending a splinter of wood flying over the bar.

Nish rolls the final barrel to a stop and sees the crazed eye of a stag jamming its head sideways into the narrow space between the concrete steps and the trapdoor. With the surge of adrenaline that comes from fear and revulsion, he manages to upright the barrel, blocking the deer's peephole and fully securing the trapdoor.

There's another thump and a rattle of barrels, but the trapdoor stays firmly shut.

Effie steps down, taking a few rapid steps away from the entrance to the cellar. They stand together, her hand on his chest, his arm round her shoulder, watching the dark space behind the bar, below which the herd of murder-deer are considering their options.

'It won't hold them for long,' Nish says.

'We need to move,' Effie says.

But they don't.

Standing under the sprig of mistletoe that hangs over the bar entrance, they turn to face each other. Not for the first time that night, Nish feels Effie's breath on his skin, her hair brushes against his cheek. Her hands slip around his waist. He brushes a strand of hair from her face and feels his heart thump in his chest. He looks into her beautiful dark eyes and feels so alive. She parts her lips and they lean closer and at long last—

'Well this is ruddy bad timing,' says a familiar voice.

And then there's the distinctive sound of a freshly loaded shotgun being snapped back together.

21

A figure stands in the shadows of the dark pub. The barrel of the shotgun that's trained on Nish and Effie is little more than another shade of black.

'So, you trapped them in the cellar, huh?' Colonel Mustard says, stepping into a beam of moonlight. There's a dark sheen of not-yet-dried blood on his face, his wireframe glasses peek from his jacket pocket, shattered and misshapen.

'We can get away,' Nish says. 'It won't hold them forever, but we can all get to safety.'

'And where will we go?'

'Anywhere. The nearest city, I don't know. You must have a car or tractor or something. We could drive to Bristol – or Swindon – or some other place that's not the dead centre of nowhere.'

The Colonel laughs without much humour. 'After all you've been through, you still don't get it do you? Your boyfriend's pretty, but there's not much going on behind the scenes. It's a wonder you've survived this long.'

'You want to protect the children,' Effie says.

'Ah, you must be the brains.'

'But there are no children down there,' Nish says.

The Colonel heaves out a disappointed sigh. 'How very observant of you.'

'We saw what was in the box,' Nish says, needled by the dismissive tone. 'We saw *who* was in the box.'

The Colonel is silent for a moment, as if torn between a decision and action.

The wind howls around the smashed edges of the building, icy and bitter. The pub is cold and a hoar frost has started to form on the furniture nearest the door, a crystalline layer that glows in the moonlight. Nish suppresses a shiver. The adrenaline has worn off and the heat from running around has long since dissipated. He's cold and tired and all out of options.

Effie puts an arm around him for warmth. He hears her teeth begin to chatter.

'Tell me, before tonight did you believe in Santa Claus?' There's a dark humour to the Colonel's question. Despite all the death, all the horror, he recognises the absurdity of the situation.

'No,' Nish says. 'I'm not five.'

'I guess I was agnostic,' Effie says. 'I'm pragmatic in the face of evidence.'

The Colonel considers her for a moment, finding something unexpected in her answer. 'Very good. Perhaps there's time yet for a story. It wouldn't be Christmas without a fireside tale and a nightcap, would it? Take the brandy and three glasses, nice and slow.'

'We don't need brandy,' Nish says, holding Effie close.

The Colonel steps closer. Faint lines of amber candlelight leaching through from between the floorboards streak across his face, revealing bloodstains turned black, the ferocious whites of his eyes, and his determined grip on the shotgun. 'It'll do you well to remember who's in charge here. Brandy. Three glasses. And make sure it's the good stuff.'

Effie picks three tumblers from behind the bar, moving slowly. When she's done, Nish scans the rows of bottles at the back of the bar until he finds the brandy.

'Show me,' the Colonel says.

Nish raises the bottle, slowly.

'Are you trying to piss me off? The only thing that's good for is flaming a Christmas pudding. The Hennessy, come on… Look, it's none of my business, and I know no one wants to be alone at Christmas, but a girl like yourself could do better than this dimwit.'

Satisfied by the next bottle that Nish holds up, the Colonel directs them towards the inglenook fireplace. The remains of the log and coals that had been on the fire have turned a papery white. It still kicks off a welcome heat, but it's dying.

'Put another log on the fire,' the Colonel says. In the dim fireside light, he looks in a bad state. A vicious bruise has blossomed behind his hairline and there's a slur to his voice. 'Not you, her. The way you've been going, you'd only snuff it out and we'll all freeze to death. Do something even you can't muck up and get us some seats.'

Effie places a fresh log on the fire. She digs it into the ashes and sends a flurry of glowing red embers shooting up the chimney. There's a basket of old newspapers. She screws up a few pages and adds them to the pyre. The papers twist and blacken. Big yellow flames soon lick around the rough edges of the log. The burst of heat is immediate, prickling at her exposed skin even while the rest of her feels like it's still in a deep freezer.

Nish arranges three chairs on the deep stone hearth – two together on one side, one facing on the other. Colonel Mustard takes the isolated chair and scrapes it back further, making sure there's enough distance to comfortably keep both Londoners within his sights.

'Pour the drinks,' the Colonel says when they're all seated.

'We could still escape,' Nish says. 'We don't need to just sit here waiting for the deer to figure a way out.'

'Don't make me repeat myself.'

Nish opens the bottle and pours a generous measure into two glasses. He hands one to the Colonel and holds the other for himself.

'I don't know what passes for manners these days in the big city and maybe I'm old-fashioned, but that doesn't seem very gentlemanly to me. Give her that glass and pour another for yourself.'

Nish opens his mouth to protest, glances at Effie, who is looking intently at the bottle.

'You'll ruddy well do as I say young man.'

Out of the corner of his eye, Nish sees Effie nod. Now that they can see Colonel Mustard by the firelight, like an armed revenant, she looks more scared than ever. Even though they've spent the night being chased by monsters, she's held firm to her conviction that they're rational. And she was right, they did want something.

But the Colonel isn't a rational actor. None of the residents of Little Slaughter have been rational actors. Driven wild by the annual cycle of death, or lockdown, they couldn't be reasoned with. They weren't open to negotiation. They happily crossed and double-crossed each other to survive. And yet, here's the last of them, returned from the dead and having lost everything, holding them at gunpoint while the vengeful reindeer trapped in the cellar need one more kill to end this year's hunt.

Perhaps the Colonel was right, Nish has been slow on the uptake. But he sees it now. They're in more danger than they've been all night long.

Nish hands his glass to Effie and pours another measure for himself.

'Well, cheers.' Colonel Mustard holds up his glass, takes a swig and watches them beadily.

Nish raises his glass to his lips, sips a little brandy. It's strong and sharp and burns as it traces its way down his throat. He doesn't know if Effie has drunk from hers, but if she has it'll be because she's realised the situation is hopeless. He would almost prefer not to know that even her quick mind can't see a route out of this.

'Let me tell you about Christmas Eve in Little Slaughter. I think she's worked this out already, so this is just for you. Now, pay attention. Do you know what time you arrived here?'

Nish shakes his head.

'Just gone nine,' Effie says.

The Colonel smiles. 'Dinner was served at nine thirty, same as every year. The landlord was worried you wouldn't arrive on time with this snow. Peacock might have been a little eccentric, but she's a devil for timing. Punctual to a fault. Except of course, now she's late forever more.' He chuckles, raises his glass again for another slug. 'Terrible mistake to shoot her, I must say. I daresay your lad Steve had just enough time to realise he was a turkey who'd voted for Christmas. How long do you suppose you've been here? Hard to keep track what with all that running around, I know. But what time would you say it was now?'

'I don't know, two... three... something like that?' Nish says. The adrenaline hasn't let him feel tired yet, but he knows exhaustion is waiting in the wings.

Effie looks at her watch. 'It can't be... Eleven fifty-nine.'

'What?' Nish turns to look at her, thinking perhaps she's got a mechanical device. She shows her Apple Watch with its display showing analogue dials fashioned to look like a vintage Rolex. He watches as the second hand counts down to midnight, only to start again.

'Every year, on Christmas Eve, Little Slaughter gets trapped in a little time bubble. Why not escape, you ask? You're free to try, but you'll find that the road out of the village just leads back into the village. You can run out over the fields, crest the hill in the distance, only to find that you're heading back down the valley into the village. There is no way out. We've all tried. Some of us went half-mad trying. One year, one of our guests was an ultra-runner. Skinny like a beanpole and with skin like leather. Told us over dinner about some mad race against a train up a Welsh mountain. He ran past the pub all night long, slower and slower, until he just stopped and let the deer pick him off.

'There's only one way to make it through Christmas Eve, and that's by letting the deer have their eight kills. It won't turn midnight in Little Slaughter until the final heart stops beating. And so some of us developed a system for counting down,' he nods towards the scoreboard. Even though Miss Scarlet couldn't tend to the score, seven marks have been chalked up. Four in the Home column, three in Away. 'Some of us might not find it so very difficult to count to eight, but the system helped others keep track. I suppose I should be ashamed...'

'You were their teacher,' Effie says. 'Mrs Peacock said something about you opening the school again.'

'Ah, you were paying attention. Star pupil. I probably should have drilled them harder on basic mathematics. But I have to admit the scoreboard does add a nice competitive dynamic. The Home team has rarely conceded a mark in the last few years. To be losing at this stage in the match is quite the upset. But there's still time to snatch a draw, eh?'

'If this happens every year, why not just go away for Christmas?' Nish says. It's such a bloody obvious suggestion and yet the remaining villagers have stayed here as if just waiting for their fate at the end of an antler. This, he thinks, will show the old schoolmaster that he's not a complete idiot.

Colonel Mustard turns to Nish and gives him a look of pure contempt. 'Why don't we go away for Christmas? What an *interesting* suggestion. Now, let me see, why didn't we all go get ourselves a nice mini-break at a hotel or spa or something? I'm told Dubai is lovely this time of year.'

'Because you were protecting the children,' Effie says, almost surprising herself with the answer.

'Yes, very good. Because we were protecting the children. Some of us are aware of our responsibilities, young man. Some of us have a sense of duty. Because the consequences of us neglecting our burden are unthinkable. It's a thankless task, but that's the cross that this village must bear.'

'Is this all because she killed him?' Effie says.

Colonel Mustard smiles, the blood cracking as his skin creases. It's not a pleasant smile. 'Well, well, well. Our detective goes for the big reveal.'

22

'I'm sorry?' Nish looks between the two of them, trying to work out exactly what game he's found himself in the middle of. 'Would you mind rewinding and maybe starting from the start? Who killed Santa?'

'Miss Scarlet,' Effie says, all the while watching the Colonel in the firelight. 'It's why the stags went for her and the Reverend up the church tower, rather than wait for us to come down the stairs. It's why they thundered past us and went straight for them when we ran back to the pub.

'She killed Santa eleven years ago. And each year since, the stags have descended on the village looking for him. The first year they arrived, one of the village mummers was dressed as Santa Claus – the original green one – and they came over to see if it was him. And, well, the play was abridged. But they come back each year to look for him, and each year they're distracted on their hunt by the urge for revenge on the person who killed him. Is that about right?'

'She was an orphan, you know,' the Colonel says, holding the shotgun steady. 'Both her parents were killed in a tragic combine harvester accident when she was five. It was an awful time for the village to lose two members of such a close-knit community. But we came together and decided how to look after her.

'I ran the village school at the time. It had always been a very small school, just about large enough for one class. I could see retirement on the horizon and the school wasn't getting any busier. So, I took her in and raised her as my own daughter.

'I thought I knew what I was doing, but raising a child is a million miles removed from teaching a child. You're intensely responsible for helping to shape them as a person, trying to guide and direct their sense of morality, steer them away from danger. She was like any young child. Enthusiastic, full of joy and laughter, kind at times, capricious at others. But materialistic... So materialistic.

'You don't realise how much advertising there is – how effective it is – until you raise a child. All these messages about these needful things – toys, dolls, cards, games, music, phones, the list goes on... Commodities well out of the reach of a rural teacher's salary.'

Nish can't help but picture Grumpy Krampus, flooding children's social media feeds with inane challenges and building a groundswell of demand that falls on the shoulders of stressed and stretched parents. He feels a pinch of remorse.

'She understood that on some level, I'm sure of it. But the other children at the school had a solution. If you wanted something hard enough, you could ask Santa. Some of the children had asked him in person, after he set up a grotto in a shopping centre in Swindon of all places.

'I knew it wasn't him, of course. That would be ridiculous – he wasn't real. And yet, as parents we become complicit in this great lie.'

Colonel Mustard seems to need to unburden himself. He takes another slug of brandy and holds out his glass to be refilled. Nish wonders if they're getting to the point of the story. But he's also conscious that once the story is over they will be back to looking down the barrel of the shotgun and contemplating their fate.

'She'd talked so much about Santa and with such excitement that I couldn't help myself. Of course we were going to go and see the big man. She could plead her case to him directly, highlight her good deeds, repent for her bad ones. It wouldn't change the fact I couldn't afford all the gifts she wanted or deserved, but it would give her hope. But fate's a funny thing sometimes.

'We arrived at the big shopping centre in Swindon to find a sea of flashing blue lights. The entrance had been barred by a pair of stern police officers in uniform. The doors opened and another pair of officers came through, leading a man in a bright red Santa outfit his hands cuffed behind his back. He fought to get free as flash bulbs went off and the policemen hit him with their batons. They got him to his feet again and the fight had gone out of him. He was pushed into the back of a police car and driven away. Shortly after, the shopping centre was reopened – this was early December and capitalism waits for no man. We'd made it so far, so I decided we should go in anyway. The grotto at the heart of the shopping centre was sealed off with blue police tape. Crime scene. Do not cross. The elves had been taken in for questioning. We had McDonald's while I tried to console her, all the while wondering what the hell had happened.

'Well, I found out a few days later in the local news… Ironic for a man who supposedly knows who's been naughty and who's been nice. Let me ask you, what kind of a voyeur do you think keeps such a close eye on children's behaviour? What kind of sick man negotiates with young children about fulfilling their deepest wishes while they sit and wriggle on his lap? What kind of creep propagates the idea that it's fine for a complete stranger to go sneaking into children's bedrooms while they sleep?'

'He was…?' Effie can't bring herself to say it, but she pictures the kind of grim predator who might fit the bill.

'That's what I thought too. But it turned out that he'd been running a fraudulent operation. The money raised from the grotto wasn't going to charity at all. The elves knew nothing about it, they were just seasonal workers doing a double shift at the local panto. Santa was planning on doing a runner with their wages too.

'But once the idea was in my head, well, I couldn't shift it. How easy it would be for someone so evil to buy her trust. And what's the first thing you do when you see a vulnerability? You take preventative action. The image of Santa being manhandled into the back of a police car was already in her head. I realised I could make sure she would never be taken in by a man in a jolly suit promising her gifts on condition of compliance. It was far better for her to be fearful and distrusting than hopeful and exploited.'

'So what happened to Santa?' Nish says.

'I see you're a believer now? It's funny isn't it, coming face to face with a myth. 'Twas the night before Christmas and all through the house we had barricaded the windows, double-locked the doors, and booby-trapped the fireplace. We used to watch Home Alone for inspiration. It was the same as any year since we saw Santa in Swindon. I was in the middle of having some work done to the house, though, and things were in a bit of a mess. The workmen had put the tools and parts as much out the way as they could, but the house was a building site.

'She never slept well on Christmas Eve. She was always worried that Santa was trying to find a vulnerability in our defences. Even when she did manage to sleep on Christmas Eve she'd have bad dreams. It sounds terrible, but it made Christmas Day all the more special. We could relax. We'd made it. But this year she had a particularly rough night and couldn't sleep a wink.

'She told me that she'd got up to go get a glass of water. I sometimes wonder... She'd been dropping hints for weeks beforehand about an iPhone. I'd say to her: "What do you need an iPhone for? You can just holler out the window if you want to talk to anyone you know." But she was insistent. I couldn't afford one, but you try telling that to a ten-year-old. I sometimes wondered, after it had all happened, if she hadn't been checking her presents. She'd been hoping so hard for something, she'd been helping round the house. She'd been an absolute angel. She'd been good as gold... Knowing what I know now, I wonder if she didn't make a reckless wish. I guess I'll never know now if she invited him in.

'Either way, she got out of bed and walked downstairs, avoiding all the mess left behind by the builders. She didn't turn on the lights because she didn't want to wake me. But when she got downstairs, she realised she wasn't alone. She couldn't see well, but she could see enough to make out a silhouette. A fat man with a big beard and a bobble hat. She knew right enough that this wasn't good.'

The Colonel takes a mouthful of brandy, swills it around, then swallows. His eyes have glazed over as he talks, as if he's reliving the memories. Nish has been wondering whether he could rush the Colonel, disarm him somehow. But to misjudge something like that would be fatal. And he's found himself strangely drawn into the story.

'So she grabbed the nearest thing to hand and hit him around the head with all the force she could manage. He went down like a sack of spuds. By the time I'd got down, he was bleeding out on the floor. I found her cowering in the corner, clutching the length of lead piping.'

'"It'll be Miss Scarlet in the lounge with the lead piping, same as every year,"' Effie says. 'That's what the butcher's wife said when we arrived. They all knew that she'd killed Santa, didn't they?'

'Takes a village to raise a child,' the Colonel says, a wistful smile tugging at his lips. 'Nothing tighter than village folk. We knew she'd done nothing wrong, really. There was a body, but who was going to report Santa missing? Picture the scene: you're ambushed by a mythical being and so you kill it. What then? Could he come back? Well, we just didn't know, so we put him in the cellar of the pub and kept a vigil.

'But nothing... Until the first anniversary, when the stags came and took our mummers. We'd thought we'd got away with it, that everything would return to normal. But nothing was normal again. We worked out the rules of the game – eight kills, each year – and kept an advent vigil to make sure he never came back.

'And you know the rest.' The Colonel is back in the room, his eyes sharp and distrusting.

'So here we are,' Effie says. 'What now?'

'You have a choice,' he says. 'One of you has to go back down there for the clock to turn midnight.'

'And the other?'

'Well, unless I can trust you to bring me eight tributes next year, I'll at least make it quick.'

23

Shotgun or antler? Christmas Eve or Christmas Day? What a way to choose how you die, Effie thinks. It's the prisoner's dilemma, but there's no least-worst option.

There had been a moment when she had thought they could escape their fate. Maybe they could have overcome Colonel Mustard? Perhaps they could have lured him down to the cellar? What if they'd never returned to the pub, ignored the siren call of the mystery?

But they are comprehensively out of options.

So she asks herself again: what's more terrifying? Antlers or shotgun?

If she chooses, at least she'll give Nish a fraction of a chance. It's better than nothing. When Colonel Mustard had been downing drinks, she could have sought the oblivion of alcohol. It would have been easy. But she didn't. Having been tempted by drink all night long, she found she could resist it. Despite all the horror of this terrible night, something has changed. And here's the irony, it's only now that she's found hope that she's having to give it up.

She takes a deep breath, ready to face her fate.

'I'll—'

'Something doesn't add up,' Nish says. 'Steve cracked you round the head with a candlestick, and here you are, holding us at gunpoint and still coherent enough to know that you need the stags to kill one of us to get through to next year. Steve wasn't exactly a small guy. What would you say, six foot, twelve stone, something like that? A swing in the dark puts you down for – well, however you measure time when time itself is frozen... But you're telling us that a scared ten-year-old girl with some building scraps killed that guy downstairs?'

'I see we have a volunteer,' the Colonel says, voice drawn and eyes hard. He flicks the gun barrel in the direction of the bar, urging Nish to get on with being sacrificed.

'See, here's what I think happened. She was scared, she picked up the lead piping, she clocked him as best she could... and maybe she got lucky. Maybe he fell badly and maybe he was knocked out for a bit.

'You wake up, hear a commotion downstairs and you come down to find her and the big guy out cold. She's distressed, of course. She thinks she's just killed a man. You're worried about her, and you send her out of the way. You just want to protect her. You tell her you'll make it all right. But when she's gone, you realise he's not dead.'

'I don't have time for this,' the Colonel says, standing and stepping back from the fireplace. He levels the gun at the two of them.

Effie goes to stand, but Nish puts out a hand to stop her.

'Time's exactly what we do have,' Nish says. 'Look at your watch, it's not getting any later. You've got us cornered. You've won. At least do us the favour of some resolution to this murder mystery. He wasn't dead, was he?'

Colonel Mustard pauses for a moment, but his tongue has been loosened by the brandy. The Londoners have conceded and it's a story he's kept to himself for a decade. 'Almost as soon as she was out of the room he started stirring. Near enough gave me a heart attack, the way he started moaning and writhing all of a sudden. Of course, I couldn't have that. I reached out for the nearest thing I could find and, well, the builders had left a few tools.'

'It was Colonel Mustard in the lounge with the wrench,' Nish says.

'Ah, if only. That would have been too perfect. Alas, it was a hammer. It was the single most horrific thing I'd ever done, and I did it all for her. I'd never imagined that it was the start of something so terrible... The beginning of a slide into an annual cycle of violence.'

Nish remembers the holes in the skull in the cellar, the remnants of a brutal attack rendered PG13 by time.

'What happens after the stags have had their kills?' Nish says.

There's a thought that has been gestating at the back of his mind, frustratingly out of reach all evening, until now. It's hatched and spread its wings and it's so awful he can't stop thinking about it. After a night of bloodshed, do the deer simply give up and vanish? Or does something else happen?

Colonel Mustard chuckles, cruel and humourless. 'Isn't that quite the question?'

'One of us isn't going to see Christmas Day,' Nish bargains. 'Might as well let us know what we're missing.'

'I was surprised enough when I first found him on the floor, writhing and alive. Imagine my surprise that first year after the slaughter of the mummers when I found him marching around the cellar.'

'He came back to life?' Effie says, shock etched on her face.

'Vampires come back at night. Werewolves come back at full moon. Only makes sense that Santa Claus comes back at Christmas.' Colonel Mustard, having overcome his reluctance, now seems to be quite enjoying his role as fireside storyteller. 'Nothing a shotgun couldn't put down, though.

'After that first year, we chained him down. Now whoever makes it to the cellar first after the final kill gets to crack him open with a hammer. Just like the first time. Adds a nice bit of tradition, don't you think? Like finding a coin in your Christmas pudding.'

'You kill him every year?' Nish says.

'To keep the children safe,' Effie says. 'Safe from a con artist who dressed as Santa in Swindon a decade ago.'

'You never can be too sure,' the Colonel says. 'Happy now? This has all been a very pleasant end to a fairly tawdry evening, but I'm afraid I'm going to need to kill you now. Nothing personal, you understand, but the deer need their blood, the big man needs a bump on the head, and I could do with getting a good night's sleep so I'm fresh for the Queen's speech.'

The Colonel pushes his chair back and stands. He steps back and levels the gun at his captives. They are out of time.

A silence of sorts settles on the pub. The wind whistles around the shards of glass, smashed wood and broken masonry caused by the night's violence. There's a snort from the cellar, muffled by ancient floorboards. The fire pops as it sends a flurry of embers up the chimney.

Nish thinks of the stags. He thinks of the dark intelligence he sensed behind those black cue-ball eyes. He thinks of the way they hunted down Miss Scarlet, the woman they thought had murdered their master all those years ago. He thinks of the herd of brooding vengeance-fuelled beasts squeezed into the cellar below with their super-sensitive hearing. He thinks of the gaps in the floorboards that let light and sound leach through to their underworld. And then he thinks that maybe he's overestimated their intelligence, because he's just coaxed a confession out of the man who's standing right above them and yet—

'You killed Santa!' Effie shouts, bold and loud.

Colonel Mustard cocks his head. 'I thought you were meant to be the clever one.'

Nothing.

Exasperated, Effie continues as loud as she can. 'And you're going to kill Santa again!'

'We have a volunteer for death by deer,' says Colonel Mustard.

The image of Santa's dulled moss-green leather flashes through Nish's mind. He thinks of the deer drawn to the mummers with their pre-Coca-Cola outfit. Of how the villagers had reacted to the use of his name, but only sometimes. And he realises it's not Santa buried in the cellar—

'You killed Father Christmas!' Nish shouts.

A pair of blades, silvered and forked like lighting, burst through the floorboards under the Colonel and through his feet. The shotgun goes off with a deafening roar. Nish and Effie duck low as plaster and brickwork showers down on them.

Pain and shock barely register on the Colonel's face before the antlers wrap around his calf and tug him to his knees. More blades burst through the floor, sending a shower of wooden shards around the pub. His arms are bound by the supple blades.

Colonel Mustard, his face contorted with pain, glares at Effie and Nish. 'What have you done?' he says, before his tethers pull him face-down to the floor.

And then his body shudders. It's like he's having a seizure, but then the antlers begin shooting out of his back. They slip out only to be thrust back in. Fountains of gore spurt into the air as the stags thrust their blades up through the floorboards.

It's only a moment before the floor gives way, but it feels like forever. There's a creak and a groan before a snap and the Colonel's body disappears into a pit that opens into the darkness of the cellar. Nish sees silver antlers flash and hears the sickening sound of flesh being pummelled into mince.

'We need to go,' Nish says.
'What about the deer?'
'I think they're pissed.'

24

Living in London, you bump into all sorts of people. Nish once met a bloke down the pub who made a living as a foley artist. Over an eight-quid pint he explained how he made a living by making things sound like other things. As he talked, it transpired that sound effects are required by not just radio, but also TV and film. And once he knew what to listen for, Nish saw foley work everywhere. Even the influencers he worked with used foley sound effects to make their videos pop.

'You might think it's a craft,' the man insisted, 'but it's more of a science.'

He went on to explain that creating the perfect sound effect required a combination of research and experimentation. Take, he insisted, the effect he'd most recently worked on.

He'd started off by hitting a coconut with a hammer, which gave a good crack, but the high note of the shell sounded a bit comical. A cantaloupe melon hit with the hammer had a good heavy *thunk*, but lacked vibrancy. A watermelon sounded disappointing and wasted half an hour in a clean-up operation. He tried smashing a Savoy cabbage with a rounders bat, but the noise was too soft. So, he moved on to white cabbage. Not enough bite. Red cabbage was better, but still too soft. Iceberg lettuce was better still, crisp, but without quite the right resonance. So, he swapped rounders for cricket and found that the *thunk* of willow against the implosion of crisp salad was just right.

This was all in aid of simulating the sound of a skull being crushed for the pilot of a Radio 4 Book at Bedtime adaptation of *A Game of Thrones*. The production would have required hundreds of sound effects, enough to keep the man busy for months on end. Sadly, the project never made it to full production, but scientific progress had been made.

Nish thinks the foley artist would probably recreate the noise coming from the basement right now by hitting several pounds of wet clay with a machete. The sound of the heavy impact is one thing, but he'll never forget the wet sucking noise of blades being removed for the next strike.

Nish and Effie edge around the crevasse in the floor, testing the floorboards as they go. Nish tries to avoid looking into the cellar, but the flashing blades draw the eye.

In the pit below he sees a pagan representation of hell. Lit by the guttering candles, the stags are in a murderous rage. Their antlers lash and flay in the flickering light. A fine mist of blood drifts into the air, like sulphurous fumes, turning the very air itself red. He can feel moisture damping his skin.

Nish is just about to pass through the door, out into the clear clean night air outside, when he hears a furious feral roar. He looks behind. Effie is a few steps back. She's nearly at the bar but has frozen with horror. One of the stags – its fur matted with blood and its eyes fixed on her – rears up from the hole in the floor.

'Effie!'

She is transfixed, held in the Lucifer-like thrall of the stag rising from the bloody pit below.

The stag's silver antlers fan out behind it in a vicious lacework crown of blood-stained blades.

Behind the sounds of meat being tenderised in the pit, there's the sound of chains shifting. No, not shifting. Falling. Like an anchor being dropped. The chains land with a rattling hiss as they slip to the concrete floor.

Effie breaks the spell and vaults over the bar. She snatches at the spirits on the back wall and for a mad moment Nish thinks she's going to start downing booze, her temperance broken by a living nightmare. But instead, she begins to throw bottles.

The first, a near-full bottle of Absolut vodka, turns a lazy arc in the air before shattering into a million pieces as it hits the stag's antlers. The stag blinks and shakes its head, alcohol stinging its eyes, and sinks back down into the pit. A bottle of Bacardi follows, then Bells, then Gordon's, each smashing around the pub. The air fills with the bitter-sharp smell of spirits, mixing with the copper scent of blood and the animal stench of the stags. More bottles sail past – Archers, Malibu, Advocaat, Sheridan's, Baileys – smashing crisply.

'Effie, come on – let's go!'

He sees an almost manic look in her eyes as she picks the last remaining bottle. It's the bottle of brandy that the Colonel turned down. The one that's only good for lighting a Christmas pudding... And then he gets it.

Effie launches the bottle, low and fast. It spins through the dark air, the amber liquid flashing in the light of the fireplace and the candles below. The brandy sails over the hell-pit and smashes into the stonework of the inglenook fireplace.

She watches where it lands like a golfer willing a ball that's landed on the green to roll closer to the hole.

But nothing happens—

In the pregnant pause Nish hears the blood-curdling cackle of a man who has remained buried for a decade and is now unshackled and free to reap vengeance. 'Mwargh ha ha ha.' There's a cough and the clearing of a throat, like an 80-a-day smoker has just woken from a long slumber. Then: 'Ho ho ho.'

—until there's a gentle *pwump* from the far side of the pub. A victorious grin breaks out on Effie's face, only to be quickly replaced by a frantic alarm. She scrambles over the bar and crosses the pub in two bounds.

Nish sees a wave of blue flames racing away from the fireplace in a short, fast wave. It tears along the floor, up the walls, down into the cellar pit. Short-lived flames shimmer blue in its wake, burning through the alcohol. But there are flickers of yellow already. The basket of newspapers. The kindling of smashed furniture. The hops strung from the ceiling beams. The ancient plastic Christmas tree, draped in equally old tinsel and surrounded by cardboard boxes wrapped to look like presents. The fire is catching and spreading with a hunger and speed that pins him to the spot.

'Come on.' Effie grabs his hand and yanks him outside.

They retrace their footsteps past picnic tables and through the gate in the picket fence – it's all that's left of the picket fence, which has been stampeded over at some point in the night, churned and smashed into the snow. They come to a stop on the snow-covered green. Up ahead is the slumped form of Mrs White. To one side is a mess of gore where Miss Scarlet and Reverend Green commingle.

'What happens now?' Nish says. 'They've had their eight

kills. They've found Father Christmas. I think he came back to life... But now the pub's on fire. Did we kill him again?'

'Let's not wait around to find out.'

From this angle, they can see the bar through the shattered front door. The pub begins to develop a welcoming honey-coloured glow, a deceptive warmth that speaks of shelter and an open fire. If it weren't for the various scattered bodies, the gaping hole in the roof, the splintered woodwork, and the snow compacted by hoof prints the size of dinner plates, The Slaughter House would be the perfect destination for weary travellers.

'Wait, what time is it?'

They both look at their watches. Effie is right. The only way to know if the ordeal is truly over is for this interminable Christmas Eve to finally pass.

'It's gone midnight,' Nish says, barely able to believe the evidence on Effie's watch.

She turns to him, eyes bright, smiling, radiant. 'Merry Christmas, Nish.'

He laughs with a joy and simple pleasure he thought he'd never experience again. 'Merry Christmas, Effie.'

And there, on the snow-packed green under the full moon and the swirling galaxies in the velvet sky, they kiss.

By the time they part, flames have begun to appear through the doorway. There's the sound of glass shattering. They stand together watching the fire lick and dance, torn between getting closer to feel the warmth and running away in case they've changed the rules of the game and the rampage is just taking a brief hiatus.

'What are we going to do? We can't stand here all night.'

'The minibus,' Nish says. 'Mrs Peacock was trying to get into it when Steve... She was faking it when we came to a stop here. I think it still works.'

Nish glances back at the pub. The flames are high now, they lap over the wooden bar in waves. Bright tongues flick at the edges of the broken window, shooting up the side of the building as they suck hungrily at the oxygen, leaving great black smudges on the building's stonework. The stags are in there somewhere, but if they're making a noise, he can't hear it over the blazing roar of the fire as it digs its teeth in.

They walk hand-in-hand, the snow crunching underfoot. They don't take the most direct path down to the road and the minibus. They feel no compulsion to see the messy end to Little Slaughter's power couple in any more detail. And there's a narrow gap in the hedgerow in the shade of one of the great bare-branched trees.

Nish takes the bank down to the road first, tracing a slippery path over the gnarled roots of the oak tree. He holds out his hand and helps Effie down. Her skin is like ice.

'You're cold.'

'You too.'

The road is dark below the overhanging trees, the snow laced with shadows as the bright moonlight cuts through the tangle of branches. The minibus is parked to one side of the road. Nish is grateful for the dark as they pass all that remains of Steve, recognisable only by his snow-ruined brogues.

A short distance from the minibus, Mrs Peacock is spreadeagled and stiff face-down in the snow, her day-glow tabard reduced to bloody shreds of fabric. By some small miracle, she's still gripping the key fob.

Nish prises the key from her cold dead hands – a phrase he swears there and then he will never use again. He presses the unlock button and the vehicle beeps, its indicator lights flashing twice.

'Okay, you ready?'

'I've been ready this whole damned night,' Effie says.

Inside, the minibus is freezing cold. A couple of windows have shattered, leaving it exposed to the night air. Nish turns the key in the ignition, praying to any benevolent being that cares to hear, and the engine sputters to life. The lights come on and Noddy Holder screams out of the speakers *'It's Chriiiist-maaaaaaas!'*

'You driven one of these before?'

'Nope,' Nish says. 'You?'

'No. It's just you seemed awful... confident. For a Londoner, I mean. Who drives in London?'

'Yeah, well my mum's going to be pissed that we're so late.'

'You know that bit at the end of the horror movie,' Effie says, 'when you think it's all over, and there's one last jump scare?'

'You didn't hear him, did you?'

'Who?'

'Father Christmas,' Nish says. 'I heard him laugh and he sounded... different.'

'Different? How?' Effie looks worried. 'Did he sound like Vincent Price? The Joker? Skeletor?'

Nish thinks about what he heard. All of the above, and none at the same time. But the laugh had changed, hadn't it? Shifted an octave down to something more traditionally jolly. It's Christmas Day and they're finally escaping. He doesn't want to worry her unnecessarily. 'Nah, you know what, I think I'm just tired and wired. I keep waiting for something to happen. But it won't. We're safe.'

He adjusts the rear-view mirror to see a shadowy form sitting behind him.

Nish whips round, heart in his mouth. But it's only the massive teddy bear, still patiently sitting with its seatbelt on, wearing its goofy grin. A reminder of a simpler time, just a few hours ago, but which might as well be a whole different era.

'All those presents,' Effie says. 'Jess and Steve must have family wondering where they are.'

'We'll find a way to find them. But one thing at a time.'

After some unhealthy sounding mechanical churning and whining, Nish puts the vehicle in gear and ever so gently eases the clutch and accelerator. There's a little motion, a pause as the wheels spin, and then a lurch forwards and they are on the road. For a moment Nish worries he's going to propel them into the raised bank, but he holds his nerve and drives them slow and steady, the headlights blazing off the settled snow.

He glances over at the pub, flames lighting up the snow through the thin hedgerow. A column of smoke stretches into the night sky, lit by the conflagration below. The fire has taken well. There will be no saving the building. He thinks of the stags trapped in the basement below.

But then he sees motion on the village green. There, bathed in moonlight, stand eight massive stags. Their vicious silver antlers liquid like quicksilver. The biggest one – a brute the size of a carthorse – looks in their direction. Nish's heart freezes as it watches them with its big black centre-set murderous eyes. The moment seems to last forever.

Until the stag shakes itself like a dog fresh out of water. The others take its lead, their fur ruffling and their antlers flashing in the moonlight. And then, all of a sudden, the antlers drop.

'They're shedding,' Effie says.

By the time the words are out of her mouth all that remain on the village green are eight rather small reindeer, grey and shaggy, with side-set eyes and dark bone antlers. They stand in pairs, as if waiting for someone out of sight to lash them together and attach a sleigh.

'That's good right?'

'It means we didn't kill him,' Effie says. She sounds relieved.

'And that's good right?' Nish can't quite get the echo of that laughter emerging from the hell-pit out of his head.

'It means it's over. Properly over. We saved Christmas.'

'Okay,' Nish says. He grips the steering wheel hard. 'Onwards.'

Effie cranks up the heating and hot air blasts through. He presses down the accelerator. It takes all his remaining willpower not to floor it. He knows if he does the wheels will just spin.

They gradually and cautiously climb the hill out of the village, Christmas music blaring across the countryside from their broken windows.

The wind whips Effie's hair around her face. She turns to look at Nish, strikingly beautiful in the crisp moonlight. As the village slips out of sight behind the hill she says: 'So, we're driving home for Christmas to meet your parents, huh?'

'Too soon?'

'Well, I guess it can't be any scarier than our first date.'

'Date? ... Wait, you're saying there's going to be a second?'

Lit by the bright winter moonlight, Effie smiles.

Join the Christmas list

Thanks for reading *Slay Ride*. If you enjoyed it and would like to recommend it, tell a friend. Or, better yet, leave a review on Amazon to help complete strangers find out about it.

And if you want to read more like this, scan the QR code to sign up to my newsletter. In return you'll get a link to download *The Mayfly*, an exclusive novella for newsletter subscribers.

Scan this...
... to get this for free

https://labirchon.com

Author's note

Thank you for reading *Slay Ride*. I do hope you enjoyed it.

Christmas can be a wonderful time of the year, but for many people it's a difficult time. I wanted to write a story that captures some of the bittersweet feelings that the festive period stirs up.

On the one hand, bright lights illuminate dark winter days, and evergreen trees crowd into our homes while the leaves outside mulch down into a treacherous sludge. December rapidly fills with reunions with friends you really should see more often, as if the world will end on Christmas Eve. It's a time for generosity and fond nostalgia.

But on the other hand, long-buried family dynamics rise to the surface, leading to simmering tensions and frustrations. Adults are transported back to their childhood, sleeping a bedroom of their teenage years that has been preserved in aspic. Ghosts assemble around the Christmas table in the form of empty chairs, the unsaid subtext of dinner-table anecdotes, and family traditions of uncertain origin. And every year it gets more and more expensive as Christmas begins to creep into our lives from September.

It's always been a big time of year for my partner's family. The women of the family would deck their respective houses with every conceivable form of Christmas decoration. You've never seen so many sparkling table dressings and snow-scene ornaments, so much seasonal crockery and festive glassware. Even down to Christmas toilet roll. (Where on earth do you get Christmas toilet roll from?)

My partner's nan (Ground Zero for Christmas kitsch) had a prodigious ability for finding the most random – and largely tasteless – Christmas-themed presents. In her honour, we each now seek out the most objectively awful Christmas-themed items to exchange on the big day. Consequently, in December our house fills with Rudolph scrubbing brushes, Santa rubber ducks, and aprons emblazoned with antler-wearing-dogs.

Midway through writing *Slay Ride*, my partner's mother passed away. It was unexpected, sudden, and – well –

complicated. So, in the year that this book is released into the world, we're feeling tender and grateful for what we have, and we're building new traditions for another ghost at the table.

So, in the Christmas spirit, I'm going to ask you a favour. Writing a book is a labour of love and it means the world to me that you've taken the time to read my work. If you enjoyed this book, I would be incredibly grateful if you could leave a review on Amazon. Reviews really are the best way of helping this book find its way to new readers.

Finally, whichever stage of the Christmas run-up or cool-down it is when you're reading this, I hope you will have/are having/have had a wonderful time. If not, remember it's just a day. There's always a space set for you at the table in Little Slaughter.

Acknowledgements

Writing a book is a strangely intimate and solitary occupation. On each bright warm midsummer morning I'd sit alone with my laptop, imagining myself into a dark wintery snowscape. But I couldn't have got this book out into the world without the help and support of friends.

D.A. Holdsworth was the great pioneer in this front, having thrown himself whole-heartedly into a post-pandemic comedy sci-fi in the grand tradition of Douglas Adams. He's been an endless fount of encouragement and practical advice. And you really should read *How to Buy a Planet*. You'll never look at a platter of crisps (or potato chips, if you're so inclined) the same way.

Special thanks are due to my partner, Lizzy, who offered encouragement and support while I puzzled with thorny questions like 'Is *Slay Ride* or *Last Christmas* a better title?'

And a shout out to Mark Stay and Mark Desvaux, hosts of The Bestseller Experiment podcast. They might have written, edited and published a book in their first year, but it took me a few more years of experimentation. To misquote one of their guests: writing is like running a marathon – it's the miles no one sees that help you go the distance.

The Rules of Time Travel

Two time travellers.
One timeline.

Rey is a time traveller. She's come back in a desperate last attempt to prevent a future disaster, even though she doesn't know if she can change the timeline.

She's overshot and finds herself in 2018 outside Daily Grind, a long-lost London cafe. In a matter of months, the cafe will be destroyed in a fire that leaves one dead.

Here's her chance. Stop the fire. Save a life. Prove the future can be changed.

But Rey's not the only time traveller in town. Someone from her past has been keeping a dark secret. And something sinister and unseen is drawing closer.

Out now

Riddle

Each day at Daily Grind ends with preparation for the next.
   Jack has already cleaned the Gaggia. Its chrome front, dials and handles are pristine.
   'Better latte than never.'
   Jack places a powder-blue disposable cup on the counter.
   Dom looks up from table he's wiping down.
   'I hope that's not instant.'
   A time traveller walks into a coffee shop.

Never mind, you'll get it next time round

Kindle and paperback editions available from Amazon

Printed in Great Britain
by Amazon